THE LADY FROM BUENOS AIRES

A WILLIE CUESTA MYSTERY

BY JOHN LANTIGUA

Arte Público Press
Houston, Texas

This volume is funded in part by grants from the city of Houston through the Houston Arts Alliance, and the Exemplar Program, a program of Americans for the Arts in collaboration with the LarsonAllen Public Services Group, funded by the Ford Foundation.

Recovering the past, creating the future

Arte Público Press
University of Houston
452 Cullen Performance Hall
Houston, Texas 77204-2004

Cover design by Giovanni Mora
Author's photo by Bill Ingram
Tango Argentino, Original Painting by Pedro Alvarez,
is available as unlimited print, size 23 x 31 ins
www.wizard.ch

Lantigua, John.
    The lady from Buenos Aires : a Willie Cuesta mystery / by John Lantigua.
    p.   cm.
    ISBN 978-1-55885-496-7 (alk. paper)
    1. Private investigators—Florida—Miami—Fiction. 2. Sisters—Fiction. 3. Disappeared persons—Fiction. 4. Missing children—Fiction. 5. State-sponsored terrorism—Argentina—History—Fiction. 6. Miami (Fla.)—Fiction. I. Title.
    PS3562.A57L33 2007
    813'.54—dc22
                                                    2007060766
                                                        CIP

♾ The paper used in this publication meets the requirements of the American National Standard for Information Sciences—Permanence of Paper for Printed Library Materials, ANSI Z39.48-1984.

7 8 9 0 1 2 3 4 5 6   10 9 8 7 6 5 4 3 2 1

ACKNOWLEDGMENTS

The author owes thanks to many people who helped during the research and writing of this book.

They include, in Buenos Aires: Victoria Donda, Horacio Pietragalla, Victoria Grigera, and Juan Cabandie, who are "children of the disappeared" and shared their stories; Alba Lanzillotto and Eugenia Paladino from the Grandmothers of the Plaza de Mayo, and Mercedes Merono from the Mothers of the Plaza de Mayo, who continue to search for such children.

Also, in Argentina, I am indebted to my journalist friends Olga Wornat, Miriam Lewin, and Joe Contreras.

In Miami, I received invaluable aid from Jane Bussey, Greg Aunapu, Mario Diament, Clifford Krauss, Julie Ferguson, and Blanca Lozano.

Gracias.

DEDICATION

This book is dedicated to the memory of Michelle Urry,
the best friend a writer could ever have.

"First we will kill all the subversives; then we will kill their collaborators; then . . . their sympathizers, then . . . those who remain indifferent; and finally we will kill the timid."
General Ibérico Saint Jean, governor of Buenos Aires, May 1976

CHAPTER ONE

On summer days I dress down—way down. This isn't just a question of comfort; in Miami it's a matter of survival. In July and August, people keel over at an alarming rate. I'm convinced that if you check with the medical examiner you'll find a pattern, at least among the guys. "Cause of death: suit and tie."

So on the morning in question I was in a long, faded tropical shirt, white linen pants, a pair of well-ventilated Mexican sandals, and amber-tinted shades.

It was early. In those summer months, if I have errands to do, I'm on the street before the heat hits. It doesn't matter what you wear, if you wait until noon, your brains will be braised in your skull.

But it isn't always easy to get up early given the hours I keep. In addition to running my own business—Willie Cuesta Investigations—I also serve as chief of security at a Latin nightclub owned by my brother Tommy. It's called Caliente—Hot—of all things. If I get out of there before four a.m., Wednesday through Saturday nights it's rare. Consequently, emerging from bed before eleven a.m. is an act of heroism.

It so happens that this was a Monday. I was not only up by ten, but I had already watered the bougainvillea and gardenias out back. I was driving to the local Cuban supermarket to buy some breakfast and stock up for the week when my cell phone rang.

"Cuesta Investigations," I cooed into the phone. When you haven't had a client lately, you tend to coo.

"Is this Mr. Cuesta?" asked a woman speaking Spanish.

"Yes, it is."

"Mr. Cuesta, the detective?"

"Well, I was once a detective when I worked for the Miami Police Department. These days they prefer I call myself a private investigator."

1

"Yes, yes. That isn't really important." She was already demonstrating impatience, which isn't unusual for women in my life. "But can you help me find a person?"

"Possibly. Finding people is one of the principal services I offer. Who are you looking for?"

As basic as the question was, it was more than she wanted to divulge over the phone.

"I want to see you," she said. "I want to talk to you in person."

"Okay. Why don't you come to my office. I'm in Little Havana."

I'd have to go home and clean up a bit. I rent a second-floor walk-up on Southwest 8th Street, the main drag of Little Havana. My office occupies the front room and I live in the back, overlooking the gardenias and bougainvillea.

A sigh of dismay escaped her. "I'm only visiting Miami, Mr. Cuesta. I don't know the city."

"Visiting from Argentina, I assume."

"That's right, from Buenos Aires."

The accent was unmistakable. The Argentines speak a lilting Spanish, apparently influenced along the way by Italian opera. To me, an Argentine always sounds as if he or she is about to break into an aria.

"Well, I could meet you somewhere late in the afternoon, after it's cooled off."

She didn't like that idea. "No, no! I need to see you sooner than that, please. It is very important. Can we meet now?"

She was talking high noon in mid-June. But if I insisted on waiting, she would call another agency. I'd be left cooing at other prospective clients.

"Where are you?"

"I'm in Miami Beach. We can meet at a restaurant called El Gaucho, on 71st Street. Do you know where it is?"

Unfortunately, I did. I said I'd be there.

"How will I recognize you?" she asked.

I described my outfit. "And I'll look hot," I said. "How about you?"

She hesitated, but for only a moment.

"I never look hot."

CHAPTER TWO

I took the Julia Tuttle Causeway across Biscayne Bay, which was always a dazzling ride. The surface of the water changed from day to day, depending on the cloud cover and the season. Right now it was an unblemished gorgeous green color, flat and smooth. It resembled an enormous table made of polished jade. Across the water, the white hotels and condo towers of Miami Beach floated a bit in the noonday sun, the way heat wavers above a sizzling tarmac.

Ten minutes later I turned onto 71st Street, the main artery in a part of town known these days as "Little Buenos Aires." Even at an early hour you can tell you are entering the Argentine barrio because you catch the delicious scent of sizzling beef left over from the night before. The area is home to numerous steak joints, and the aroma hangs in the air for blocks around. The Argentines in Miami left behind the *pampas*, but not their propensity for preparing the best beef in the world. They had the Atkins diet down long before there was an Atkins.

I found a parking space, fed the meter, and drifted down the street toward the blue-and-white umbrellas that marked El Gaucho restaurant. Music spilled out onto the sidewalk. A brokenhearted Latin guy sang about how the lonely night spoke to his heart and how he hungered for the dawn of a new love.

I was walking by the umbrellas, wending my way toward the air-conditioned interior, when someone behind me said my name. I turned and saw a woman seated by herself under an umbrella.

"You *are* Mr. Cuesta, aren't you?"

"Yes."

"I'm Fiona Bonaventura. I'm the one who called you. You never asked my name."

She was right. It was a minor instance of miscommunication, although it hadn't been the only one. Over the phone she had told me that she never looked hot. Well, there wasn't a bead of perspiration on

3

her, but she was still way above room temperature from my point of view.

In her mid-forties, I'd say, she was wide-shouldered and slim-hipped. She wore light weight gray slacks, a pink silk blouse, and a tasteful silver necklace that had the looks of a family heirloom. Her skin was as pale as cream, her wavy hair was jet black, the eyes were the deep blue of the southern Atlantic, and her full lips were painted a reddish, brown hue. She was an Argentine Ava Gardner. Elegant, cool . . . hot.

She gestured me toward the chair across from her.

I hesitated. "Why don't we go inside and get out of this steam bath."

She batted her eyes once and didn't move. "I just came from Buenos Aires where it is quite cool this time of year, Mr. Cuesta. I like the heat." She pulled out a chair for me.

I don't get paid to argue with prospective clients, so I took my seat. Propped across from her in my tropical duds, I looked more like her cabana boy than a professional investigator.

The waitress walked over. The Argentines make a perfectly acceptable beer named Quilmes, but it was much too early. So after she asked for iced tea, I ordered a lemonade.

"How did you get my name?" I asked.

"I found you listed in the telephone directory. It said you speak Spanish and that you are an expert in international investigations."

And that was true. During my last years in the Miami Police Department I served in the intelligence unit. My job was pursuing foreign criminals whose careers had brought them to Miami. They included both common crooks and political operatives. I handled quite a few extraditions and visited a variety of Latin countries. Miami was one of a handful of American cities that had a need for its own FBI *cum* CIA, and I'd been part of the local unit.

"Yes, I've worked international cases. So who are we looking for?"

She went into her purse and pulled out a faded color photograph.

"This is my sister. Her name was Sonia."

The woman in the photo appeared to be about twenty, although the shot had been taken a long time ago. She had long, black, straight hair and the same dairy-fresh skin as the lady sitting before me. Where she was different was in the eyes. They were darker, deeper, and more somber. But she was still quite beautiful.

"You said her name *was* Sonia."

"That's right. She's dead."

"I'm sorry. So who is it you're looking for?"

"Her daughter."

"Do you have a photograph of the daughter?"

She shook her head. "No, unfortunately I don't.'

I frowned. "What's her name?"

"I don't know that either. You see, I don't know for sure that my sister ever had a daughter. She may have had a son, and there's a slight chance the child didn't survive at all."

I flicked my eyebrows, as if it had all come crystal clear. "I see. You want me to search for someone who may not exist and maybe never existed."

"Possibly."

I brightened. "A piece of cake. I handle this kind of case all the time. I've found Tinkerbell, the Tooth Fairy, Big Foot. It's my specialty."

The lady across from me wasn't amused. Her beautiful eyes narrowed.

"I'm not crazy, Mr. Cuesta, and this isn't a laughing matter."

We didn't speak again until the drinks arrived. I sipped mine and gave the waitress a chance to move away.

"I wasn't laughing," I said. "I'm just easily confused. Why don't we try it again and start at the beginning."

She put down her tea and tapped the photo with a long, red fingernail.

"My sister was twenty-one years old, a university student in Buenos Aires, when she joined the political movement against the military government in my country. That was more than twenty years ago. It was a dangerous thing to do, Mr. Cuesta. Military intelligence agents had a history of kidnapping the enemies of the government and sending them to secret detention centers and torture facilities."

She glanced up and I nodded. "Yes, I remember what went on. It was in the newspapers here in Miami."

"My sister was married, and her husband Mario was a leader of the movement at the school. She became pregnant and was eight months along, just as the kidnappings increased. My father had once served in the civilian government. In fact, he had been an assistant cabinet minister for foreign relations. Through old contacts he received word that the government wanted to grab Mario. The family decided that Mario and Sonia should go into hiding until the danger passed."

I glanced at the photo of the dead girl. "I assume they didn't hide well enough."

She shook her head. "The place wasn't the problem. A small apartment was found for them. They were the only ones hiding there, and they moved to it in the middle of the night. Only the closest friends and family members knew where it was, but none of us went, afraid we might be followed. Mario and Sonia never left it. They had plenty of food and didn't need to move.

"But just three days after they took refuge, government agents showed up, kicked in the door, put hoods over their heads, and dragged them away. Neighbors told us later that the agents went right to the apartment. They seemed to know exactly where Mario and Sonia were."

She paused and I sipped.

"What happened then?"

"Mario was tortured and murdered within hours. His body, what was left of it, was found much later buried near a military installation outside the city."

"And your sister?"

"Sonia was taken to a separate secret detention center. A naval facility right in Buenos Aires. Another student who was captured and tortured at the same time saw her there that same day. He lives here now. He and others have told us that Sonia was put in a special section for pregnant prisoners. From the stress of being captured, she went into early labor and gave birth. She was eventually disappeared. You know what it is to be disappeared, don't you?"

"Yes. It means no body was ever found."

"Exactly. Many families never know for sure if their loved one is alive or dead. In the case of my sister, we know. A document was later found at the detention center, a list of prisoners who had been executed. They were injected with drugs, placed on airplanes, and dropped into the ocean. The sharks were the coconspirators of military intelligence and made sure that the bodies would never be discovered. My sister's name was on that list."

I winced. I'd heard before of that Argentine practice for prisoner disposal, but it still was difficult to absorb. There was a surgical neatness to it, with the sharks as the surgeons.

And despite all the years that had passed, I could see it remained difficult for Ms. Bonaventura to recount. She paused and I didn't press her. To watch a woman so obviously well-to-do and sophisticated tell such a terrible story caused a deep sense of dislocation. These sorts of things weren't supposed to happen to anyone, but especially not to people who looked like her. Not in Argentina, not anywhere. I'm sure she felt the same way.

"What happened with the baby?" I asked finally.

"The same thing that happened to many other babies. My sister wasn't the only woman captured while she was pregnant. In fact, the government put a special policy in place. The women were allowed to give birth, and then they were eliminated. The other inmates at the prison would hear the newborn child cry but never see the mother again, or the child for that matter. The infants were given away to military families or other individuals with government connections."

"Is that what you think happened with your sister's child?"

She nodded. "Yes. Those persons raised the babies as their own. The children were never told about their true mothers or fathers. But in a number of cases, the real families, especially the grandmothers, have used DNA evidence to identify the children and claim them.

"We also know that some of those people who ended up with the babies escaped Argentina. They did it in order to avoid being accused and have the children taken away from them. They went to various countries. I believe that the couple who took my sister's child may be in Miami."

I kept nodding. I did that a lot when I wasn't quite sure what to say. I had heard the story of the Argentine babies. The "children of the disappeared" was what they were called, a strange phrase that made them sound like the offspring of ghosts—which in a sense they were. I'd never met anybody caught in the middle of that awful story. The thought left me momentarily speechless.

Fiona Bonaventura broke the silence.

"She was my only sibling, Mr. Cuesta. Her death broke the hearts of my parents. They both died shortly after. I have been searching for her child ever since."

She stared deep into my eyes, or rather, let me stare deep into hers.

"Who are these people who you think have the girl?"

"Their names are Manuel and Felicia Navarro."

"Do you know where they might be?"

"I know exactly where they are." She mentioned an address nearby on a street named Marseilles.

That surprised me. "How did you find them?"

"It wasn't I who found them. It was a friend of mine who was visiting here. She was walking down this very street in front of us, 71st Street, when she saw the child. She had known Sonia and was startled by the resemblance. She was also aware of what had happened to my sister, knew of my search, and thought right away, 'That could be Sonia's child.' She ran home and phoned me in Buenos Aires. I found a flight and came right away."

"Have you seen the girl?"

She nodded once. "I have. Yesterday, I went to that same spot where my friend had seen her. I waited for almost four hours and I spotted her. She is apparently studying somewhere because I saw her get off a bus with books in her arms. That was at five-thirty.

"I followed her to a building near here, watched her enter an apartment, and I read the names on the mailbox. After a while she came out again to speak on her cell phone. From across the street, I watched her again."

"And?"

Her eyes narrowed as if she were peering into a great distance.

"It was as if I were seeing my sister again, Mr. Cuesta. Not just the way she looked, but the way she moved, her expressions, her mannerisms. Everything. It was like seeing Sonia. I'm sure it's her child."

Of course, if you'd come all the way from Argentina, maybe you saw what you wanted to see. But she did have a look on her face of someone who'd seen a ghost, a ghost whom she loved.

"Did you try to speak to her?"

She shook her head. "No. Of course I wanted to very badly, but it might alarm her. Also I didn't want to warn those people who have her."

"So what do you want me to do?"

She leaned forward. "I need you to find out who they really are and where they come from. I want you to prove that the child is not really theirs, that they took Sonia's baby after she was born at the detention center. I need you to get her back for me. I also want to know if they were involved in my sister's death, because if they were, I want them put in prison."

I raised my eyebrows. "That's all?"

"Yes."

She didn't catch the irony.

"That will probably take a few days to accomplish, and I can't promise anything."

I told her my daily rate, and her face went even more pallid. She bit her lovely lips, and her accent had even more aria in it than usual.

"I'm here with my husband, Mr. Cuesta. He didn't want to make this trip to Miami. He always opposed the political activities of Sonia and Mario and believes that we will never find any child. I am refusing to go on with life, that's what he says to me. It is his money that I am using to pay you, and he is losing patience. Please do what you can in a few days."

She transformed those dark blue eyes into pools of woe. They were like patches of Biscayne Bay, and I was like a stiff with a chunk of concrete chained to my foot. I jumped in and sank right to the bottom.

CHAPTER THREE

I dropped Fiona Bonaventura where she was staying, a condo complex a few blocks away on Collins Avenue.

It was one of those seaside palaces occupied by rich Latin Americans. They were looking for somewhere safe to invest their money and also someplace secure they could escape to, just in case their countries' political systems collapsed. Similar buildings stretched up and down Miami Beach. I imagined that being in one was a bit like visiting a posh country club in Cali or Caracas.

I waited for her in the car. The parking valet at the door eyed my aging red Le Baron convertible with barely concealed disdain. I sneered back at him.

A few minutes later she came back down and handed me a two-day advance. A short, slim man in an off-white suit, holding a briefcase, stood behind her.

"This is my husband, Eduardo Estevez. He would like to have a word with you."

She gave me an apologetic roll of the eyes.

"Sure," I said, to put her out of her misery.

She disappeared inside, and Estevez climbed into my car without asking.

"I'm in a hurry to reach a business meeting. We'll speak right here if that is acceptable."

What was acceptable was asking first.

In addition to the suit, he wore a crisp, sky-blue shirt with a gold tie and a jeweled gold wristwatch. His hair was blond, and his eyes were light brown tinged with gold as well. It was as if he had eaten the stuff since childhood—gold, that is. It would have made me feel better if he looked gaudy. But he didn't. He had the continental polish of most upper-echelon Argentines. He was a golden boy.

"I want to assure myself that my wife isn't being taken advantage of," he said, toying with the combination lock on his briefcase. "As you

10

must have heard already, this is a matter of great emotion for her."

I shrugged. "If you want, I'll give you a list of Miami police officers who will vouch for the fact that I'm not a crud. They may not have much else to say, but they'll tell you I'm not a sleazebag."

Estevez didn't respond to that exactly.

"I want you to understand that I, like Fiona, want to find this child if it exists. But I think it is very unlikely we will do so. I can't afford to finance what you Americans would call a fishing expedition."

As a matter of fact, he looked like he could bankroll the whole South Florida fishing fleet and have some left over. But he didn't give me a chance to mention it. He became agitated.

"Do you know how long this has been part of my life, Cuesta? Twenty years! I live in a world of ghosts. Fiona and I had been married only a short time when all this occurred. She and her sister were not close at the time. We were barely acquainted with Mario Murillo, Sonia's husband. But these people who I hardly knew, who I had nothing in common with, who have been dead for two decades, are still present in my life."

"I take it that you didn't agree with their politics."

He shook his head hard. "Definitely not. It was irresponsible and stupid of them to become involved in all of that. I told them it put us all in danger, and my wife agreed with me.

"But then Sonia and Mario disappeared. The moment that Fiona found out that her sister's child might have survived, her life changed completely. We have no children of our own, and that child became the central preoccupation of her existence. I've lived with this search all these years."

The fact they didn't have kids went a long way toward explaining Fiona's obsession. But I didn't say that.

"Your wife told me you didn't want her to come here."

"No, I didn't. What happens the next time someone sees a girl who looks like Sonia? Will it be here, or in New York, or London or Africa? Will we go there, too? I want to put it to rest once and for all. We can't sacrifice our entire lives to this."

"I'll do my best to resolve it quickly."

I said it because it was true, but also because his cologne had become a bit cloying in the close confines of the car.

"For the money you're charging, I certainly expect you to."

I gave him my best smile and he got out.

Since I was already in the area and already hot, I drove back to check the address Fiona Bonaventura had given me for the Navarros. It took me past the El Gaucho restaurant again and past a Latin supermarket that had been there a long time, even before the Argentines had arrived. They were advertising sales on *yuca, malanga* root, and one-hundred-pound sacks of rice. If you had any doubt you were in a neighborhood that had turned Latin in recent years, all you had to do was go to the corner and try to buy a frozen dinner. Good luck.

The address was on Marseilles Street, about a half mile away. It was a complex of garden apartments, although given the recent heat and lack of rain, the only "garden" the place had going for it was some brown grass in the central courtyard and a few curled crotons in the flowerbeds.

The complex backed up to a canal that fed Biscayne Bay. The buildings were coral-colored stucco, built in the Art Deco style, with some baroque touches, including fluted columns framing the entranceway. For some reason it was called the Colonial Arms, although it looked about as colonial as an aluminum beach chair.

I passed through the portal into the courtyard and found two stories of apartments on each side. A row of mailboxes was built into the wall near the entrance. All the names were Latin—Mendoza, Rosas, Duarte, Galindos.

Taped on the box for Apartment 12 was a strip of yellowed paper. Written on it was the name "Navarro." I looked up and saw that Apartment 12 was on the second floor, across the way, overlooking the canal. At least they had a nice view.

I crossed the courtyard, climbed the stairs, and drifted slowly by the door. The blinds were slightly open but I didn't see any movement inside. I didn't hear anything either.

The rest of the apartments were closed and quiet as well, it being the middle of the workday. But there was life down at the rear of the courtyard. Near the edge of the canal, a woman sat at a round metal table equipped with an umbrella.

A dried bougainvillea bush grew on the edge of the canal. She had picked up a handful of the red petals and was dropping them one by one over the railing into the canal, where they floated slowly toward the bay. Before her sat a small pitcher and a couple of glasses, as if she were awaiting company.

I walked down the stairs to her. *"Buenas tardes."*

My greeting surprised her. When she looked up I saw she was a woman around sixty, with a large head and a thick halo of salt-and-pepper hair. Her skin was bronzed and her features were strong, especially a long straight nose and high cheekbones. Her face looked as if it might have been chiseled from stone by a sculptor. Her most salient feature was a large pair of glinting, granite-colored eyes.

She dropped the last petal into the canal and fixed on me.

"You're hot," she said.

"Just a bit."

She poured the second glass full and pushed it at me.

"Sit and have some tea."

I wasn't the person she was waiting for, but I guess I was good enough.

On a chair next to her were a textbook for the teaching of Spanish and a pile of test papers that she was in the process of grading. People of all kinds, who came running to Miami from Latin America, managed to scrape out a living teaching Spanish. Given the glut of Spanish-speakers, the pay was low, and the life wasn't easy. The pile of papers was thick.

I sat, tasted the tea, and we introduced ourselves. Her name was María Terán.

"You shouldn't be out in this sun," she said, with an accent that was distinctly Argentine.

"My feelings exactly."

"Who are you looking for?"

"The family of a friend of mine. Their last name is Navarro."

She pointed up to Apartment 12. "But they're not home."

"I'm not certain this is the right family. Can you tell me where they're from?"

"Buenos Aires."

I nodded. "Yes, this family is also from Buenos Aires."

She shrugged, as if there was no other place to be from.

"Are you from there as well?" I asked.

"Oh yes. Although I've already lived in this country for some time."

She didn't seem too happy about that state of affairs. She gazed at the canal where water moved slowly, as if it were the passage of her life.

"You would prefer to be in Buenos Aires?"

She rolled her eyes. "How can you ask such a question? Of course, I would. Don't misunderstand me, people here in Miami have been kind to me. But compared to Buenos Aires, Miami is a fishing village. The fishermen dance *salsa* and *merengue* very well, but compared to my city, it is still a village."

She shot me a look, as if she knew she was being a bad girl.

"Buenos Aires is certainly a beautiful city," I said.

She brightened. "You've been there?"

"Very briefly."

Years before, I had flown down for two days on an extradition expedition. From the airport I'd traveled to the hotel, the next day I'd made my way to the Marcos Paz prison to pick up my prisoner and then back to the airport. I'd taken only one side trip: the first night, the FBI liaison at the U.S. embassy had invited me to see and do some late-night tango dancing. He'd spent most of the night laughing at my style.

But I had seen the wide, European-style boulevards of Buenos Aires and appreciated its classical architecture. I understood how a twentieth-century city like Miami might not be María Terán's cup of tea.

"So why did you leave beautiful Buenos Aires and come here?"

She reflected on that a moment. "Let's just say I came following someone I loved."

"Well, at least you left for a good reason."

She pursed her lips and nodded wistfully. I had the feeling her voyage north in search of love had not worked out the way she'd wanted. Maybe that was why she was dropping bougainvillea petals into the canal.

Age has its privileges. One of them is speaking to total strangers about the tragedies and longings of your life and being listened to, at least for a few moments. But there was work to do. I pointed up at Apartment 12.

"Do you know what Mr. Navarro did in Argentina? Was he a soldier or in the government?"

She shook her head. "I don't believe so. He told me that he drove a taxi."

"I see."

Of course, if you were the right Navarro, you didn't tell neighbors that in Argentina you had worked as a war criminal or a kidnapper of babies.

"The man you're looking for, what does he look like?" she asked.

"Oh, I've never seen him or his wife. I only know their nephew, if it's the right Manuel Navarro."

She arched an eyebrow. "I've never heard them mention a nephew."

"He told me he had a cousin, a girl who's quite beautiful."

Now she frowned at me. She obviously didn't like my interest in the girl. Maybe I'd made it sound as if the imaginary nephew lusted for his female cousin, which wasn't acceptable behavior. Or possibly she thought I had designs of my own, and I was distinctly too old for her. The girl would be around twenty and I'm twice that.

"Yes, she's very beautiful, but very young," she said firmly. "Anyway, they're not home. The father and mother are at work and Elena studies. She's an art student, very talented, and she works very hard."

She said it pointedly, so that a lusting lout like me would lose interest in her.

"I guess I'll have to come back later."

"Who should I tell them was looking for them?"

I didn't want to leave a business card imprinted with the word "investigations."

"Just tell them I was looking for the Navarros and that I'm a friend of their nephew."

She gave me a curt nod, and I walked off with my tail between my legs.

CHAPTER FOUR

The waning afternoon brought no relief from the heat. At five o'clock I was back in the neighborhood, sitting in my car only partially shaded by a palm tree. My air conditioner raced like a patient with his blood pressure way out of whack.

A music store across the street pumped out tango tunes. At the moment a crooner—maybe the same one I'd heard earlier outside El Gaucho—was complaining of a femme fatale "dressed by night and moonlight," who had used him and abused him and left him for dead. Argentine men seemed to have a very rough time of it, even worse than most.

I was doing surveillance. I wanted to get a look at the girl, so I was parked near the spot where Fiona had first seen her. That was on 71st Street near the bus stop.

"She got off the bus with books in her arms," Fiona had told me. "That was at five-thirty."

The photo of Fiona's late sister lay on the seat next to me. I watched several buses stop and pull away. People got off, most of them somber after a day's work.

In Miami, given the history of Latin America over the past fifty years and all the people who had come running for their lives, you never knew who you were looking at. Was the old guy with the lunch pail a former general, now working as a janitor? Was the woman with the highlighted hair a one-time Latin debutante, now doing business as a beautician? You never knew. Identity was a very fluid matter in Miami.

A few minutes after five-thirty a bus pulled up and several people got out. The last of them was a slim young woman with jet-black hair, wearing faded jeans speckled with paint stains and a sleeveless black top. She had on a small backpack and carried books in one arm. The light changed and she crossed the street right toward me.

As she approached I looked down at the photo and then back at her. I understood right away why Fiona Bonaventura's acquaintance had

16

phoned her in Argentina. The girl was a twenty-first-century version of the woman in the photograph. It was like looking at a beautiful young ghost.

She glanced at me as she went by, and we made eye contact. Given her ravishing looks she had to be accustomed to guys gawking at her. She threw her hair over her shoulder and glanced away. I turned and watched her go down the street. She didn't look back. I guess I didn't do it for her.

I started the car, drove around the block, and turned onto Marseilles Street, just in time to see her enter the Colonial Arms. She crossed the courtyard, climbed the stairs, and disappeared into Apartment 12.

I parked across the way at an angle. From there I had a clear view through the arched entranceway to the apartment door. Reaching into the back seat, I grabbed my camera bag, brought out my camera body, and snapped a longish lens in place.

A catamaran was cruising up the canal on the far side of the building. A blond woman in a very small red bikini was stretched out on the near pontoon. I adjusted the lens and brought her into excruciatingly clear focus. I snapped one of her. Then I let her sail away and I focused on Unit 12. I brought the number into clear view and snapped a picture of the door just for the record. Then I put the camera down and waited.

The lady who I'd spoken to earlier, María Terán, was no longer in evidence. She had been replaced by several children splashing in a plastic pool at the rear of the courtyard.

Just short of six p.m. I saw a black car pull into a driveway behind the complex. Moments later I saw two people emerge from that driveway, enter the complex, and walk together across the courtyard. They appeared to be a couple.

The man was square-shouldered and stocky, powerfully built, with short bristly gray hair like a steel brush and a grim expression. The woman was shorter, extremely thin, with bottle-blond hair to go with a very pale complexion. She wore aquamarine-colored hospital scrubs, like those a nurse's aide or orderly might wear.

They stopped at the mailboxes. Through the lens I saw the man open number 12 and lock it again. As they climbed the stairs they were facing me, and I took several frames of them. They then walked down the veranda and entered the last unit.

I could see their faces fairly well through the long lens, and I noticed no resemblance between either of them and the girl. But if they were Manuel and Felicia Navarro, the alleged baby stealers, there wouldn't be.

I did the math. Each appeared to be about sixty years old, which meant they would have been approximately forty when they had taken the child. The chronology made sense. Maybe they had tried to have their own children and failed. It didn't excuse anything, but it was an explanation.

A minute later something strange happened. The door opened and the young woman stepped out by herself, dressed as she had been earlier. She walked very deliberately to the end of the veranda and leaned against the railing. She looked over the canal to the bay beyond.

She stood perfectly still for several minutes, like a young wife waiting for a sea captain husband to sail back from years on the oceans. Or maybe a young widow who knew her love would not return. There was something tragic in the tilt of her shoulders and in the intensity of her stillness. In fact, for a moment I thought she would jump into the canal.

She didn't. The kids carousing in the plastic pool were calling to her, and she finally turned. They waved at her, but she didn't wave back. Instead she headed once again into the apartment. As she did, I took her photo.

I sat for some time waiting to see if anyone else showed up. The sun sank in the west, so that the windows of nearby buildings went all iridescent. José Feliciano's version of "Light My Fire" played in my head.

I was still there, dazzled by the light, when I saw one of the little girls get out of the pool, climb the stairs still dripping water, and knock on the door of Apartment 12. After a few seconds she knocked again, but no one answered. Finally she gave up and padded away barefoot to her own house.

I had seen the entire Navarro family file into the apartment less than an hour earlier. Now nobody was answering. It was still too early for prime-time television, so the possibility that they were glued to the tube was unlikely. Of course, there could be other reasons for their being unwilling to come to the door—dinner, showers, naps—but the scene made me nervous.

I put the camera down, climbed out of the car, crossed the street and courtyard, took the stairs, and walked to Apartment 12. The blinds were now closed. I stopped and listened, but heard nothing. So I knocked.

I figured when someone came to the door I could claim I was in the wrong apartment complex. Or maybe the moment Manuel Navarro looked into my eyes he would know the jig was up. He would spill the whole sordid story. Such was the inescapable weight of truth and justice in my baby browns.

I waited for the door to open, but it didn't. I put my ear against it and couldn't hear a thing: no television, no radio, no nothing. I knocked, this time much harder, but no one responded. So I tried the knob and it turned.

The moment I walked in I knew they were gone. The unit had a back door beyond the kitchen, and it stood wide open. Through it, I could see stairs heading down. I went to the landing and found that the staircase led to the rear driveway, where the black car had pulled in. You could take that driveway toward the canal, turn left, and reach the next side street. The car was gone, and that was certainly where it had gone.

I went back into the apartment. On the sofa in the living room lay a small suitcase left behind, with clothes strewn next to it and on the floor.

I walked into the two bedrooms and found bureau drawers gaping open. Closets were devoid of clothes, with tangles of wire hangers underfoot. Cheap art still hung on the walls, including a faded print of a gaucho chasing a steer across an Argentine plain. And the furniture was still there. But all personal items—photographs, toiletries, fuzzy slippers—were gone. The Navarros had taken it on the lam.

The girl obviously had occupied the smaller bedroom, the one with the single bed. Glossy posters of American and Latin musicians were tacked to the walls, and a couple of oil paintings hung up there with them. They were portraits, but with wild brushstrokes and colors, so that the people seemed to be coming painfully apart at the seams. I looked closely and saw the signature—"Elena." That was it, no last name. Well, if you were an art student on the run your whole life, maybe that was the way you saw people, as coming apart at the seams.

I searched the drawers and found nothing to help me, except for a transcript from Miami School of Art and Design. Elena Navarro had gotten three A's and two B's in her previous semester. As María Terán had said, the girl studied hard and didn't have time for a lout like me.

I did find one thing on the bureau in the larger bedroom: it was a flyer from a dance joint called the "San Telmo Tango Club" in Miami. On the back were written a combination of letters and numbers: "GT—332." I had no idea what that referred to, but I pocketed it.

I drifted back to the kitchen. Everything there appeared to have been left behind, including two large ceramic gourds, the kind that Argentines use to brew their *mate*, a sort of tea.

I poked around a bit more, but found nothing to indicate where they might have gone. Given that Navarro might be a wanted war criminal, they most likely had done this before. I remembered how the girl had come out of the apartment and looked longingly out over the canal. She had probably just heard that they were moving again. I wondered how they explained the moves to her. It must have been quite a story.

But right then I was more concerned with the fine story I would have to spin for my client. Somehow I'd managed to tip off the Navarros. It had taken Fiona Bonaventura twenty years to find the girl, and I had lost her in one afternoon.

CHAPTER FIVE

I left, closing both the back and front doors to the deserted apartment. I walked across the courtyard to the mailboxes, identified the one belonging to María Terán, and knocked on the door of Apartment 2.

She answered the door dressed as she had been before, with a small vase of flowers in one hand.

"Yes?"

"Ms. Terán, I'm wondering if you were able to reach Mr. or Mrs. Navarro and tell them I was here earlier."

She shook her head. "No, I didn't. I haven't had time."

"Are you sure?"

I was ticked off, and my tone wasn't too friendly. She frowned.

"Why do you ask me this?"

"Because they've taken off."

Her frown deepened. "What do you mean?"

"I mean they're gone, moved out. And I can't figure out why they would leave unless maybe you told them something."

She didn't like being questioned and called a liar on top of it. Her chin came up and her gray eyes grew flinty.

"I told you I didn't communicate with them. And why would they run away just because you came looking for them?" Her eyes narrowed. "Or maybe you weren't telling me the truth about who you are and what you are doing here."

She was treating me like a bill collector. I started to protest, but she waved a hand in an authoritative manner, brushing me away.

"This has nothing to do with me. Please, leave me alone." She closed the door in my face.

I was going to pound on it again, but she might call the cops. That would only make matters worse.

Instead I headed for my car. As I stalked off the premises, I saw a sign posted on the outside of the building. It identified the company that

21

managed the complex, Gold Coast Realty. According to the sign, the offices were located at an address on 69th Street. So I drove over there. I found the place about five blocks away. On one side of it stood a Latin convenience store, its front window full of phone cards that could be used to call everywhere in Latin America, from Tijuana to Tierra del Fuego.

On the other side was a travel agency. It advertised cheap flights to all the same locales, when a telephone call just wouldn't do the trick. That same business offered money orders, passport photos, translations, and immigration counseling, an all-purpose supermarket for immigrants.

Squeezed between those two businesses was the realty office. In the front window were faded Polaroid photos of apartments and condominiums with bilingual descriptions of their conveniences. Seasonal rentals were available.

It was now past normal business hours, but a light was still on inside. I took the opportunity to duck in.

The office turned out to be not just a realtor's operation, but a management and maintenance depot as well. In addition to two gray metal desks, the room contained a couple of refrigerators, several air conditioners, and half a dozen wooden doors leaning everywhere against the walls. The numerous portals gave the place an "Alice in Wonderland" flavor.

I was trying to decide which door led to the Mad Hatter when one of them opened and a guy came out drying his hands. A small, narrow-shouldered, gaunt man, he was bald, with a pate that was extremely shiny. In fact, it looked like he waxed it. Around it was a sparse fringe of gray hair.

He wore a dark gray suit with a pale yellow shirt and a tie in a stained-glass design. His thick glasses caught the reflection of the fluorescent lights, so when he looked at me his eyes were momentarily full of an otherworldly light.

"I'm sorry but the office is closed," he said in the same Argentine accent I'd heard all day. "You will have to come back in the morning."

"That's alright because I'm not here to rent or buy anything."

I produced my wallet and flashed my investigator's license. He looked down at it, and his eyes flared a bit. They were bloodshot, with dark rings around them, as if he didn't sleep a lot. He appeared to have bad nerves. I couldn't imagine why. The real estate market was booming.

"Are you the owner of the agency?" I asked.

"Lord, no. I'm only the property manager."

He said it as if he hoped that would get him off the hook. At the same time he moved behind the desk. I saw business cards propped there and picked up one that identified him as Benito Corral.

"I'd like some information on two of your tenants, Mr. Corral."

He frowned. "Which tenants are you referring to?"

"Manuel and Felicia Navarro."

The pronunciation of those names produced a marked reaction in the little man. He crooked a finger and ran it around the collar of his yellow shirt, which wasn't tight to begin with. Then he glanced at all those doors around us, as if he would like to disappear through one of them, except he didn't know which one was real. Finally, he came back to me, shook his head, and took a transparently false stance on the issue.

"It would be wrong of me to say anything about tenants. I can't give out private information."

"I'm glad you're so concerned about the interests of your tenants, Mr. Corral. I wish these particular individuals were as loyal to you as you are to them. They just moved out of Apartment 12 at the Colonial Arms, and I doubt they gave you notice. The place is empty."

Corral didn't believe me. He stalked over to a filing cabinet, went down on one knee, opened the bottom drawer, rifled through the contents, removed a manila folder, and brought it to the desk. He found a phone number and punched it into the phone with a shaky finger. He glanced up at me, and I gave him my sunniest smile.

Nobody answered and he hung up. Then he picked up a two-way radio from a charger behind the desk. He called someone named Pedro, asked if he was working near the Marseilles building, and dispatched him to the Navarro unit.

I took the opportunity to sit down in a swivel chair across the desk. On the table against the wall I noticed a *mate* gourd, much like the ones I'd seen in the Navarro's apartment, except this one was made of wood. A metal strainer sat next to it.

"You're from Argentina, aren't you?" I asked.

He said he was, although he didn't seem any more enthusiastic about that than he was about anything else at the moment.

"Been here long?"

He didn't bother to answer.

Pedro called back a couple of minutes later. I could hear the crackling voice over the radio.

"The place is cleaned out, Corral. They're gone. No clothes, no luggage. No nothing. Over."

Corral placed the radio back in the charger, dropped into his chair, and swiveled back to me. The news didn't make him mad, as I'd expected it would. At first it left him deep in thought, almost as if he were meditating. Then he seemed apprehensive. For a landlord, the reaction was unexpected. When he spoke finally, his tone was totally altered.

"Why were you looking for them?" he asked, trying to sound offhand.

I decided that we were on the same side and honesty would be the best policy.

"I believe Navarro is a war criminal from your country and that he and his wife may have stolen a child, one of the children of the disappeared."

That shocked him, as I figured it would. Given his nerves, it also scared him. "Why would you think that?"

"Because their daughter, or at least the young woman they call their daughter, may have been born to a woman who was murdered by agents of the government in Buenos Aires twenty years ago. Navarro may have been involved in killing her. The dead woman's family believes that is so. After seeing the Navarros and the girl, I think it is a distinct possibility."

He folded his hands in front of him, as if he was praying, and shook his head.

"*Dios mío*, will this never end?"

"Will what never end?"

"All this about the dirty war. It goes on and on."

The "dirty war," I knew, was what Argentines called that nasty period in their history when Sonia Bonaventura and her husband had been killed. They used that terminology to distinguish it from other wars, which were never very clean to begin with.

"Were you there during that time?" I asked him.

He nodded absently as if his mind were elsewhere.

"Did you leave because of it?"

His head came up and he fixed on me. "No, I came much later. And like most people, I came looking for work, trying to earn my daily bread. But I think everyone who left my country has, in the end, had to leave because of what happened during those days. I believe we, as a people, are all being punished because of those times. It's a kind of curse, an Argentine corner of hell that came into being after Dante."

He fell silent again and stared at his folded hands. Corral was apparently an educated man, with much more intellect than was needed to keep track of tenants and refrigerators for a real estate company. Again, identities and destinies were very fluid in Miami.

"Well, Mr. Corral, Navarro may have been one of those who created that circle of hell," I said. "You could help me by telling me what you know about him and his wife."

Corral shook his head nervously, like a hummingbird, a bald hummingbird.

"I don't know anything about them."

"Really? Your firm rented an apartment to them. You don't know if they were serial killers or bagpipe players?"

"I only rent people some room. I can't look into their souls."

His hands were folded so tightly his knuckles were white. He seemed scared, maybe of me, but maybe of somebody or something else. Maybe of Navarro.

I smiled again. "I'm not the secret police or Argentine military intelligence, Mr. Corral."

But that didn't reassure him. He shook his head harder.

Just then the radio squawked, and he swiveled to answer it. The Navarro folder lay open, and I saw a form labeled "Rental Application." While Corral was distracted, I slid the folder noiselessly to me, turning it so I could read.

The application listed Manuel and Felicia Navarro as the renters, and a daughter, Elena, as the only other tenant. It said that Manuel worked as a "clerk/driver" at a place called International Protection Services, an ironic employer for a man who may have helped murder quite a few people.

Felicia, according to the rental application, was a nurse's aide at Jackson Memorial Hospital.

It also listed two personal references. The first was "Sara Ingram" and under relationship it said "cousin of Manuel Navarro." The second was "Sergio Villarreal," who was identified as a diplomat at the Argentine consulate in Miami. They both had phone numbers listed next to them, and I quickly jotted them down in a notebook.

I had just finished the second one when Corral swiveled back, glared at me, grabbed the folder, and closed it. Righteous indignation filled his bloodshot eyes.

"You must leave now. I'm closing the office."

I figured I'd have to add Corral to the long list of people who would never rent to me.

I got up and headed for the door—the real door, not one of the Wonderland ones. As I did, the small man murmured something that seemed strange at the time—strange and just a bit scary.

"God bless you," he said.

CHAPTER SIX

I climbed back in my car and reviewed the phone numbers I'd copied from Corral. The consulate would be closed by now. So I dialed information and got an address for Navarro's cousin, Sara Ingram. It was in a town called Glades Springs, about thirty minutes northwest of Miami. There was a chance that was where the Navarros had headed.

I dropped the film I'd shot at a pharmacy and then I headed north. The traffic had dried up. I made good time and pulled into the burg of Glades Springs even sooner than I'd figured. It was a well-to-do suburban bedroom enclave divided into communities—some gated, some not—with names like Commonwealth Corners and Tudor Heights. Despite the short distance I'd traveled, I had left Latin Miami way behind and might as well have been in another world. My chances of being able to buy an empanada or a chorizo in the town was very small. At least it looked that way.

I passed several of those communities before I found Fairweather Road where the cousin lived. It was in a subdivision called The Fountains because each house had one on the front lawn.

There was no guard at the entrance, but a private security vehicle drove by me as I searched for the house, and the driver gave me a long look before pulling away.

I found the Ingram residence, a split-level palazzo toward the rear of the housing development at the end of a cul de sac. I didn't see Navarro's black car anywhere. In fact, there were no vehicles in the driveway.

Instead, four teenage boys played basketball at a hoop against the garage, which was illuminated by a spotlight. I walked past a conch-shaped fountain on the lawn and managed to get the attention of a tall, crew cut boy who had just shot a layup.

"I'm looking for Mrs. Sara Ingram."

"My mom's not here, she's still teaching," he said, dribbling the ball between his legs.

"Teaching?"

"At the dance studio."

"Where can I find that studio?"

He pointed vaguely to the west. "It's in the shopping center."

"I see. Her cousin Manuel isn't around, is he?"

He shook his head, dribbling behind his back. "No, Uncle Manuel and Aunt Felicia haven't been here lately."

I thanked him, headed back toward town, turned into a mall just off the main drag, and spotted a sign for the Galaxy Ballroom dance studio on the second floor. I parked, took a narrow interior staircase up, and heard the dramatic strains of tango music, particularly an accordion, filtering down to me.

At the top of the stairs I passed through a glass door, then a thick black curtain, and found myself in the salon. A spacious parquet dance floor was surrounded by mirrored walls. Hanging at the center of the room was a mirrored ball, and, as it rotated, beams of light swirled around the space. Thus, the Galaxy Ballroom.

Just inside the door stood a rack marked "Women's Tango Shoes." On it were about thirty pairs of high heels, all of them in brilliant glossy black, one with more straps than the next. In polite society, these were known as "procreation pumps." If you were a woman and didn't understand what tango was really about, the shoes would sure make it was clear to you.

A few folding chairs were lined up against one wall, but no one was in them. On the dance floor were five couples, although two of those couples were comprised of women. A shortage of males was obvious, as it was in most dance classes.

All the students appeared to be Anglos. The couples were arranged in a straight line, posed in a variation of the classic tango position—clutching each other with one arm and with the other arm extended.

Standing apart from them was the teacher, who I assumed was Sara Ingram. She had the same swarthy complexion as her cousin Navarro, but with short black hair. Probably in her early forties, she was petite, well-proportioned, and well-toned. She wore a black sequined top, tight black pants, and black heels. She was reflected in the mirrored walls everywhere you looked, multiplied again and again. She was a one-woman chorus line.

The music in the background was brooding and dramatic. Her voice was feminine but firm and rose above the music.

"Remember, you are not dancing with your legs You are dancing with your hearts and your souls. More than anything, your passions. Ready now . . ." She waited for the right beat of the music and called out, "One, two, three, four . . ."

The students paced the traditional tango steps. They stopped at the end of an eight count, as their teacher called, "Turn!" Then they glided back in the other direction.

Some of them pulled off the tense tango pose better than others. One of the men, a hulking guy who looked like a former high school linebacker, appeared more constipated than commanding, as he led his partner through the passes.

"Feel it!" Sara Ingram called out as the orchestra took the music to a crescendo. "Act as if you are great dancers already. That is the only way you will ever dance tango."

At one point she grabbed one of the better male dancers and did a demonstration. She led him, more than he did her, moving precisely and sinuously, with a simmering sensuality. At the end of one step, she pointed her toe, then wrapped her foot around his lower leg, arched her back in an act of submission, and stared deep into his eyes. The swirling lights played over her sequins and made her gaze boil with intensity. By the time she pulled away again, the guy was on the brink of a stroke. You got the feeling that Sara Ingram enjoyed playing the tango temptress with her white suburban students.

She put her class through a few more paces, straightening backs, adjusting the placement of men's fingers along the women's spinal cords, and adjusting tango attitudes, too. Finally she called it quits.

"Wednesday at the same time. Ciao."

The students gathered their stuff and filed out, until I was finally left alone with her. It was only then that she noticed me.

"Would you like to sign up?" she asked. "We need men."

"I'm not ready to sign up quite yet, although it looks interesting. Are you Sara Ingram?"

"That's right."

"I'm sorry to disturb you, but I'm an investigator from Miami. I'm looking for your cousin Manuel Navarro."

Her mouth fell open. The juxtaposition of her cousin's name and the word "investigator" clearly made her less than comfortable.

"Is there some kind of trouble?" But from the look of fear in her eyes, I think she knew there was trouble. Maybe there always had been when it came to her cousin Manuel. We both were reflected endlessly in the mirrors all around and the look on her face, multiplied many times, appeared like a deep history of fear.

"Do you know where he is?" I asked.

"He doesn't live here in Glades Springs."

"Yes, I know that, but . . ."

A voice came from behind me and cut me off.

"What is it, Sara?"

I turned and found a man standing just inside the curtain. He was a large man with close-cropped graying hair, a florid complexion, and a widow's peak. But it was his outfit that really distinguished him. He wore white riding britches, high leather boots, and a red pullover shirt with a large white "3" on the front. He was dressed a bit like a jockey, except he had to be at least six foot two and weigh two hundred pounds. It would be a very sorry racehorse that had to carry this guy.

He approached us, and we were all reflected in the mirrors. A strange threesome we were: the lady in sequins, the extra-large jockey, and me, the cabana boy.

"What's wrong, Sara?"

"This man is asking about Manuel."

"Can I help you?" he asked.

"Are you Mr. Ingram?"

"That's right."

"As I was telling your wife, I'm looking for Manuel Navarro and his wife and daughter."

He nodded once. "And as Sara told you, they don't live here."

"I know that, but they disappeared suddenly today."

That made him frown. "Who are you?"

I took out my wallet and showed him my ID.

"So you're not a policeman. You're private."

"That's right, and I was hired to find them. But right after I did find them, they disappeared. They cleaned out their apartment on Miami Beach. That was this afternoon."

He folded his big arms across his chest. When he did, I was able to read a patch on his right shoulder—South Florida Polo Club. That explained the outfit.

"And just why were you hired to find them?"

"It's a very delicate matter."

The big man rocked on the heels of his riding boots. "We can take it."

So I told them, as delicately as I could. I didn't mention Fiona by name, and I didn't accuse the Navarros of anything illegal. I only raised the possibility that, unknowingly, they had adopted a child born in captivity.

Even before I finished, Ingram was frowning and shaking his head. "We don't know what you're talking about. They have Elena's birth certificate. It says Manuel and Felicia are her parents. What you're saying is all horse manure."

I turned to Sara Navarro. "Could Manuel and Felicia have children of their own?"

I thought she started to shake her head, but Ingram cut her off before she could speak.

"Sara, don't say anything to this man."

He was almost twice her size, the kind of difference that gives some of us graphic visions of other people's sex lives. But there was nothing sexy about the scene. She was scared and he was angry. I had the feeling that Sara Ingram might be able to twist men around her finger—or her leg—on the tango floor, but at home hubby was the boss.

"I've told you we don't know anything about what you're asking," he said. "And we don't like you coming here, accusing our family members of crimes."

"I'm not accusing them of anything, Mr. Ingram. Just because Manuel was in the military doesn't mean he did anything wrong during the troubles down there. He was in the military, wasn't he?"

I turned back to Sara. She didn't respond to my question. "Have they called you? Do you know where they are?"

Again she didn't respond, but at the back of her frightened gaze I saw a truth trying to hide.

From the back pocket of his britches, Ingram had extracted a leather riding crop, and he held it clutched in his right hand, as if he were ready to whip me out the door. I was lucky he didn't have his polo mallet with him.

"I told you we don't know what you're talking about. We're locking up now."

Again, it wasn't worth doing anything that would attract the police, or a riding crop to the side of the head. I eased a business card from my shirt pocket and placed it gently on a chair next to his wife. Then I decided to get out of the suburbs and head back to the inner city, before I got hurt.

CHAPTER SEVEN

I got home and poured myself a rum and tonic with a twist of lime. Then I took from the refrigerator a fish I'd bought that afternoon on my way back from Miami Beach. I stoked up the grill in the backyard and phoned Alice Arden, Esquire.

"It's me."

"Uh-huh."

"I think I've fallen in love with a mahi-mahi."

There was only the slightest pause as she processed the news.

"Is it mutual?"

"Yes, it is."

"How do you know?"

"The way she looks at me. She can't take her eye off me."

"Well, don't get in over your head. Are you inviting me to dinner?"

"If you haven't already eaten, yes."

"I haven't. I just got in. Is that all you want?"

"No, I need your legal expertise. I'm on a case that will interest you."

"I'll be there."

Alice lives not far away, in a condo overlooking the Miami River. She arrived twenty minutes later wearing black tights, a T-shirt from the Sorbonne, and bearing a covered salad bowl.

Alice Arden is a handsome woman, tall, lean, with shoulder-length straight blond hair, brown eyes the color of root beer Lifesavers, slim hips, and colt's legs. When she worked as a public defender, they called her "the snow queen," in part because she defended lots of low-level cocaine dealers, but also because she's pale.

These days she's in private practice doing immigration law, representing refugees from all corners of the earth, and performing pro bono human rights litigation on the side.

Alice looked down at the fish. "I understand the attraction. You've always liked bony women."

"Bony and cold-blooded, like you."

"I'm not cold-blooded, just discerning."

In the past, I have expressed my attraction to Alice. She, in turn, has told me she has no interest in younger men. I don't know exactly how old she is, but the difference between us can't be more than a handful of years. I think the real issue is that she prefers not to mix business with pleasure. I can't argue with that. I've worked various cases with her over the past several years, and we work well together. But she's still good-looking.

I poured her a glass of white wine while she took a knife to her competition. I do the buying, she does the cooking. When she finished, two filets lay next to each other on the plate, looking like the wings of a fleshy butterfly. We went out back, laid them on the grill, and sat. The sun was down now and the worst of the heat had passed.

"So how was your day?" I asked.

She shrugged. "Nothing exotic."

By that she meant she had handled immigration problems for her usual array of Haitians, Cubans, Colombians, Venezuelans, and other assorted Latins and Caribbeans. For Alice, exotic meant Manchurian or Muritanian.

"How 'bout you?"

"I had a torrid encounter with an Argentine beauty."

"Do tell."

So I filled her in on the noontime meeting with Fiona Bonaventura, the story of her sister and the alleged niece. Even though she had heard lots of lurid and tragic stories in her career, Alice still winced at the details. It's one of the things I admire about her. Despite the "tough lady" exterior and the fact that she is a fierce litigator, she still feels other people's pain.

"I've handled oodles of Argentines over the years," she said crossing her attractive bare feet on the grass. "In the early 80s, it was individuals running away from the goons in the military government and trying to get asylum here. These days most are coming for jobs. The political cases are kind of rare, but I know the family members of the disappeared women are still searching for those kids."

"Well, I may have one."

"But you're not sure if the girl *is* the niece."

"She looks a lot like the photo, but absolutely sure, no I'm not. I'm told the people who are passing themselves off as her parents are in possession of a birth certificate."

"That means nothing. The military supplied phony birth certificates when they delivered those babies. You'll need DNA testing."

I thought that over. "We don't have any blood samples or any other remnant from the deceased sister. She's long dead."

"No matter. If you can get a strand of hair that belongs to the girl, you can match it with that of your client. As long as the hair has the root still attached."

"Even if she's only the aunt?"

"That's right. The aunt will have enough similarities in the helixes with the dead mother. It can be done."

I sipped some more rum and tonic and thought it over. "I don't have a hair from the girl. In fact, I don't have hide nor hair where she is."

"That's not good."

"Of course, I could go back to the apartment and collect a sample. Manuel Navarro has short gray hair and the mother's is bleached blond. The girl's would be the only long, dark hair. I could check her bed, her bathroom."

"How will you get into the apartment?"

"Well, I imagine I'll have to break in. It was open when I was there earlier, but by now the caretaker has probably locked it up."

Alice put her wine down and placed her hands over her ears.

"I'm an officer of the court and I didn't hear that. But if you're going to do it, you better do it tonight before they clean the place."

CHAPTER EIGHT

We finished our fish and washed it down—Alice with wine and me with beer. I got ready to drive back to Miami Beach. Alice said she would go home but wait to hear from me before she went to sleep.

"As your attorney I want to give you one piece of advice: Don't get caught."

I thanked her. Then I crossed the Julia Tuttle Causeway again and eventually entered Little Buenos Aires, where the aroma of grilling meat was even stronger. The sidewalk cafes, including El Gaucho, were crowded with meat eaters. Loud Latin rock—it sounded like Maldita Vecindad—rose toward the heavens.

I left the crowds and noise behind and turned onto Marseilles Street. I passed the Colonial Arms slowly, saw no lights in Apartment 12, cut my own lights, eased into the alleyway behind the building, and parked among the cars of the other tenants.

I took from the glove compartment a penlight. From my wallet I withdrew a thin strip of metal. Long ago I had peeled it off a vacuum-packed can of Bustelo Cuban Coffee, and it served as the perfect door jimmy.

I took the backstairs as silently as I could, looked around, and saw nobody. From the apartment next door I heard a television playing, some kind of comedy show in Spanish. It was on loud, mostly canned laughter, which was good because it might cover any noise I made.

I tried the knob of the backdoor, but it didn't turn. Pedro, the handyman who Corral had spoken to, apparently had locked it. I produced my metal strip, introduced it into the door jam, moved it down against the tongue of the lock, jiggled it, and opened the door.

I stepped in quickly, closed the door behind me silently, and swept the beam of the penlight around the apartment. It looked the same as I'd left it that afternoon. Apparently no one had started to clean it.

I didn't dally. Following the beam up the short hallway, I entered the girl's bedroom. The musicians taped to the walls stared at me

35

through the darkness. I turned down the pink comforter that was still on the bed and scanned the pillow with the light. I found a couple of long black hairs and held them up, but neither of them had roots.

I left them there and entered the bathroom. Elena had not left her hairbrush, which would have been extremely convenient. But I trained the light on the trash basket just below the mirror. There I found a small clump of hair that she apparently had cleaned from the brush.

I picked it up, held it in front of the penlight, and clearly saw several roots amid that tangle. I pulled from my pocket a ziplock plastic bag Alice had given me, deposited the clump in the bag, sealed it, and slipped it back in my pocket. I turned off the penlight and headed for the door.

Just as I did, I heard a noise down the hall.

I froze and listened. Was Pedro coming back to clean the place? No, that was unlikely at this late hour. Had they possibly left a pet behind that I hadn't seen earlier? No, I hadn't seen a water dish or food.

Or was it Navarro? Had he forgotten something and come back?

My mind raced. I had the DNA evidence in my pocket, and I was willing to bet it would prove who the girl really was. Navarro was definitely on the run, acting like a guilty party. I figured I better take my best shot right then to grab him, before I lost him again.

In darkness and silence, I reached to my hip and realized I hadn't brought my gun. I had to assume he wouldn't surrender without a fight, and there was a chance he was armed. I much preferred to encounter him with a weapon, hopefully get the drop on him. So I tiptoed back down the hall and toward the living room.

The lights were still out, but I saw the front door slightly ajar. It hadn't been that way when I'd sneaked in from the rear. Somebody was on the premises besides me, inside or outside. I turned away from it, made for the kitchen, headed for the backdoor, and, hopefully, for my gun.

But I didn't make it.

I was slipping by the refrigerator when I sensed someone next to it in the dark. Before I could bolt for the door or even turn, I saw the shape of a person and then a dark object coming at me at eye level. A split second later I took a tremendous blow on the side of the head. I heard something crack and shatter—possibly my skull.

I slammed into the kitchen counter to the right of me and slid to the floor. I didn't lose consciousness, but my cerebral cavity, and every other bone in me, resonated with the blow. My eyes jittered with the vibration.

When I looked up I could see a shadowy human standing right above me and I knew another blow was coming. I lifted my arms as the wraith gathered himself to go at me again. My head wouldn't survive a second hit. Whoever it was raised his arm. He held something else in his hand to finish me.

Suddenly the television next door went mute. Even above the canned laughter, the next-door neighbors apparently had heard the blow or had heard me hit the floor. The blurry shadow in front of me froze. I'm sure he was weighing the risk of finishing me off. I could hear him breathing—that's how quiet it was.

Voices of real people, not television voices, sounded from next door. A woman complained about "ese escándalo"—that ruckus—in the next apartment. They fell silent, waiting to hear what came next.

That decided it for him. He dropped what he held, stepped over me, hurried for the backdoor, and ducked out.

I sat in silence a few moments and then the canned laughter from next door started up again. I lay back on the floor and listened to it. After a while, the world stopped vibrating. I pulled the penlight from my pocket, struggled to my feet, and stepped on something that crackled underfoot. Shining the light on it, I saw ceramic shards all around me. They were pieces of a large tea mug that I had seen earlier in the kitchen. Someone had mugged me—literally.

I felt my pants pocket and found that I still had the plastic bag with the hairs in it. I wondered what Navarro, or whoever the other person was, had come searching for. But I didn't think about it long.

On shaky legs, I snuck out the backdoor before somebody else showed up. For an empty apartment, the place was as busy as a bus station.

A half hour later I was at Alice's place, and she was ministering to my wounds. She leaned over me, wielding a bottle of alcohol and a cotton swab. In the background a woman was singing in Spanish about an eclipse of the moon and something even darker, "an eclipse of your love."

The guy who'd hit me had almost "eclipsed" me. The mug—and by that I mean both the implement and the attacker—had broken the skin on my head. I had dropped a couple of painkillers to ease the throbbing.

"Okay, now tell me," she said, "who or what did you damage with this skull of yours?"

"The mug got the worst of it," I insisted. I explained what I knew.

"Well, you shouldn't have gone in there."

"You didn't say that before I left, and you're my attorney."

"That's because I didn't know you'd return as damaged goods. Did you get what you went looking for?"

I handed her the plastic bag with the hairs in it.

"Perfect," Alice said, forgetting about my injuries and focusing on the hairs. "I'll call the lab in the morning and tell them you're coming. I'm their best client. Most of the people I represent have to prove they are related to U.S. citizens in order to stay in this country. I send droves of people to that lab, and they'll be sure to take good care of you."

I dabbed at my own scalp. "If it turns out this girl was taken from her mother at birth, that she really isn't the daughter of the Navarros, what legal steps can we take?"

She thought it over.

"If the Navarros brought her into this country under false pretenses, that alone will put them in very hot water. Of course, it will help if the family—the true family—can get them charged with kidnapping back in Argentina."

"Kidnapping and possibly murder."

"That too . . . my God!"

"What's wrong?"

"If this girl doesn't know any of this, it's going to come as an enormous shock."

"No kidding. Finding out the people you think are your parents may have been party to the murder of your real parents."

"Exactly. It's like a Greek tragedy."

I tried to read the concern in her eyes. "Do you think it's wrong to reopen this case, to expose the girl to this big of a shock?"

She shook her head hard. "Not at all. The girl has a right to know the truth about her history. Almost always the truth is the best way, and it seems to bubble up from underneath the surface anyway. I see it all the time in my practice. People who came here and thought they'd left marriages behind, children behind, whole lives behind for good."

She shook her head. "Life just doesn't work that way, boyo," she said, gazing at the bag with the long black hairs in it. "No, it doesn't."

CHAPTER NINE

I squeezed a few more minutes of sympathy out of Alice, then I headed home. At that hour, it's a five-minute drive. I was almost there, when I took out the flyer I'd found in the Navarro's apartment and read the address. It was on South River Road, just a few blocks west from where I live.

I was curious and I figured the longer I delayed looking for Navarro, the farther away he might get. I delicately probed the dent I'd gotten on my head. It was going to hurt much more in the morning, so I'd better get some work done now.

The upstream stretch of the Miami River, where the club did business, was night and day from the more gentrified area where Alice lived. The river was narrower here, and the neighborhood was industrial and maritime. Ramshackle Caribbean freighters were tied up all along its docks.

It was also a high crime area. If you lived around there, you put bars over your windows, and you didn't leave anything lying around outside your home. If you did, your belongings—anything from bicycles to birdbaths—soon would be aboard a freighter heading anywhere from Port-au-Prince to Panama City.

That area right along the riverbank also featured a selection of bars where seamen could find female companionship, and nearby were some extremely sleazy hotels with hourly rates where their "romances" could be consummated.

The San Telmo Tango Club seemed like an intermediate stop, a place you might go for a quick drink and a dance before you did business.

I pulled into its dusty gravel parking lot and found a few cars there, even though it was Monday night. In Miami, somebody is dancing somewhere, seven days a week.

The building, which was right on the river, was made of old pocked white stucco, with a red barrel-tile roof in bad condition and a wide doorway lighted by a rusting, wrought-iron lamp.

I walked in and found a low-ceilinged place, again with white stucco walls, lighted by dim bulbs in old sconces. Tin tables were tucked into shadowy cubbyholes along the walls. In the middle of the room was a good-sized dance floor. It was made of wood, which over the years had been worn smooth and shiny by shuffling dancers. A rusting chandelier hung over the center of it.

At one end stood a weathered bar, and behind it hung a long, blemished mirror.

It looked like a rough place, but I got the distinct feeling it was supposed to give you that sensation. The tango had been invented in the roughest riverside barrios in Buenos Aires. It was designed to exude danger. Passion might explode at any moment—romantic or violent. That was the idea.

Of course, most people who danced the tango didn't dip into the dark side of it. They were more like Sara Ingram's intermediate students. But the people in this place seemed to be looking for the full experience.

About a dozen couples were in attendance when I got there. Half were on the dance floor and the others were curled around each other in their cubbyholes. Tango music played. At the moment it was a torch song about a man who stood outside a woman's house unable to reach her:

> *Your caress and my desire,*
> *but no windows, no doors.*

The couples dancing shared plenty of caresses and desire. The way they were locked together was nothing like Sara Ingram's students. When these people moved to the music, tracing the classic steps, it was as if one body moved. Their skins had seemingly been grafted together, so that they melded into something that seemed even closer than sex.

Some of them dressed the parts of desperate lovers. The women wore black, spiked heels, skirts slit up the side, net stockings and daring decolletage. The men were dressed in "ruffian chic"—zoot suits, fedoras, and two-tone shoes. It was a bit of a costume party. During the day they might be accountants and dental hygienists but by night they were tango toughs and their molls. The whole place had a "den of thieves" flavor.

None of those couples paid me any attention as I made for the bar. The bartender, a sallow guy with a sharp nose and kinky hair, served me a beer. As he did, I noticed he had a mechanical hook instead of a right hand. I tipped him well and then asked him if he knew of an Argentine man named Manuel Navarro who maybe hung out here. I showed him the photo I'd picked up at the pharmacy.

He glanced at it, and then his eyes glazed over.

"If you have questions about customers, you have to ask the boss."

"Where do I find the boss?"

His eyes darted to a doorway that led to a veranda overlooking the river. I walked over that way and found a man sitting by himself at a table. He peered out at the slow, dark current of the river drifting downstream on the slack tide. From where he sat he could also see through a window into the bar, to make sure matters progressed smoothly.

He was a small, olive-skinned man who wore a long-sleeved, black silk shirt, a white cravat knotted at his neck, and a black fedora. He looked like he hadn't shaved in a few days—once again the ruffian look. He had a shot glass of clear liquid in front of him—vodka, tequila, or maybe ouzo. This was a bit of Argentine theater, and he was both a character and the impresario.

He looked up at me languidly. "Can I help you?"

"I'm told you're the owner."

He studied me as if trying to see me from different angles without moving. Then he shrugged. "That depends on why you want to speak to me," he said in a gravelly voice that seemed to barely escape his throat.

I smiled. "I'm not the police, and I'm not a bill collector."

"Then there is a chance I'm the owner. My name is Oscar Porta."

I told him my name, and he invited me to take a chair. A launch with a small motor on the back pulled up to the pier just below us. A young black man in cutoff shorts and a flowered shirt was at the tiller. His cargo was covered in canvas, and I got the impression from the look he flashed at Porta that it was some kind of contraband. Porta waved him off and told him to return later. The kid motored off and disappeared into the dark.

"So what can I do for you," Porta asked sipping his drink.

"I'm looking for a man, another Argentine. His name is Manuel Navarro."

He stopped in mid sip, but didn't answer. His eyes drifted to a dock just upriver from the bar. A freighter was tied up there and near it a shipping container that looked too large for the vessel.

"Do you know him?" I asked.

He shrugged. "Navarro, it is a very normal name, and there are too many Manuels."

I showed him the photo and told him Manuel Navarro might have been in the Argentine military. He studied it without a glimmer of recognition on his dark face.

"Why do you want to know about him? Has he done something?"

Given the location of Porta's club, the probability was that lots of people who walked in there had "done something." Drug traffic, prostitution, smuggling of goods and of people, those were all aspects of daily life where he did business.

"I think he might have kidnapped a child from Argentina," I said.

Porta's dark eyebrows came together. That was a crime he didn't encounter every day.

"I don't know anyone who steals children," he said, and he drained his drink.

He yelled out in a rough manner to the bartender, who came scuttling over and poured him a refill. It was ouzo, and he had another one poured for me. The bartender's mechanical hand clicked when he let the glass go. It needed oiling. I sipped my drink.

"Of course, this man Navarro wouldn't tell you if he'd stolen a child, would he, Mr. Porta?"

He met my gaze. "But I would know anyway. I know many things I'm not supposed to know. It is impossible to have secrets from me in this club, and there is not much I don't know in this neighborhood. Especially the dark alleyways and the crimes that happen there."

He flicked his eyebrows at me cleverly. I was willing to believe that he was a repository of certain knowledge. Club owners had to know their clientele, especially any possible criminal activities. I had become wise to that from my own brother Tommy and his club, Caliente.

But at the moment, Mr. Porta sounded more like a tango tune come to life. Maybe that was the inevitable result of living in such surroundings day in, day out. But it was more likely just part of his mafioso act. I wanted to bring him out of that act and to the matter at hand.

"This has to do with the 'dirty war.' The girl is one of the children of the disappeared. The guy I'm looking for maybe killed her mother."

That got his attention. The phony sneer turned into genuine repugnance.

"We don't serve that species of person in Oscar Porta's club."

He was letting me know that he might play at being a "tango tough," but that there were some lowlifes who were lower than others. The military killers, like Navarro, were below him and his customers.

He knocked back his drink and slammed the glass on the table.

"Why do you come here looking for a bastard like that?"

I took out the flyer I had found in Navarro's apartment and showed it to him.

"I found this where the bastard was living up in Little Buenos Aires. I thought it might mean something."

He shrugged it off. "Those flyers are everywhere where Argentines live."

I flipped it over and showed him the cryptic inscription on the back: "GT 332."

"Does this mean anything to you?"

He glanced down at it. For the first time since I'd sat down at that table I saw fear in his dark, liquid eyes. Suddenly he wasn't tough at all. He was a businessman with an angle, and something about those letters and numbers punctured the mystique and scared him right out of his impersonation of a rogue. But he wasn't going to tell me why. In a moment the sneer was back in place.

"That means nothing to me and now I have things to do."

He got up and waited for me to do so as well. Just as I had in Glades Springs, I left a business card lying on the table. As I headed for the door, couples were still pacing the dance floor to the strains of violins and another agonized tango singer:

What does it matter
the fear that life brings
if I find the kiss
for which my soul is searching.

CHAPTER TEN

I woke up the next morning with a jackhammer in my head. Ceramics and skull bone are a bad combination. I dropped painkillers into my mouth as if they were depth charges and didn't move until they started to work. I finally dragged myself out of bed and showered, flinching when the water hit the gash. Later I combed my hair delicately over that area.

Alice called early and told me that the DNA lab could take the hairs and some of Fiona Bonaventura's blood any time in the early afternoon. So I called Fiona and said I needed to see her. It was important.

A half hour later I walked into the condo building where she and her husband were holed up. The lobby featured a large grotto made out of coral, with water tumbling into it from a spout made out of a conch shell. It was surrounded by lots of big tropical plants and mirrors.

The security guard called up, and I got in the elevator for the fifteenth floor. The maid let me in, and I found my clients waiting for me in the living room. It featured more plants and mirrors and a sea view. They spared me another grotto.

Fiona and her husband were dressed stylishly, as if they were part of a magazine ad for this tropical time-share. She was in black jeans and a black silk blouse. Estevez wore only a bathing suit and a white sport shirt unbuttoned down to his golden chest hairs. He had a golden body tan and looked as if he had just come from the beach.

I took a seat on a sofa that overlooked the ocean. The sea stretched to the horizon in beautiful bands of color that advanced from aquamarine to deep blue. Right then I wished I were sailing over that horizon.

"So what have you learned?" Estevez asked. He lit a cigarette with a silver table lighter and sat down on the far arm of the sofa.

"I've learned that the Navarros have friends here who tipped them off that I was looking for them. They're gone."

That drew different reactions from them that shattered the chic of the magazine ad: shock on the part of Fiona and anger from Estevez.

"What do you mean gone?" he demanded.

"I mean they packed up and left late yesterday afternoon. They took all their clothes and personal belongings. The place is empty."

The look on Fiona's face pained me almost as much as it had to pain her.

"But why?"

"I told you, someone tipped them off. I don't know who. I spoke to only one person at the apartment complex yesterday, and she insists she didn't tell them."

"So I've lost her again," Fiona moaned. "Twenty years searching, I see her once and I lose her again."

Those were exactly the words I had anticipated and dreaded. It was as if the girl were dematerializing right in front of her eyes.

"We don't know if she is your niece," Estevez said. He turned on me. "But we might have known if you hadn't done something stupid."

I told them exactly how I'd proceeded the previous afternoon, including my conversation with María Terán. Estevez stood up and started to pace.

"Well, maybe that woman is lying. You shouldn't have been so obvious, asking questions to other Argentines."

"She says she didn't tell them."

He made a sound of disgust. "All I know is we've come all the way here, spent money to fly, to rent this place, and paid more money to you. Now the people we came to investigate are gone."

I was about to offer him a complete refund. This was a radical move given the hit on the head I'd taken, but Fiona cut me off.

"It's always about your money, Eduardo. From the beginning it has been that way. Money is all that matters to you."

Estevez stopped pacing. "That's not true."

She glared at him. The sadness had disappeared, and all her upper class hauteur was in evidence now.

"Yes, it is. Twenty years ago when you opposed Sonia's political activities you said it was because it put her, me, and you in danger. But you were really worried about your business, your reputation as a businessman, your contacts in the government that helped you make money."

He wanted to protest again, but she waved a red-nailed finger at him. Those deep-blue eyes of hers were angry, like stormy waters off Buenos Aires.

"Don't try to tell me differently. I've been married to you for more than twenty years. I know you. Lately, you are acting just as you did back then. Well, it isn't about your money. There are matters more important than that. It's about finding my sister's child. If we have to spend money, we'll do it. Don't make me do that on my own because I will find a way."

Reading between the lines of that statement was easy: if he didn't cooperate, she could divorce him, take a good-sized chunk of his net worth, and continue the search on her own. Estevez seemed to comprehend that. He watched her warily as if the balance in his bank account were diminishing in front of his eyes, one digit at a time.

But Fiona wasn't finished: "Don't make me question your loyalty, Eduardo, because we don't know where that will lead."

The marital knives were out, at least hers were. She sounded like a queen calling into question the fealty of a commoner, a subject in danger of having his head chopped off. They stayed staring deep into each other's eyes.

That last phrase of Fiona's, about loyalty, seemed to mean something to both of them, something a third wheel like me wouldn't understand. The easy interpretation would be that Fiona was accusing Estevez of garden-variety infidelity. But given all that had happened in their family, maybe it was something else. I couldn't know.

Fiona finally turned away from him. Lucky for me, most of the irritation she felt at the escape of the Navarros she had leveled at her husband. I didn't quite understand it, but queens didn't have to explain their inexplicable behavior.

"If they are running, it means that they are probably the people we are looking for, Mr. Cuesta. Is there anything we can do now?"

"I went to the realty office that manages the property. I got some leads on other people they know and I'm checking them out. I'll work as quickly as I can."

I pulled from my jacket pocket the plastic bag containing the hairs.

"And we can go to a DNA lab, you can give some blood, and we can hand over these hairs from the girl. They can tell us definitively if she's your niece or not. We'll eventually need that proof for the courts. But as soon as we get it, we can get the police looking for them too."

Estevez looked at the bag suspiciously.

"Those belong to the girl? How did you get them?"

I shook my head. "Given that you're paying me, it's better for legal reasons that you not know."

Fiona leaned forward. "I'll go to the laboratory whenever you want. I'm sure she's my niece and we'll prove it. And you should do whatever it takes to find her. I have paid you for two days and if you need more, you will have it."

It was clear she was speaking not just to me but to her husband. We sat in silence several moments. That silence was like a fourth person in the room, a very large person who knew them much better than I did.

I told Fiona I'd pick her up at one p.m. to go to the lab. Then I left them sitting there—Fiona, her lowly subject Estevez, and that giant silence.

I hurried out of the building before they changed their minds and fired me. I had hours before we were supposed to be at the lab, so I started to follow the meager leads I'd mentioned to Fiona.

International Protection Services, where Manuel Navarro worked, was located in an industrial park north of the airport. It was a large steely warehouse and over the entrance hung a long billboard bearing the company name. Beneath that were painted the words "Professional Armoring," and next to it a drawing of a medieval knight covered in armor.

Again, it seemed ironic that Navarro might have anything to do with shining armor.

I parked and entered a small business office. It contained a service counter and an empty black metal desk. Above that desk hung a poster of the pope, who was riding in an open car, blessing the faithful from inside a bubble made of bulletproof glass that protected him from possible enemies. Beneath that was printed a logo:

"When people depend on you, depend on IPS—International Protection Services."

The implication was that the company's business efforts were blessed by the pope.

On the counter I found a pile of brochures, and I leafed through one briefly. The company's main business was making vehicles that couldn't be pierced by any kind of projectile. The brochure illustrated for me how thick armor plating was welded into vehicles, behind their doors, under their floors and roofs. It also told me that bulletproof glass could offer "360 degree protection from terrorists and common criminals."

The company offered all sorts of extras for the individual who was conspicuously security conscious—electronically charged door handles to foil would be carjackers, reinforced front and rear bumpers if you had to ram your way out of a tight spot, and emission systems that could lay down a smoke screen if you were being chased. At that point I started to wonder if I had wandered into a low budget James Bond movie.

I still was standing there when the back door to the office opened and a gray-haired man ducked in momentarily. He wore a white shirt, a skinny tie, and a plastic pocket protector with pens in it. He saw me with the brochures in my hand and introduced himself as Bob Shields, the manager.

"I'm with another customer giving him a tour of the operation," he said. "Why don't you join us?"

I said that was fine with me, and I followed him into the warehouse. It was a good-sized, high-ceilinged workspace, crowded with about a dozen vehicles. Most of them were big, shiny, new SUVs, but there were also a scattering of Mercedes, BMWs, and a Jaguar.

The vehicles had been partially dismantled, with their doors, hoods, and flooring removed. Several welders, equipped with welding hoods and visors, were busy installing sheets of steel into the chassis. So many torches blazed at once that it looked like the Fourth of July.

Shields was explaining the different options to his other customer.

"You want to protect yourself from teenage thugs playing with 9-millimeter pistols, you use a quarter inch of ballistic steel all around," he said. "If it's Colombian guerrillas gunning for you with AK-47s or worse, you go with the half inch. I'll show you why."

He led us both to a strange black compartment standing by itself at the very back of the warehouse. A bit bigger than a telephone booth, it was lined inside and out with steel, except for a narrow, horizontal slot at eye level. It was just big enough for the muzzle of an AK-47 to pass through.

"Cover your ears," Shields said.

We did, he stuck the muzzle through the hole and unloosed a full 30-round clip into a piece of steel that stood about twenty feet away across the rear of the warehouse. Even with my fingers stuck in my ears, the burst was deafening.

Shields put down the weapon, we left the booth and walked to the steel. Flattened AK-47 rounds lay scattered on the concrete floor, like the slugs used to cheat parking meters. The backside of the steel panel had puckered a bit but not one round had passed through.

"You see what I'm saying?" Shields shouted over the loud sizzle of the welding torches and the echo of the gun-burst. "It's the difference between breathing and being road-kill."

The other customer asked a question about gas mileage given the weight of the steel.

Shields rolled his eyes and grabbed the guy by the tie.

"Listen, buddy, this isn't a question of miles per gallon. It's how many miles you stay alive and how soon you're willing to die. Dead guys get great mileage because they don't go nowhere no more. Ya get me?"

He tapped the customer on the chest. "We'll throw in a remote starter free of charge so you can avoid the big bang. That's what we call a car bomb."

He sounded a bit like the Avon lady, throwing in a free lipstick.

His customer told him he'd think it over. They shook hands, and the other man hurried out before something happened to him. Shields then turned all his avid attention to me.

"So what can I get you? Armoring? Bulletproof vests? A couple of Delta commandos to guard your daughters?"

He made me smile. "As much as I could use your services, I'm not in the market at the moment, Mr. Shields." I handed him my card. "I'm looking for a man who works for you. Manuel Navarro."

He studied the card long enough to read it three times. "What did Navarro do to have you on his tail?"

"Maybe nothing. It may be the wrong guy, but I'd like to talk to him about a missing persons case I'm on."

"Well, he isn't here right now. He's out of pocket.'

"Do you know when he'll be back?"

Shields shook his head. "He called here last night and left a message on the machine. He said he had a family emergency and would be gone for a few days."

In a way, Navarro had told the truth. But the family in question was the Bonaventuras, a family he had helped devastate two decades earlier.

"Do you have a cell phone number for him?"

"I do, but he's not answering it. And no, I can't give it to you. I don't think Navarro would want that. But he'll be back soon."

"Are you sure?"

He gazed around his warehouse where sparks flew.

"He better be. I need him here. We have a couple of cars going through customs at the port of Miami right now, and I also have a lot of incoming work."

"What exactly does Navarro do here?"

"I have plenty of clients in Latin America. They're having a hell of a time down there with kidnapping gangs and carjackers. A real war. But I don't speak any Spanish, so Navarro handles the translating with clients, all the paperwork with the customs officials in those governments. He gets the vehicles to port here with all the right permits. He's even drummed up business for me in Argentina, where he's from."

"A very valuable employee," I said. "Do you know what Navarro did down in Argentina?"

"He was in the military."

I tried not to betray my investigative pleasure. "I see. Do you know what he did while he was in uniform?"

"He told me he was in supply."

True, but what he'd supplied was torture and suffering.

"How about Navarro's wife? Did you ever meet her?"

"Yes, she came in here a couple of times to help with paperwork when he had to work on the weekends. But I finally told him not to bring her."

"Why was that?"

He got a pained expression. "Because the truth is I didn't like the way he treated her. She's a quiet, nervous woman, at least when she's around him. And he's very rude to her. One time I even saw him slap her. I figured I'd give the woman a break and let her stay home by herself. She'd be better off."

Shields didn't vanquish Navarro for hitting his wife, but he did try to keep her out of harm's way. I guess that was as close to a real knight in shining armor as I would get in that place.

"How about their daughter, Elena. Did you ever meet her?"

He shook his head, and just then his cell phone rang. He answered it and found a client on the other end.

"Well, which one is it? The Hummer or the armored Land Rover? Who are we up against, dude?"

I slipped a business card into the plastic protector in his shirt pocket and shot him a salute.

On the way out, I noticed a shipping container next to the warehouse. It was embossed with the letters "IPS." I stopped, studied it, and realized I'd seen one just like it the night before. It had been sitting in a lot just upriver from the San Telmo Tango Club.

Somebody else might have considered that a curious coincidence. But Mrs. Cuesta didn't raise her younger son to believe in curious coincidences. I figured somewhere down the line I'd get a chance to check it out.

CHAPTER ELEVEN

I was already on the Miami side of the bay, so I headed for the second address I'd copied from the rental application: the Argentine consulate.

On my way over I called the Jackson Memorial Hospital personnel department. I heard just what I thought I'd hear: Felicia Navarro had not shown up for work. They had not heard from her and had no new contact information.

The consulate was located in a glass tower on Brickell Avenue in the heart of Miami's international banking corridor. I don't do much international banking, but I like being on Brickell. It's sleek, clean, and clogged with beautiful international women in business dress.

The building in question was no exception—a polished marble lobby, lots of modern angles, and a few feminine angles as well. The directory informed me that the Argentine consulate could be found in Penthouse One. I took the elevator up to the top floor of the tower, and it deposited me right at the double mahogany doors.

The reception area resembled a doctor's waiting room with chairs along the walls, except that a blue-and-white Argentine flag hung from a pole in the corner. A photo of a man—smiling with a blue-and-white sash across his chest—hung next to it. He was, presumably, the president of Argentina, and he seemed pleased with himself.

The remaining décor consisted of travel posters—a wide boulevard in downtown Buenos Aires, which I recognized from my one visit there; a man on horseback in the Argentine *pampas*; a very large waterfall; and, right next to the service counter, a couple clutched in a steamy tango.

I had never taken to the tango. Being of Caribbean extraction, I was born to *salsa* and the *merengue*. It had always seemed to me that the tango was just a bit too tense and dramatic for my tropical blood. But after seeing Sara Ingram wrap her foot around her student's leg, seeing the couples the night before moving as sinuously as they had, and looking at the beautiful woman in this poster with ecstasy in her eyes, I was starting to reconsider.

I was still thinking that when it became my turn at the counter. The attendant was a woman about forty, with long, dark-red hair, an olive complexion, and black horn-rimmed glasses. I've always liked women in horn-rimmed glasses. They seem to be saying, "Be warned, buddy, I have brains."

This one was no different. She seemed to know what I'd been thinking. Her brown eyes were smiling, and her full red lips had a humorous curl to them.

"Can I help you?"

"I hope so."

She glanced at the poster and back. "Do you want to learn to tango?"

"I'm not sure. I like the way they're looking at each other, but I don't know about the dance."

Her eyes narrowed. "If you want the look, you have to do the dance."

She made that sound like a life philosophy.

I shook my head. "Unfortunately, I can't tango right now. I'm here to see a Mr. Villarreal."

Her playfulness disappeared from one moment to the next. She pursed her lips as if she were folding them away for another occasion.

"Mr. Villarreal is the vice consul," she said.

"Is that so?"

"Do you have an appointment?"

"No, I don't."

"Then I don't know that he will be able to see you. Mr. Villarreal sees no one without an appointment."

I handed her a card and she read it.

"Can you tell him it's very important? It concerns three Argentines who may be missing."

"Maybe someone else can see you."

"No, it needs to be Mr. Villarreal. It's extremely important."

She held up a finger and disappeared through a door into the inner sanctum. I turned and smiled in the direction of about a dozen people who sat with documents clutched in their hands, waiting for passports, visas, trade permits, whatever. They looked like they had been waiting quite a while.

I wondered what it must have been like at that consulate during the awful "dirty war" in Argentina, especially if you were one of the Argentines running for your life. Could you come here for help? Could you trust them? Could I trust them now to help Fiona, given the diplomat's name on Navarro's application?

A door leading to the inner offices opened. Out came a long-legged, craggy-faced man with windblown hair, wearing a blue jumpsuit. He shot me a chilly look from icy blue eyes and kept going out the door. He was obviously not a diplomat and not who I was looking for. I wasn't to his taste either.

The attendant was gone less than a minute and came back shaking her head.

"No, he can't see you. He says he's very busy."

"He says?"

She rolled her eyes. I got the impression that she didn't like her superior, Mr. Villarreal, very much, maybe because all the people had to wait forever and got angry with her. I leaned close.

"Tell him it's a security matter."

Her head was still shaking. "He says he cannot. You can speak with another officer here, if you please. Take a seat and you'll be called in turn."

She gave me a conciliatory smile and turned to her next customer.

Smile or not, I had hit a bureaucratic wall. I could try to walk right in on him, but that might get me shot. Consular stations everywhere had terrorism concerns to one degree or another, and security tended to be tight.

I took a seat and thought it over. I stared at the posters of Argentina and an idea occurred to me. It wasn't a very decorous idea, but there were moments when you just had to apply "diplomatic pressure" of your own.

I took out my cell phone, punched in a bunch of random numbers and then acted as if I was waiting for someone to answer. The lady behind the counter glanced at me out of the corner of her eye.

When I spoke, I did so in Spanish and loud enough for everyone in the room to hear me.

"Hello, Roberto. . . . Yes, it's me . . . I'm at the consulate in Miami. I've told them that your family members are missing, but they don't seem to want to listen . . ."

I waited and then raised my voice a bit more. "Yes, yes, I've told them that they are Argentine citizens and they may be in danger. But it isn't doing any good. They have me here waiting as if I were applying for a dog license."

I grimaced and pulled the phone away from my ear as if someone had screamed on the other end. The lady in the horn-rimmed glasses was now giving me her full attention. I met her gaze as I spoke into the phone.

"Don't yell at me, Roberto, and don't use that kind of language. It isn't my fault. And it isn't the fault of the attendants here either. They are very courteous, very lovely people. It is the diplomats themselves who seem to have no concern for the safety of their fellow Argentines in a foreign land. Your relatives could be dead as far as these guys are concerned."

All around me, those fellow Argentines, tired of waiting for those same diplomats, were listening with rapt attention and sympathy.

"Yes, Roberto, it might be a good idea to call the Foreign Ministry yourself and ask to speak with a high official. Hold on, I will ask the attendant for the number."

But I didn't have a chance. As I said, I've found that girls in horn-rimmed glasses are generally quick studies. This one was no different. She turned on a heel, disappearing through that same door she had before.

I spoke into the phone. "Hold on, Roberto, the attendant is away from her station. How is the weather there?"

He didn't have a chance to tell me. She reappeared moments later at the second door.

"The vice consul will see you now."

I said goodbye to Roberto and folded my cell phone. Such are the powers of diplomacy.

She ushered me in and led me to a corner office with windows facing west. It overlooked downtown Miami and, in the distance, the airport and the Everglades. A photograph identical to the one hanging outside was hung here as well, the same smile still frozen on the president's face.

The man who occupied that office wore a charcoal gray suit with light gray stripes, a bright pink shirt, a crimson tie, and a red carnation in the lapel. He was about fifty, short and chunky, with hangdog cheeks, a flushed complexion, which matched his shirt, thin hair that he combed over, and a dark moustache that hugged his top lip. He had a continental air to go with his continental width.

Unlike his president, he wasn't wearing a smile, and he didn't offer me his hand, which didn't seem very diplomatic.

"Yes, what can I do for you?" he asked with official brusqueness. When he spoke, I saw he had small gaps between his teeth.

I glanced at the chair in front of his desk. He gave me a look that let me know I was taxing his patience, but gestured me into the seat. He sat down as well. I looked just over his head out the window.

"Nice view you have here. You must get nice sunsets over the Everglades."

All he wanted was for the sun to set on my visit.

"Can I help you?"

"I hope so. I'm trying to find an Argentine man who lives here in Miami. His name is Manuel Navarro."

I watched his eyes as I uttered the name to see if recognition dawned there. But diplomats are trained not to display what they don't want to display.

"I don't know that name."

"He rented an apartment on Miami Beach and he gave you as a reference."

He tilted his bulk and leaned back in his chair. "Many people from Argentina come here to the consulate. Many use the consulate as a reference. We try to serve our citizens. That is our policy."

"Yes, but he named you personally, so I figured you might have had dealings with him."

He shook his head. "You can't expect me to remember every single person I meet Mr . . ." He glanced down at the card the attendant had given him. "Mr. Cuesta. As I said, large numbers of people pass through our doors."

I produced the photos I'd taken of the Navarros.

"As I said, the man is named Manuel Navarro. His wife is Felicia." He took the photos, examined them briefly, and shook his head. "I don't recognize them."

"I'm here because they're missing."

He appeared dubious. "Missing? What do you mean missing?"

I told him about the Navarro's sudden evacuation of their apartment, and he shrugged.

"People move, Mr. Cuesta. They change apartments. That is their right."

"These people packed and moved in a matter of minutes, as if the building were on fire. And they did it a short while after I went there asking about them. I think they're running from me."

He smiled, as if the idea that I might scare somebody was ludicrous.

"Why would they be afraid of you?"

"Because I went there to ask if their daughter is really theirs, or if she is one of the children of the disappeared, taken from her mother, a woman who was later murdered by government assassins, military killers."

That made him purse his lips. I had dealt with diplomats many times during my years in the intelligence unit of the Miami P.D. They represent the most refined, civilized, and positive aspects of their peoples, not child stealing. Diplomats don't like to discuss their countries' dirty laundry. Their job isn't to justify the past, but to get their nations past those dark patches, those falls from grace. In other words, a guy like Villarreal might prefer to shovel a bit more dirt on a grave than to open it.

Diplomats, in general, also are not plain speakers. They don't like words such as "murdered" and "assassins." But I'd known that when I'd opened my mouth. A fellow like Villarreal could fend you off with diplomatic refinement if you let him. I didn't want to give him wiggle room, and he didn't wiggle. He just stared at me with a curdled look on his full face.

"You've heard of the children of the disappeared, haven't you, Mr. Villarreal?"

"Yes, of course. What makes you think these people are mixed up in such a thing?"

"A client of mine told me they were."

"And who is that client?"

"I'm sorry, I can't tell you that."

"I see."

"But that person is an Argentine, currently here in Miami."

Given his name on Navarro's rental application, I couldn't very well identify Fiona to him. You never knew where people's interests lay, especially a government official.

He took that in and swiveled a bit in his chair.

"Over the years, many people in that position have thought they saw children who are related to them, Mr. Cuesta. One has to understand that these individuals want to see certain things but that the reality is often different. Human beings, totally unrelated, resemble each other."

I took out the photos of both the late Sonia Bonaventura and of the girl and laid them before him.

"This is the woman who was killed and this is the girl who lives with the Navarros. We believe Manuel Navarro was in a position to receive the child when she was an infant. I think you can see why my client suspects the girl may be a blood relative."

He studied the photos, again without any outward indication of his thoughts. Then he handed them back to me and elected to take evasive action.

"The accusation that you are making is a very serious one, Mr. Cuesta. But this is the consulate of Argentina, and we are here to serve Argentine citizens. I can't do anything unless your client comes to me."

He stood up to signal that the audience was over, plucked a business card off his desk, and held it out so that I had to stand up to reach it. When I did, he stepped around the desk nimbly, put a hand on my back, and exerted diplomatic pressure in the direction of the door. I could sense that he was a good tango dancer. He had the moves.

"Tell your client to come see me. Tell her anything she says to me will be held in the strictest confidence." He gave me a last gentle nudge and closed the door behind me.

I exited through the waiting room, took the elevator down, and was halfway back to my car when I stopped in the middle of the sidewalk. A thought had occurred to me, one that made me wince.

Villarreal had referred to my client as "her." "Tell her anything she says to me . . ."

But not once had I mentioned Fiona or that my client was a woman.

CHAPTER TWELVE

I called Fiona, and she was waiting for me when I pulled up in front of her building. She was wearing white pants, a navy blue blouse and tortoise-shell shades. She looked very glamorous for someone who was about to have blood taken out of her.

As we headed back across the bay I filled her in on the morning's interviews.

"Have you ever heard of this guy Villarreal?"

She searched her memory. "I told you my father had served in the civilian government before the military took over. He was in the foreign relations ministry, and he once had an assistant on his personal staff named Villarreal. I guess it could be the same man. If it is, I didn't know he was here."

"Well, I wouldn't try to make contact with him. He may not be on our side."

I told her just how I had found Villarreal's name, as a reference for Manuel Navarro, and that worried her. I also told her that he seemed to know more than he wanted to reveal.

"Do many people in the government back in Buenos Aires know you're looking for your niece?"

"Oh, yes. I went to every government official I could go to, and I've spoken to the press as well."

"So Villarreal could know you are here?"

She shook her head. "No. I didn't tell anyone I was coming here. Once my friend called me and told me about seeing my niece, I told no one what I had planned, except my husband. I needed to do this secretly."

I didn't like that at all. How did Villarreal know my client was a woman? Did he guess? Did he figure out that only a woman would go so far to find a child? Or did he have informants, just as the Navarros seemed to have? Why would an official of the Argentine government protect a goon from the old regime? Was it that he didn't want to dig up the gruesome past, or was there another reason?

We arrived at the DNA lab, which was off Biscayne Boulevard in Little Haiti. Among the various Miami ethnic groups, it was most often the Haitians who needed DNA testing in order to keep from being kicked out and shipped back to Haiti. If you could prove you were the immediate relative of a Haitian who was already a citizen, then you could stay.

For that reason, the down-at-the-heels neighborhood had become a weird, unlikely locale for genetic technology. In this particular clinic, the walls were hung with bright Haitian voodoo flags, tapestries made of bright cloth and sequins and featuring spooky, doll-like figures. I guess, to Haitians with a certain sensibility, DNA testing was just the newest kind of voodoo.

But other people, in addition to Haitians, availed themselves of the service as well. The waiting room was full.

"I hope we don't get caught in the crossfire," I said to Fiona.

She scowled at me, not able to figure out what I meant. So I explained.

"When some guy finds out that Junior isn't Junior, he might get mad. I can see the headlines: 'Private investigator gunned down in paternity conflict.'"

But that didn't happen. A young Haitian woman who worked the reception desk welcomed us warmly. I guess Alice Arden really did have powerful pull at the place because the girl recognized our names and ushered us right in. We met with a Dr. David Sanger, the owner of the clinic, a thin, white guy, with frizzy red hair and a thick moustache, wearing rimless glasses and a white smock.

I presented the black hairs in the plastic bag. He beamed at them as if he were gazing at a newborn baby.

"I've always wanted to work on one of these Argentine cases."

"You've heard about what happened down there?"

"Oh, yes. Everyone in the DNA field knows about the missing children from Argentina. DNA experts have been able to track some of them down and get them back for their real families. It's one of our consummate successes."

He glanced at Fiona. "You're possibly the aunt of the girl in question?"

"Yes, I think so."

Sanger held up the bag with the hairs, jiggled it, and smiled in a "mad scientist" way.

"Well, let's go find out. We'll draw some blood and begin unraveling those helixes."

"How long will it take?" I asked him.

"Because the relationship isn't that of parent and child, a definitive report would take at least a couple of weeks. But I can learn enough in two days to give you definite guidance."

Fiona followed him into an examining room. I sat and waited for her and made nice with the nurses. The two of them came back out after a couple of minutes.

Sanger held up a vial of blood and flashed that big, ghoulish grin again, as if he were a vampire and about to drink it

"I can get to your case tomorrow," he said. "I'll let you know as soon as I can."

I was ready to leave, but Fiona had a last question.

"How much will this cost, doctor?"

Sanger shook his head. "A case like this I perform pro bono. No charge."

A ghoul, but a ghoul with principles. I liked him.

As we drove back across the bay, Fiona fell silent. She stared out across the azure water, at the shimmering skyline of Miami Beach. Worry was etched on her beautiful face. The scenery wasn't doing it for her, and I thought I knew why, but I was wrong.

"Are you afraid the test will show she isn't your niece?"

She shook her head.

"No, it's something the doctor said that disturbed me."

"What's that?"

"It's true that in my country doctors have been able to find some of the lost children with the DNA tests. They are all over eighteen now, and they have a choice. They can join the family of the real mother, or they can stay with the people they have always thought were their parents. In some cases, the children choose those people, even though they aren't their true blood."

I thought about what Alice Arden had said, about how tragically complicated a case like this could become for the people involved. For Fiona Bonaventura, it already had. I could see in her eyes that, after twenty years of searching, the possibility of rejection suddenly had risen before her. She had been so involved looking for the girl that she had never considered that before.

I watched her out of the side of my eye as I drove. "Are you afraid that will happen in this case?"

She shrugged, but said nothing.

"Maybe the girl is going to have to make the same choice," I said. "I don't know what a court will say about her options. But all you can do is tell the girl the truth and give her a chance to choose a future. That's all you can do for any child, Fiona."

She nodded, lost in her thoughts. I watched her pondering her possibilities, and I wondered if it did happen, just what she might do.

When we had crossed the causeway and reached Miami Beach, I brought her out of her spell.

"You told me the first time we met that there was a person here who had been arrested and tortured at the same time as your sister."

"That's right. His name is Miguel Méndez."

"Will he talk to me? We may need him to go before a judge and identify Navarro."

She tried to picture that possibility and obviously had her doubts.

"He's extremely cautious. It would be better if I go with you."

She dug in her purse and produced an address down on South Pointe, at the foot of Miami Beach.

"Will he be there now?" I asked.

"Yes, he is always there. He is a technician for a computer company, one of those people you talk to if you have trouble with your machine. He does the work by telephone from his house. He is on call all night and sleeps during the day. He almost never goes out and lives by himself as well."

She didn't say why, but the implication was that after the torture he had been through years before, Miguel Méndez was afraid to walk the streets and meet real people. As we drove I asked her about it, and she told me just how badly Méndez had been treated in Argentina's secret prisons. It wasn't pretty.

We reached the neighborhood and found the address. It was in a condo complex called "South Pointe Harbour," a creation of developers who were better with bricks than they were with spelling.

About four blocks off the beach, it was surrounded by a tall stucco wall, with large shards of seashell set in the top, in place of broken glass or barbed wire. An armed guard was posted at the gate, unusual for South Pointe, which was, in general, more laid back. Méndez obviously had security concerns.

Fiona gave the guard her name, he phoned ahead, and we were allowed through. We found Méndez's unit in the last building, at the very back of the complex. Fiona knocked, and moments later the door opened, but only a bit because it was on a chain. A man peered out.

I could see only a narrow wedge of his face, but he was about forty or forty-five years old, mid-sized, with a pale unhealthy complexion and pitted skin. His eyes were close set, brown but almost black, skittish, but also with a hint of meanness, the kind of meanness a dog might exhibit if it had been mistreated.

He must have had the air conditioning turned down to fifty because a cold draft of air wafted out at us.

Fiona smiled at him. "Miguel? It's Fiona Bonaventura, Sonia's sister."

The eyes didn't respond because they were busy staring at me. Fiona hadn't given my name to the guard, and Méndez wasn't happy that I was there.

"This is Mr. Cuesta," Fiona said. "He's trying to help me find the people who killed Sonia. He's a friend."

That didn't convince Méndez. So I produced my card, and he took it from me with sparrow-like fingers through the narrow crack. He stared at it with his jittery eyes, as if the words on it were some kind of code for something else, something menacing.

"I assure you anything you tell me will be kept in the strictest confidence," I said.

As I uttered that standard disclaimer I wedged my foot in the door. It was a habit from my police days, and in this case it was also a mistake. He glanced down at it as if that had been done to him before— probably by the Argentine goon squads. When he looked back up, he was even more spooked. Fiona sensed it too.

"Don't," she said under her breath.

I took my foot from the door.

"Excuse me, but I'm not the police," I said as calmly as I could. "I'm trying to find Sonia's child, and in a small way you might be able to help."

He read the card again carefully. Through the opening of the door, I could see over him into a sliver of his apartment. On the corner of a desk stood a *mate* gourd. Like Navarro, you could take the boy out of Buenos Aires or the *pampas*, but you couldn't take them out of the boy.

The only other thing I saw was a computer. In fact, two of them sat side by side on the same desk. They both had chessboards on the screens. Méndez appeared to be in the midst of two games with faraway opponents. I guess if you had been tortured, you wanted any opponents to be far away. As I watched, one of the pieces on a screen suddenly jumped to another square, and the computer chirped.

You got the sense that he had fled from his demons and this was where he had finally stopped. The problem was you could sense the demons right there with him. You could see them in his eyes as well.

"Fiona tells me you were held in the same secret detention center as Sonia."

He nodded, but said nothing. We were still standing outside, and so far he hadn't said one word to me. I certainly had a way of putting people at ease.

I brought out the photo of Manuel Navarro, which I'd taken as he entered his apartment at the Colonial Arms.

"Can you tell me if you recognize this man?"

I proffered the photo, and he plucked it from me with his birdlike fingers. He gazed at it, and I could see his memory working, or trying to work.

Fiona seemed to be trying as hard as he, attempting to know something she couldn't know by herself.

"Please try to remember, Miguel," she said.

A torture victim like Méndez might have wiped out a lot of memories, like erasing a hard drive, just to keep from reliving them again and again. On the other hand, some people never forgot. They couldn't.

He still stared at the photo. If he didn't recognize Navarro, it wouldn't kill the case, but it might make it all that much harder.

"Remember, it's twenty years since you've seen him," I said. "Don't look at his gray hair or his weight. Look at his face, his features."

He squinted hard for a good thirty seconds, and I sensed that I would come up dry. But then I saw his eyes flare just a bit. It was as if he had lifted a creaking trapdoor in the deepest cellar of his tortured memory and was peering into that dark, dark space. He looked up at us with eyes that were pried open with fear, and he spoke in a whisper:

"Yes, he was there. Is he here now?"

I didn't answer. I didn't have to. Méndez knew.

A moment later he shoved the photo at me, glanced one last time at us as if we were carrying the plague, the terror plague, slammed the door, and locked it from the inside. The interview was over.

CHAPTER THIRTEEN

Minutes later I dropped Fiona off at her condo complex. The visit with Méndez had helped her bounce back from the doubts she'd expressed earlier.

"If Navarro was there, he almost certainly stole my sister's child," she said as I pulled up to the building. "Now we just need to find them. We know what they look like now and we know what names they are using."

I told her that was true and didn't do anything to douse her optimism. But as I pulled away and headed home, I wracked my brain about what to do next.

First I had to find Navarro again, which was going to be a trick. If I did find him, Miguel Méndez might identify his former jailer before a judge.

On the other hand, given his reticence to even open his door, it might prove difficult to get Méndez to testify. And even if he went to court, he was obviously a very frightened individual who, faced with his former torturer, might choose that moment to forget he d ever laid eyes on Navarro. It had happened before with such villains and victims.

I needed more on Navarro than Miguel Méndez. By the time I reached home, I knew who to call.

Jeff Callahan had been the FBI liaison at the U.S. embassy in Buenos Aires, the one who had helped me on an old extradition case. He was now stationed at FBI headquarters in Washington.

I got him on the phone, we briefly exchanged pleasantries, and he taunted me about my tango dancing.

"So what can I do for you, Willie?"

I told him I needed information on a possible child stealing case. I gave him Navarro's name.

"Can you put me in contact with someone in Argentina who would have access to military records?" I asked.

"No problem. But it will be easier if you go online and look for him. The Argentine human rights organizations, over the years, have managed to get their hands on the old military and police personnel files. The victims who survived have supplied information on the crimes committed by hundreds of kidnappers and killers. Many of the 'dirty war' fugitives from those years are listed on websites. Some of them even have photos. That way the public can help find them. You can track down torturers right at your desk, Willie."

He gave me a couple of web addresses.

"If it doesn't work, call me back and I'll get in touch with Buenos Aires. Good luck."

I thanked him, hung up, poured myself a strong rum and tonic, with half a lime, and signed on to the first website. It featured only text, no photos. But it was an astounding document.

It listed hundreds of names, with their military or police ranks, units to which the alleged criminals belonged, the secret detention centers where they were stationed, and their activities. It was a hair-raising catalogue of war criminals and their crimes.

Some of the descriptions were short, others more detailed, especially in the case of actual torturers. It listed the number of known victims and methods, one worse than the next—electricity, water, darkness, and all kinds of instruments. Torture seemed to bring out the creative streak in some creeps.

As I read, I found myself picturing Sonia Bonaventura and Méndez in military torture chambers being put through the different methods. I wondered what the beautiful Sonia had suffered, but I didn't wonder too hard. It was grisly reading.

The files also included the last known whereabouts of the torturers, or suspected whereabouts. A number were thought to be in hiding in Latin American countries apart from Argentina or in Spain. A few, according to the site, were rumored to be in the United States.

The list gave you an idea of just how large and dirty an operation the "dirty war" had been.

Finally, I went to the "N's," scanned down, but found no listing for the missing Manuel Navarro. That wasn't good. The list seemed to include every private and corporal, as well as officers, who had cooperated in the carnage. Why wasn't he there?

I signed off that website and onto the second. This one included similar lists of sins next to the names, but some of them were accompanied by snapshots, official mug shots, probably taken for military and police IDs. Some were goons from central casting—gruff, jowly, with hooded eyes. But many others looked like wide-eyed, innocent children—as if they were amazed at their own evil. It made me realize that not only had some of the victims been very young, but also some of the butchers.

I scrolled down toward the "N's" again, but never reached them. In the middle of the "M's," a familiar face stopped me. The last names next to it were "Martínez Navarro," the first names "Antonio Manuel." But it was certainly the man I knew as Navarro. He had taken his middle name and his maternal last name and devolved a new identity. In the old country he had probably been known as Antonio Martínez. Now he was Manuel Navarro. But it was the same man.

The photo was at least thirty years old. He was heavier and grayer now, but even in his youth Navarro had not looked innocent. He was depicted in a military uniform with a lieutenant's insignia. His hair was black, and the mouth already had a cruel set to it. A deadness lay in the depths of his eyes. He had never been an angel.

I wished I'd had the photo when I'd gone to see Miguel Méndez. On second thought, the actual face, as Méndez had seen it back then, might have scared him to death.

The account of Navarro's service was more complete than most. It started with his days as a prep school cadet at the Argentine Military Lyceum. He then graduated to El Colegio Militar, where he took at least one course from a former German military officer who had participated in atrocities during World War II. A great way to begin a military career.

His initial service was as a quartermaster for an infantry regiment. Maybe that explained what he'd told Shields at International Protection Services, about being a supply officer.

But apparently that work had not satisfied Navarro, because before long he had transferred as a junior officer to military intelligence. His first years of service in that section had come under a civilian government. But in the mid-1970s the generals had taken command in a military coup.

According to the electronic files, by that time Navarro was an administrator in intelligence. As the abductions, disappearances, and deaths began, he had been instrumental in converting military and police facilities into secret detention centers and torture chambers in the province of Buenos Aires. He was involved in "equipping," "supplying," "staffing," and "administering" those facilities.

In other words, he had recruited torturers and signed their paychecks. He was a bureaucrat in charge of blood spilling. His ledgers kept track of suffering and death.

According to the report, he worked directly with the "*Grupo de Tareas 332*"—Task Force 332—which performed the disappearances.

"This subject also participated in the torture of certain, high-profile prisoners at various detention centers, including those of the Air Force and Navy." That was how the report ended. It made me wonder if he had been directly involved in the torture of Mario Murillo and Sonia Bonaventura.

There was no mention of his having stolen the babies of disappeared women, at least not in this file.

But it was still quite a resume. This was the kind of guy who was now living in Miami, or at least he had been. This was the guy who was on the loose and who wouldn't like the fact I was searching for him. This was, almost certainly, the murderous shadow who had almost cracked my skull the previous night and who would have finished me off if he'd had the time.

I looked over the file again, and my attention was drawn to the task force that had disappeared people: *Grupo de Tareas 332*. I stopped for a moment, then I reached into my pocket and took out the San Telmo Tango Club flyer I'd turned up at Navarro's apartment. I flipped it over.

Written on the back were five ciphers:

"GT 332."

Alice called that night, a while before I went to bed.

"You're very highly thought of at the DNA lab in Little Haiti," I said.

"I'm a helix 'ho."

"A what?"

"A helix 'ho. I'm into helixes."

"Dr. Sanger says he'll have preliminary results in no time."

"Good. What else did you detect today?"

So I told her about the visit to Miguel Méndez, his positive identification of Navarro, and my eventual perusal of the Internet files.

"This Navarro sounds like a sweetheart," she said. "You always get involved with such tasteful individuals."

"I have high standards."

"It's good that this guy Méndez remembers him. There's nothing like a victim pointing across a courtroom and saying, 'That's the dirty dude.'"

"We'll see how much pointing he does."

We signed off and I hit the sack, but I didn't close my eyes right away. I was thinking about an article I'd read years back in one of the Miami papers. It listed all the former dictators and military strongmen from Latin America who had retired to the Miami area. It told you where they lived, where they played golf or dominoes, and their favorite haunts.

Given how many dead people they were responsible for "haunts" was the exact right word.

It was impressive list. Miami was the preferred destination for such individuals—guys who had closets full of Latin skeletons—to spend their golden years. How did one know when it was time to retire from blood letting? Did the satisfaction suddenly go out of it?

Rumor had it that those retirees sometimes got together for social occasions. One wondered what the conversation was like at the canasta table.

If I stayed on the Argentina case, I would soon be able to write my own addendum to that article. But I didn't want to think about the subject at all right then. I didn't want to give myself creepy dreams.

I cleared my mind and closed my eyes, but it didn't do much good.

CHAPTER FOURTEEN

During the week, when I'm not working at the club, I like to catch up on my sleep. That night I wasn't in luck.

It was 4:10 a.m. when the phone rang. I forced my eyelids apart, fixed on the digital clock, cursed like a sailor on the Miami River, reached for the phone, trying to strangle it, and made a barely human noise into the receiver.

"Willie?"

"Who's this?"

"It's Lester Grand."

Grand was a detective sergeant with the Miami Dade Police homicide squad. Once an All-American offensive guard at the University of Florida, he had blown out a knee before he could turn pro. He had eventually turned policeman, working his way up to homicide.

"Uh-huh, Lester. Did you call to let me know you're a big boy now and can stay up late?"

"No, I called to tell you to get out of bed and come down to 69th Street on Miami Beach."

The address made my eyes come open again. "Why would I do that at four a.m., Lester?"

"Because there's a dead man here lying on his back and he's using your business card as a tie clip. I thought you might enlighten me on how that came to be."

"Who is it?"

"You'll see when you get here." He gave me the address.

"How about if I get there after two more hours sleep, Lester."

"You can come, or I can send someone to get you. They'll show up with the sirens on, Willie. Make you real popular with your neighbors."

"I'll be there."

At four-thirty a.m. about the only people on the road were those just leaving nightclubs. In Miami that can still cause a traffic jam, but it didn't that night. I made good time.

The terrified face of Miguel Méndez was floating in my mind's eye. When he had found out Navarro was in Miami, it obviously had frightened him to the bone. He had gazed at me in terror.

But the address Grand had given me wasn't in South Pointe where Méndez lived. It was in Little Buenos Aires—more specifically, the offices of Gold Coast Realty. When I arrived, I found four police cruisers parked and yellow crime scene tape decorating that side of the street, like sagging crepe paper.

One of the uniformed officers, a slim black woman, told me I couldn't pass. I told her Lester Grand had woken me up expressly to stumble by her looking like a Latin zombie. She finally let me by.

I found Lester in the front room of the realty office, bent over a body on the floor.

I advanced and looked over his shoulder. Stretched out flat on his back was the real estate property manager, Benito Corral. He had been shot or clubbed in the back of the skull. A large circular pool of blood surrounded his head, like the halos they used to paint around the heads of saints. Except this one was blood red.

He wore the same outfit he had worn when I'd spoken with him about thirty-six hours earlier. Lying on his chest, just above his shirt pocket, was my business card. It looked like it might have slipped out of the pocket when he fell. I couldn't think of any reason somebody would put it there, unless they just wanted to screw with my sleeping patterns.

I looked around. The extra doors still were leaning against the walls. It seemed the murderer might be behind any one of them. But I figured the police had already checked that possibility. The killer, apparently, was long gone.

Lester turned and looked at me.

"The man himself."

"Under protest."

"Not as much protest as this guy," Grand said, glancing down at the dead man. He pointed at the card. "You see what I'm saying?"

"Can't miss it, can you? And it was lying just like that when you arrived?"

Lester frowned at me, which, given his size, was worrisome.

"You're not accusing me of tampering with a crime scene, are you, Willie?"

"Wouldn't think of it. How'd you find him?"

"A guy on patrol saw the light on, got curious, and took a peek through the window."

I crouched down next to Corral and got a closer look. His eyes were open, and they were full of frozen fear. He was even more scared of me in death than he had been in life.

"Shot in the back of the head?" I asked.

"Yes, but look at his neck too."

Corral's chin was wedged against his collarbone. Wound around his throat, partially concealed by the folds of flesh, was a set of white plastic rosary beads threaded onto a chain. The small silver crucifix attached to them could be seen dangling down into his coat collar. There was minor bleeding where the beads had pierced the skin. It appeared someone had strangled him with the beads, or at least grabbed him by them before shooting him. It made the hit look like a ritual death.

I rocked on my heels. "That's a new one on me."

"Me too," Grand said.

"Maybe that narrows the suspects down to Catholics. Of course, the city is full of Cubans, Nicaraguans, Colombians, other Latinos, and Haitians too, most of whom are Catholics. But you can at least eliminate the atheists."

"Maybe, but why is your business card here?"

You couldn't distract Grand with talk of the world's religions. He knew a real clue when he saw one.

"I came here to talk to him two days ago."

"About what?"

"A case I'm working on."

"What case is that?"

So I told him I was on a missing child case and that the girl was Argentine. But I didn't give him much detail or feed him the name of Fiona Bonaventura.

"So what did this guy tell you?" Grand asked gazing down at Corral.

"Nothing much at all. Certainly nothing that would have gotten him knocked off. Maybe my case had nothing to do with it. Maybe somebody just came in here to rob him."

"If they did, they didn't do a very good job. There's money in a bag in the desk drawer. He has more in his wallet, and they left his watch."

With the toe of his very large shoe, Grand nudged the sleeve of Corral's suit jacket to reveal a gold wristwatch.

Grand's radio squawked just then. It turned out that Corral had lived in a condo run by Gold Coast Realty, just two blocks away. Grand had sent his partner, a young white guy named Prosky, over there to notify any family members. Prosky's voice crackled out of the radio, which looked tiny in Grand's big black hand.

"You read me, Grand?"

"Yeah, I read you."

"He lived by himself. I woke up the super, and he told me that. He let me into the apartment too, and I looked around. There's some stuff over here you should see."

"Stuff? What does stuff mean?"

"Just come. You'll see for yourself."

Grand turned, rumbled out the door, around the cruisers and down the block, until he found me at his side. He stopped.

"Where you think you're goin'?"

"I'm goin' with you. If I see anything relating to my case, you'll want me to tell you."

"Is that right?"

"Yes, it is."

Prosky met us at the glass front door of a nondescript building two blocks off the bay. He led us upstairs to a boxy, antiseptic one-bedroom apartment on the second floor. The super, a short, Latin man with tousled hair, wearing a terry cloth bathrobe and a bitter expression, was waiting for us. He seemed more perturbed by the loss of sleep than by the sudden breaking of the lease by the murder victim.

Grand took a quick tour of the place, and I followed him. The living room was furnished with a bare coffee table, as well as a couch and one stuffed chair, neither of which looked like they'd ever been sat on.

The bedroom contained a narrow single bed, a night table, and a crucifix. In the rug under the crucifix were two worn spots that looked like they might have been made by knees. Either that or someone had spent a lot of time standing right there.

That was all. The place was spartan and spotlessly clean.

The super had followed us into the bedroom.

"How long did this man live here?" I asked him.

"Three years."

"Doesn't look like he threw a lot of wild parties. In fact, it doesn't look like he breathed in here."

Prosky summoned us to the closet across from the bed. Some clothes hung there on hangers, and he slid them to one side. Behind them stood a narrow wooden table. On it sat a gold chalice and a missal, as if the table were an altar where mass was said. Hanging next to it on a nail was a black cassock and also a Roman collar.

"They're priest's clothes," Prosky said.

"I can see that," said Grand.

He reached around Prosky and picked up from the floor of the closet a wide black leather briefcase. Sitting on the bed, he emptied it of documents and also of a folder containing photographs. I stood behind him as he leafed through them.

Most of the photos showed the man I'd known as Benito Corral, but in them he was dressed as a priest. He was posed with other priests or parishioners—men, women, and children.

But in one snapshot he was surrounded by soldiers posing outside a barracks. Most of them were young, but standing next to him, a bit taller than the small priest, was a stocky, middle-aged man in an officer's uniform. It was the individual I knew as Manuel Navarro, and I bit my lip in order to keep from whistling.

The paperwork told us that Corral's real name was Father Francisco Pérez and that he had been ordained in Buenos Aires thirty years ago. He later had served as a chaplain to the Argentine armed services.

As Grand reviewed the rest of the documents, I stared at the walls of the monastic apartment. I wondered just what had caused Corral to give up the cloth, come to Miami, and live under another identity.

I also wondered what it had to do with the case of Sonia Bonaventura, because I knew there had to be a connection. Corral was connected to Navarro, Navarro was connected to the girl—Elena—and she, I was pretty sure, was connected to Fiona and her family. At this point, they were all connected to me.

I also thought of the last words Corral had said to me as I walked out of his office. "God bless you," he'd muttered.

They had been worrisome words when he'd said them to me, and they were even freakier now. As it turned out, it was he who'd needed the Lord's protection.

Grand interrupted my musings.

"Any reason to think this is connected to the case you're working on?"

I shook my head. "Not that I can see."

"I'd like to talk to this client of yours just in case."

"I'll let her know."

I picked up the photo of the priest with the soldiers.

"I'll just borrow one of these so I can show it to her. Maybe it will jog her memory."

Grand packed up the rest of the priestly paraphernalia, and we made our way back to the murder scene. The coroner's man was there and had confirmed that Corral—or Father Pérez—had perished as a result of a single shot in the back of the head. Time of death was between five and eight hours earlier. Roughly between nine p.m. and midnight.

That wasn't news. But another cop had managed to contact the woman who worked as a receptionist at the office.

"She says she left at five-thirty. Just before she took off a guy came in and got into a big fight with the dead man."

Grand liked that. "Who was he?"

"She didn't know. Never seen him before. She said they argued in Spanish and whoever it was sounded like he was from Argentina, just like the dead guy. She speaks Spanish, but the door was closed and she couldn't hear what they argued about. She said it was nasty."

"What did he look like?"

"Blond hair, short, expensive looking. That's what she said. And that he wore too much cologne."

Grand turned to me. "Sound familiar?"

I shook my head, something I was getting good at.

"Probably just somebody who wouldn't pay the rent," I said.

I told Grand I'd be in touch, and I headed back to my car before he asked me something else I had to lie about. On the way home I tried to decide who I would talk to first.

Would it be Fiona Bonaventura? Or should I go directly to her husband Eduardo Estevez? Because I knew that was who Corral had argued with shortly before he died, and it probably wasn't over the cologne.

CHAPTER FIFTEEN

It was light out when I got home and too late to go back to bed. I ate breakfast, waited until eight a.m. and called Alice, knowing she'd be awake.

"You're up early," she said.

"You don't know the half of it."

I told her about the wake-up call from Grand, the body, and the hidden identity of the dead man.

"Wow!"

"Now you tell me what role a priest could possibly have played in all this."

I didn't think she'd have an answer to that. But being Alice Arden, of course, she did.

"There were priests who served as chaplains to the death squads."

"You're kidding me?"

"I don't kid about such things. They started as chaplains attached to certain military units, and they stayed loyal to those units even after the kidnapping and killing began."

"So they knew those things were going on?"

"Yes. In fact, in some cases they even blessed the prisoners before they were executed."

I pictured Father Pérez sketching a cross over Sonia Bonaventura before she was loaded on a plane to be fed to the sharks.

"The priests were fanatics," Alice continued, "and later on when it all leaked out, they explained that since all enemies to the military regime were considered communists and communists were godless, that the people killed were better off dead. After the military government fell, the priests sank out of sight."

"That's all been proven?"

"It's in the official government records. It's gospel."

I drank that in. It took a few gulps because it was another one of those moments in Latin American history that boggled the mind and the soul.

"And maybe that's why Father Pérez sank out of sight here in Miami," I said finally.

"Probably. I have to run. We'll talk later."

She hung up, and I was left staring at the phone. I now knew what Corral had to do with Navarro. I had the old photo of them together right in front of me. But that still didn't explain how Eduardo Estevez knew Corral, the former Father Pérez. And if Estevez knew the priest, did he also know Navarro? Could he know where Navarro was hiding? Could it be Estevez who had warned Navarro? Did he have reasons for not wanting to find him and the girl? Was that why Fiona Bonaventura doubted his loyalty?

At nine I picked up the phone again and called the number I had for Fiona and Estevez. The maid answered. *El señor y la señora* were not at home. Fiona had gone to exercise, and Estevez had gone down to the beach.

I thanked her and hung up. Then I showered, shaved, slipped my handgun into a hip holster under my jacket, and shoved off.

I drove to Collins Avenue, parked a ways down from their condo building, took the public access to the beach, and slogged across the sand.

The shoreline was already littered with vacationing Europeans, but also with South Americans who were escaping the cooler weather down in the next hemisphere. Most of them lay baking in the sun, which was already strong enough to toast your average tourist. Covered with greasy tanning oils and lying dead still, they looked like basted birds scattered on the edge of the continent.

I wandered among those birds trying to find Estevez. He had that golden tan, and this was probably where he was burnishing it. I finally found him lying by himself on a patch of sand behind some rocks. He wore only his scant swim trunks and a white plastic pince-nez that serious sun worshippers used to cover their eyelids. They made him look like a zombie.

"Good morning, Mr. Estevez."

He grimaced, pulled off the pince-nez, and propped himself on an elbow. He wasn't thrilled to see me, but he never was.

"What is it? Can't you see I'm busy."

Lying in the sand passed for "busy" among some people.

"This is important."

The golden boy seemed to have his doubts that anything could be more crucial than his tan.

"What is it?"

"I'm wondering where you were between nine p.m. and midnight last night."

"And why do you want to know that?"

"Because the police will want to know. That's why."

"The police?"

"Where were you?"

"I was north of here visiting a friend. We went to have drinks and dinner. I didn't arrive home until almost one a.m."

"You can prove that?"

"Yes, of course. What is this about?"

"I hear you were friendly with Benito Corral, or rather, Father Pérez, as he was known to his torturer buddies."

I saw surprise momentarily cloud the contempt in his eyes, but he didn't respond. I wasn't interested in being cute or cagey with him. I wanted to pin him to the sand.

"Although you weren't friendly with him yesterday. You went to see him at the real estate office and you argued. What was it you argued about?"

He turned away and gazed toward the sea.

"I don't know what you're speaking about."

"Well, maybe this will help you remember. Father Pérez was murdered last night, and the police want to know who was arguing with him a short while before he was shot dead."

Estevez's fine mouth fell open. He seemed even more surprised now, but you could never tell how good a liar someone was on short acquaintance. And sometimes killers were surprised they'd killed someone. Few people ever expect to be murderers.

"How did you know Pérez?"

The news, or maybe the mention of the police, had taken some of the defiance out of him, at least for the moment.

"I used to live near the church in Buenos Aires where he celebrated mass."

"Was that before he became chaplain to the death squads or after?"

His face stormed over. "I didn't know anything about that!"

"I thought everyone in Argentina knew. That's why he was hiding here in Miami."

"We only found out later. My wife and I went on holidays to church. Pérez said the mass. That's all I knew back then."

"Is that what you were arguing about yesterday? About how he said mass? Is that why you shot him?"

He freaked again. "I had nothing to do with that. I told you, I can prove it."

Of course maybe the coroner's man was off by an hour. Maybe the priest had died closer to one a.m. It only took a second to shoot somebody, a quick detour, like buying a loaf of bread. Then you headed home just a few blocks away.

"Why did you go to see Pérez in the first place?"

Estevez shook his head in exasperation. "I wanted him to help resolve all this. I thought he might know these people, the Navarros, and know if the child was really theirs. Then I could tell my wife and we could go back to Buenos Aires."

"How did you know where to find him?"

"A friend back home has contacts in the church and knew he was here. When I told the friend I was coming and why, he found out where the priest was."

Fiona Bonaventura said she had told no one in Buenos Aires about the trip. Her husband had been less discreet.

"So what did you argue about with Father Pérez?"

"He grew angry with me for going to that office. He felt my contacting him put his position here in danger. He said some other men with problems in their military pasts had been deported from here so they could be put in prison in their home countries. He was afraid it would happen to him. In fact, he was terrified."

"So what did you do?"

"I didn't do anything. He refused to help me and told me to take my wife home and stay there. He said I didn't know who I was getting involved with. That they are dangerous men. Then the meeting was over and I left. It was somewhere around six o'clock."

Pérez had been right: they were dangerous men.

"Did he tell you he knew the Navarros? That he rented to them?"

Estevez's eyes widened. "No, he didn't."

"Well, he did."

Now the priest was dead, and Navarro was nowhere to be found. All I had was the elusive Estevez, whose upper lip was beaded with sweat—maybe from the heat, but probably more from nerves.

I remembered again our last meeting and the cryptic words his wife had uttered about his loyalty. I decided to twist the screws one more turn.

"Twenty years ago, did you know where your sister-in-law and her husband—Sonia and Mario—were hiding?"

The question curdled his expression even more. "No. I didn't."

"Are you sure?"

"Yes, I'm sure. The rest of the family knew, but I wasn't told."

I could see that even now, two decades later, that rankled him. And I rankled him too.

"Are you implying that I betrayed them?" he asked.

I didn't say a word. He stared at me in disbelief, then jumped to his feet.

"Get out of here!" he shouted. "Get out! I didn't come to Miami to be accused of murder. Not last night or twenty years ago."

He turned, stalked off, and waded into the water. The other basting birds were all scowling at me. I was creating a disturbance, messing with their quiet absorption of ultraviolet rays, and they weren't happy.

Before leaving I yelled something at Estevez's bare back.

"GT 332!"

He stopped and stared back at me.

"Do you know what that was?" I asked.

Estevez stayed stock still for several moments, the water up to his waist. He seemed about to speak, but didn't. Instead, he turned, dove into the sea, and started to swim, headed vaguely for the horizon. I didn't wait to see if he made it.

CHAPTER SIXTEEN

Unfortunately, I wasn't getting paid to piss off my client's husband. In fact, if I wanted to get paid at all again, I had to find the girl. So I did the only thing I could think of. I cranked up and drove toward downtown to the Miami School of Art and Design. Now that Navarro was on the run, the girl, Elena, might not be continuing with her education, but it was the only lead I had.

The campus was located a few blocks north of the city center, just a block off the bay. It occupied an old shopping mall that had failed and been converted to an art school as part of an urban renewal project. I'd passed it, but I hadn't been inside since the transformation.

A few minutes later I walked in and found myself in the same cavernous lobby that had been there when the place was a castle of commerce. Back then it had sold everything from girdles to ghetto blasters.

Now all signs of the retail world were gone. Instead the walls of that lobby were crammed with paintings, collages, assemblages—artistic visions of all kinds. Some were big, others small. Some of them abstract, some not. Many wildly colorful, others subdued. The good, the bad, and the ugly. All together, in one space, it seemed like a universe that had been exploded and then hung up in disparate pieces all around me.

Hanging from the ceiling by piano wire, above all those other creations, flew a black metal archangel, larger than a human being. It was full of holes, which were meant to be bullet holes. It seemed to say even angels can get caught in antiaircraft fire. I guess if you were young in the post 9/11 world, that was how you saw the cosmos—as an exploding universe, dangerous even for the angels.

I knew that in recent years many young artists had come to Miami from Latin America, and the names attached to the works were mostly Latino. The transformation from a bankrupt American shopping mecca to a haunted warehouse where Latin American dreams and nightmares were stored was both weird and beautiful.

I walked along the first floor, which had once been occupied by shops. Now the dark spaces were classrooms, school offices, and art studios. You could see through the front windows to the students, either listening to lectures, or painting, sculpting, and assembling. I didn't see Elena Navarro.

I reached a larger space that once had been a department store in the mall, but, like the lobby, it was now a gallery given over to the work of the enrollees. I drifted through it, and eventually my attention was caught by a wall of four paintings that looked familiar.

They were full-body portraits, two men, two women. They all featured the same wild brushstrokes, partially in black but also in strident colors, that I had seen in the girl's bedroom at the Colonial Arms. I read the signatures on the paintings before me. They all said "Elena."

I stepped back from them. They weren't beautiful, but their dark energy attracted and held your attention. I noticed something about each of the figures that I hadn't noted the first time I'd seen her work: they didn't seem to be standing on anything. They were all suspended in space. Or, possibly, falling through thin air as if dropped from a plane.

There was no way Elena Navarro could have known how Sonia Bonaventura had died, not as far as I knew. But still she painted those suspended, tortured figures. That made them much, much spookier.

I left the gallery, kept walking, and reached a back entrance to the school. The question was where to put myself so that I might catch a glimpse of Elena Navarro. I thought of going to the registrar's office and asking where I might find her. But the folks there probably wouldn't tell me. And they certainly wouldn't do so without alerting the girl. They might mistake me for a stalker.

I sat on a bench in the main hallway. It was summer and attendance was light. The people I saw were young, stylish, and artsy. Some had hair dyed the colors of the rainbow. It had been a couple of years since I'd visited a local school. I noticed a slight decrease in tattoos and a small uptick in body piercings.

I couldn't help but think how different this school was from the one where Sonia Bonaventura, Elena's mother, had matriculated. Here you didn't have to look over your shoulder for lurking kidnappers. Only for lurking detectives like me.

I finally decided where I might best bump into her. I went to the cafeteria, because everyone had to eat, including me.

I found it at the end of that first floor, in a space that had once been a Chinese restaurant. I stood in line and purchased a coffee and a blueberry muffin. Then I sat with my back against a wall, under an abstract painting that looked both like stalks of bamboo and the bars of a jail cell, with haunted eyes staring out from behind them. From that seat I could see anybody who came in.

I had finished the muffin and was working on the coffee when I saw Elena Navarro walk into the cafeteria. She was wearing the same small, black backpack she had the first time I'd seen her, but she wasn't carrying books. She also wore an extremely unhappy expression on her beautiful face.

She passed through the line, purchased an iced tea, and said hello to several other students at a table not far from me. But she sat at a separate table by herself. Two minutes later, a tall, good-looking, serious young man entered the cafeteria, his dark, curly hair tucked under a baseball cap.

He crossed to her table, gave her a peck on the lips, and sat down next to her. I was willing to wager this was the boyfriend.

They fell into intense conversation. It was clear that the girl was distraught, and he was trying to console her. Of course, if you'd been forced to flee your home just two days ago, for reasons that probably had not been truly explained to you, you had cause to be disturbed.

In fact, if that had happened to you previously, so that your life felt like a floating crap game, you had plenty of reason to be upset. And maybe the Navarros were planning a move out of Miami altogether. In that case she would probably lose her art school and her handsome boyfriend. Not a happy prospect for a girl her age.

I watched them talk, and the young man kissed her some more. Finally, they got up. The guy exited in one direction and the girl in another. I threw my trash into a nearby bin and shadowed Elena. She wandered down the main corridor and disappeared into a faculty office.

I sat back down on a bench and waited some more. I spent the next half hour the way I'd spent most of my time in school, either staring into nothing or glancing at girls who passed. I think my years in school prepared me for my profession. Back then I had done much more surveillance than studying.

About a half hour later, Elena Navarro emerged again. She didn't look any happier than when she'd gone in. I wondered if she was notifying a professor that she was dropping out. I also wondered what kind of reason she gave. The real cause was that her "father" was a war criminal, but she probably didn't know that.

She walked down the corridor, and I fell in behind her. Passing under the perforated black angel, she left the building. She walked a block and planted herself at a bus stop. I drifted up as well and dropped thirty-five cents in a machine to buy a Miami Herald. I hid my face behind the paper, just in case she had a very good memory and might recognize me from that one glance we had exchanged in Little Buenos Aires. As long as I had it in front of me, I read the city page. But of course there was no mention of the murder of Father Pérez. It had been discovered too late.

We didn't wait long. After a few minutes, a 48 bus pulled up. The girl allowed an elderly woman to get on first and then followed her. Two other guys got on, and I brought up the rear. I didn't have change and ended up paying two bucks for the bus. I asked for a transfer because I'd seen the girl take one.

Elena sat by herself in the middle. I made my way farther back, which would allow me to keep her in sight. There was no empty bench back there, so I sat next to a small, gray-haired lady in sunglasses. She smiled at me gaily, as if maybe I was trying to pick her up. I smiled back, but let the opportunity of romance pass.

After a while, we pulled into a bus depot on Douglas Road, and the girl got up. I did the same and followed her off the bus. We waited another few minutes at the depot. When the 72 bus swept in, she got on. I boarded right behind her.

This bus was more crowded. She walked almost all the way to the back and then sat down. In order to keep an eye on her, I stopped in the middle and remained standing—a straphanger.

We headed west and made our way into Coral Gables. In fact, we entered the most exclusive enclaves of the Gables, passing big plots occupied by pink and white Spanish colonial stucco palaces.

As we approached the corner of Anastasia and Granada, the girl got up. She came toward the door at the middle of the bus. I, gentleman that I am, allowed her to get off first. I followed.

The bus pulled away, and she crossed the street, walking east under an arbor of banyan and poinciana trees. I made as if I were heading in the opposite direction. That was west toward the Biltmore Hotel, which was only two blocks away. But then I stopped and watched her. She shuffled along the way a little girl might walk, as if a part of her—the part that had never understood all the moving and running—had never grown up. Just the way she walked was enough to break your heart.

She went one block and then turned south. I jogged in that direction and reached the corner in time to see her turn into a house about a hundred yards down. It was one of the smaller houses on the block, done in umber-colored stucco, with a barrel tile roof and an archway over the drive. But if this was where the Navarros were now staying, it was a big step up from their last lodgings.

I gave her time to get inside. Then I drifted by the place, just so I could write down the house number. Parked in the drive, toward the back of the house, was the same black car I had seen arrive at the Colonial Arms two nights ago. It had to be Navarro's.

I thought about staying right there and not moving, so that I wouldn't lose the girl again. But that wasn't realistic. I couldn't get anything done that way. And eventually the Coral Gables cops would pick me up for loitering and weird behavior.

So I kept going around the block, walked over to the Biltmore, found a cab, and asked to be taken back downtown. I'd been on the case about thirty hours. I'd lost the girl and found her again. I was back where I'd started—except one man was already dead.

CHAPTER SEVENTEEN

I picked up my car and headed home. I intended to check databases and find out just who owned the house where the Navarros were holed up.

On the way, I heard a report on the radio about the murder of the former priest Francisco Pérez, alias Benito Corral. Grand was asking anyone with information to contact Miami-Dade homicide. There were no other details about the murder that I didn't already know.

I wasn't quite home when my cell phone rang again. It was Fiona Bonaventura. She didn't give me a chance to get a word out.

"What did you say to my husband? What did you ask him about Sonia? He came back here and he was crazy."

"I found the girl again," I said, figuring that would bring her back on board.

But it didn't. Her tone didn't change. I thought I'd gotten myself out of trouble with my client, but I was apparently in even deeper hot water. Something had a hold of her now, something other than her quest to find the girl.

"I want you to come here now," she demanded. "I need to talk to you."

She hung up.

I pulled up to the condo twenty minutes later and saw her sitting in the lobby next to the door, wearing the same tortoise shell shades. She sprang up, stalked out, and climbed in next to me.

"Drive. We need to get away from here before my husband comes looking for me."

I did what I was told, driving several blocks and pulling onto a side street that offered a view of the aquamarine sea. I hoped she might take a moment to enjoy it and calm down, but she didn't. She took off the shades and bore down on me.

"Now, tell me what you said to my husband."

I shrugged. "I didn't say anything. I asked him a question."

"Which question?" But she seemed to know already. Her hands had clenched into claws.

"I asked him if he knew where Sonia was in hiding twenty years ago and if he told anyone."

Her face twisted in agony and her clawlike hands bunched into fists. A sound escaped her that was angry and anguished.

"You have no right to ask that of him. I didn't tell you to ask him that. I didn't tell you to speak with him again at all."

"I had to speak with him."

"Why?"

"Because the police want to talk to him about a murder."

That stopped her. Outside the car, people in bathing suits passed, heading for the beach. Just feet away, we were speaking of disappearances, betrayals of the innocent. Radically different realities—brightly colored beach umbrellas and torture chambers—had a way of coming together in my home city. It made the world come unhinged in a particular way that doesn't happen in most places.

"An Argentine was murdered here on Miami Beach last night. Your husband was one of the last people to see him alive . . . if not *the* last. Did you know Father Francisco Pérez?"

She sank way into herself, into some alleyway of memory in the area of her sister's death. But finally she nodded.

"Yes, I knew Father Pérez."

"He said mass in your local church in Buenos Aires."

"That's right."

"Did you ever speak to him about your sister, Sonia, and her political activities?"

She shook her head once. "No, never."

"Did you know that he was also chaplain to one of the death squads?"

"We only heard that later."

I brought out the copy of the photo of Pérez posed with the soldiers.

"That was him, wasn't it?"

She studied it and nodded.

"Do you know who that is standing next to him? It's Manuel Navarro."

She stared in horror at the photo.

"Your husband went to see Pérez yesterday."

I told her about the priest's using a phony identity, his connection to Navarro through the rental company, and Estevez's argument with him. Then I told her how her husband had explained it to me and of Pérez being found dead less than twelve hours later.

"Did your husband tell you all that? Did he tell you Pérez was here?"

She didn't answer.

"Why wouldn't he tell you, Fiona? Why didn't he want you to know? Who tipped off Navarro that I was watching him? How did Navarro know to run?"

Fiona was shaking her head as if she had the same questions in her mind, but was trying to dislodge them.

"Your husband knows things about all this that you don't know, Fiona."

She bunched her hands into fists. "You're trying to destroy my marriage."

I didn't answer, but given what I suspected, there wasn't a real marriage to destroy. In many marriages secrets existed, places one didn't pry. They often had to do with past mistakes, but they didn't reach this degree of seriousness, of tragedy. They didn't continue to haunt the respective lives. I didn't know what Estevez had done or hadn't done, but it was enough that Fiona Bonaventura was afraid to ask.

She turned on me.

"You weren't there when my sister and Mario were kidnapped. People were disappearing all the time. Everyone was terrified. Eduardo was trying to protect me."

"I know he's your husband, but even you have suspicions about him. I heard you say as much to him. What did you mean by that?"

"Eduardo had friends in the government, the military, and at the embassies—that's how he knew the danger we were in personally. I know he hated Mario, and at times I thought . . ."

She stopped, unable to utter the accusation. I finished it for her.

"That he betrayed Mario and Sonia?"

Her face stormed over, the way her husband's had earlier. "Not Sonia. Maybe she only died by mistake."

I could see that deep inside she was still trying to picture what might have happened all those years before. She had probably done so hundreds of times over the two decades. But the main characters, Mario and Sonia, were dead. She was like a frustrated director whose actors never said their lines intelligibly and died before the movie was finished. It seemed there was no way she would ever know for sure.

"But you think maybe he handed Mario over to military intelligence?"

She shook her head hard. "I suspected that in the beginning because of how much he and Mario had argued. But I never really believed it. He wouldn't do that. He was trying to protect Sonia and me, all of us. And he has protected me ever since."

"And you think he's trying to protect you now by not telling you where your worst enemies are hiding?"

She tried to find an answer for that question but couldn't. Finally, she dug her long fingers into her thick, black hair.

"Since I received the call telling me my niece might be here in Miami, my husband has acted differently. In the past Eduardo has always helped me follow the leads we had. But this time he told me he didn't want me to come. It was the first time anyone actually acquainted with my sister had contacted me saying they had seen her child. It was very important to me, but the moment Eduardo heard it meant coming to Miami, he was totally against the trip. It's something I never expected."

It was something I hadn't expected either. If I were going to help her reclaim her niece, I couldn't be fighting someone close to her. Maybe, for his own reasons, Estevez didn't want it to happen. Maybe he hadn't wanted to come to Miami because he *did* have secrets. Maybe Miami was the one place they could be revealed. Maybe. But right then I let it go.

"I found the girl again."

She heard me this time, now that she wanted to escape her doubts. "Where is she?"

"She and the Navarros are in a house in Coral Gables. I need to find out who owns it. I'm starting to think that other members of the old gang are here in Miami, along with Navarro and the late Father Pérez."

That frightened her. The murder of Pérez was proof that the old "dirty warriors" were still willing to shed blood.

"We have to get Elena out of there before something happens to her," she said.

We had finally hit on something we could agree on

"Yes, we do, Fiona. Yes, we do."

CHAPTER EIGHTEEN

I dropped Fiona off and told her to stay in touch with me. I had to keep a closer track of her as the connections between the Argentines started to come clear. If Estevez had contact with the war criminals, they might know where he was living. That meant they would know how to find Fiona. I didn't like that.

It also meant they might be keeping track of *me* through Estevez. I didn't cotton to that either.

I was halfway home when my cell rang again, and I saw a number I didn't recognize. I answered and heard a woman speaking very softly, almost in a whisper.

"Mr. Cuesta?"

"Yes."

"This is Sara Ingram."

I hadn't slept much, and it took me a moment to remember that Sara Ingram was the cousin of Manuel Navarro. She was the tango dancing woman from Glades Springs with the polo-playing husband who didn't like me.

"Yes, Mrs. Ingram. How's your husband? Does he still want to whip me to the finish line?"

I don't think she understood the reference. She hesitated. I heard a radio on in the background.

"I'd like to know if you've been in contact with my cousin Manuel," she said.

"No, I haven't."

I hadn't actually seen Manuel Navarro at the Coral Gables address. I also didn't know if Mrs. Ingram was in touch with her cousin. She might be spying for him, helping him stay out of my way. Her life seemed to have nothing to do with his, but they were family. In Latin culture, cousins are often just as close as siblings. And in most instances, blood is thicker than the law.

"I see," she said.

"Have you heard from him?"

"No, we haven't." She was still speaking in a near whisper.

"Is your husband there, Mrs. Ingram?"

"No, he isn't."

"Then why are you whispering?"

Again she hesitated. I wondered if Sara Ingram didn't whisper all the time in the shadow of that big husband of hers.

"Did you call me because you want to talk to me about your cousin, Mrs. Ingram?"

She didn't answer directly. "I understand that Father Francisco Pérez was killed. I heard it on the radio."

It was also clear that the news had scared her.

"Yes, he was. Did you know Father Pérez?"

"No, not personally, but I'd heard of him. Can you tell me how it happened? Do they know who did it?"

She wanted information from me, for whatever reason, and I wanted her knowledge of Navarro.

"Why don't we meet," I said. "I don't like speaking about these matters over the phone."

She made a barely audible whimpering sound, as if that too scared her.

"I guess I can meet you, but it will have to be somewhere outside of Glades Springs."

I proposed an Argentine bakery in North Miami Beach called Marco's that also operated a small café.

"In a half hour," she whispered.

I whispered back, said I'd be there, and hung up.

I arrived before she did and stood in line. The place was small, but wall-to-wall Argentina. Full wine racks reached to the ceiling crammed with Argentine malbecs, cabernets, and merlots. The compact grocery section featured strings of blood sausage, large wheels of cheese, some made from sheep's milk, and shelves of tinned native delicacies, including a dizzying selection of *mate* teas. Bright Argentine soccer banners hung from the ceiling.

All of this surrounded the bakery counters. They were laden with butter cookies and Napoleons and tarts filled with custards, caramels, chocolates, and jams. Cheesecakes were glazed with sugared fruits, one more extravagant than the next. They were baroque baked goods for which the Argentines were famous. And they looked almost as dangerous as the desperate men I was investigating. Behind those counters sat an espresso machine almost as large as a locomotive.

In the background, music played. A male singer was remembering a passion that had "dragged him like the winds into the storm of love." The bakery and the music went together. That kind of passion had to leave one with a big appetite and a need for sugar.

I resisted the more extravagant selections, ordered an *empanada* and espresso, and found a table just next to the *gelato* counter. On the wall next to me hung a poster advertising a polo match. It said the Argentine National Team, "the current world champions," were arriving that weekend to play a squad of American players. It listed the members from each team. The name of one member of the U.S. squad was instantly familiar: David Ingram. It appeared that the big man did more with his riding crop than threaten people.

The café section was fairly crowded. From what I could overhear, most of the customers were speaking Spanish. For the affluent South American crowd—especially Argentines, Chileans, and Brazilians—Miami in the summer wasn't just a way to escape the cold back home. It was also a tactic to avoid all the criminal troubles. These days you could take a break from the kidnapping threats by spending a couple of weeks on the sands of Miami Beach.

The tables on each side of me were full, and as I nibbled I thought I overheard someone speak the name of Father Pérez. The news of his death was on the radio, and, given his notoriety, that news would spread quickly.

I was sipping my espresso when Sara Ingram arrived. She wore a fancy sweat outfit in baby blue, white sneakers, a baseball cap with a long brim, and shades with oversized, bright red rims. She was no longer the tango siren I had seen at the dance studio. She had left her house looking as if she were just nipping off to the gym in Glades Springs—not to meet a private detective, not to talk about the secrets of her Argentine past and the bloodshed there. It was a strange and deceptive world we lived in. Yes, it was.

We ordered her an espresso. Then I pulled a chair out for her and she sat down. She looked around a bit to make sure nobody she knew was in evidence. Then she took off her shades and turned to me.

"You didn't tell me this would be an Argentine café," she said in a whisper. "I don't usually do this kind of thing."

"Neither do I. I try to be off the streets this time of day in the middle of the summer. What can I tell you about the death of Father Pérez?"

"How did he die?"

I told her the simple facts of where, when, and how.

"I see."

"You didn't know Father Pérez?"

She shook her head. "No, I didn't."

"But you knew he might have been involved with your cousin Manuel back in Argentina."

She nodded.

"Are you afraid that Manuel did it?"

She feigned shock. "Why do you say that?"

I brought out the photograph of the priest grouped with the soldiers, including Manuel Navarro. I laid it before her.

"That's the priest standing right next to Navarro."

She studied it, shading it with one hand so that the people at the next table couldn't see it. She had run from her country's history and her cousin's history all the way to a house in the U.S. burbs, but she hadn't been able to hide. She could protest all she wanted. We both knew what she was afraid of.

"Manuel Navarro was mixed up with some very bad people when he was in the military, wasn't he?" I said. "And he is mixed up with them here."

She met my gaze. "He was a soldier. He did those things because it was his duty."

She said it, but I had the feeling she was simply repeating something she had been told, like a school child repeating a rote answer. Administering torture chambers wasn't legitimate work for a soldier. Manuel Navarro was no hero. But I hadn't brought her there to make her repent for her family's sins.

"He was in charge of secret detention centers in Argentina," I said. "In that position he would have known about the birth of children to female prisoners. In fact, he would have been in a position to take possession of such a child. Did Felicia want one of those children?"

She shook her head. "It wasn't like that. I was close to Felicia back then. I lived with them for a time. You have to understand that Felicia was always a very simple person. Manuel made her stay at home. She knew nothing of politics or of the problems our country was passing through. I doubt she even knew of the disappeared. But she wanted a baby very badly."

"And they couldn't have one of their own?"

"No, they couldn't. Felicia knew she herself was capable of conceiving. She had tests done. But Manuel couldn't have children."

"He's sterile."

She barely nodded. "Yes, although he doesn't know that. He always said it was Felicia, and she never told him the truth."

"So they took one of the children born at the detention centers?"

"I don't know that. Felicia asked Manuel about adopting a child, and he didn't want to do it. But she begged him and begged him until finally he gave in."

She looked around suddenly as if someone might be trying to hear what we were saying. Then she leaned closer to me and her voice dropped to an even lower whisper.

"All I know is that one night Father Pérez showed up at their house with the baby. She was only hours old. He told Felicia that the child had been found on the steps of a church."

"Father Pérez?"

"Yes."

I pictured the priest holding a swaddled infant.

"So Pérez knew where the child came from."

She nodded.

"So he could have testified in court against Navarro, not just about the child but the whole dirty business."

She didn't answer because she didn't have to.

"Does Navarro know who the child really belonged to?"

She shrugged. "I assume, but he has never spoken about it. The truth is Manuel tries to act as if Elena doesn't exist. He has never been kind to her. And now that people are after him because of the girl, it has made matters even worse for Felicia and Elena."

I was the one "after" Navarro. I was the one apparently making things worse. But what she said made me better understand where she was coming from. Her concern seemed to be more for the mother and daughter and less for Navarro. That could help me.

"You're afraid Manuel might have killed Father Pérez, aren't you?" I asked.

Her glance skittered around the café in all directions, as if she were looking for a way to escape. But it was a question she couldn't avoid. It was why she had called me in the first place. She came back to me, her eyes full of fear.

"Did he kill the priest?"

"I don't know, for sure, but I think so. At least one other man seems to have had problems with Father Pérez." I thought of Eduardo Estevez.

Her face momentarily filled with hope. Maybe it hadn't been a member of her family who had murdered a man of the cloth.

"Who is that?"

"It doesn't matter," I said. "You wouldn't know him. When was the last time you spoke to Manuel?"

"He called us over the weekend."

"Us? Does he speak with your husband too?"

She flinched and shook her head nervously. "No. My husband has nothing to do with all this. Nothing. He just wants to help Manuel because he's my family."

I pointed at the poster. "Where did he pick up polo?"

"In Argentina. That's where we met. But I want my husband kept out of this."

"What did Manuel tell you?"

"He said someone was looking for them again and that made him angry. He didn't say anything else, and the next thing I knew, he, Felicia, and Elena were gone. Then you came to see me."

I frowned. I had only started on the job Monday. So Navarro had known, had been tipped off, even before I was hired. Once again my thoughts turned to Eduardo Estevez.

The espresso machine issued a burst of steam, like a locomotive. It startled Sara Ingram. She slipped her oversized sunglasses on quickly and got up.

"I better go now."

She had been nervous the entire time. But when you had family like Manuel Navarro, maybe you were nervous all your life.

"If you find them, please call me," she said.

"If you hear from them, will you do the same?"

She nodded hesitantly. But given how frightened she was, I didn't really believe her.

CHAPTER NINETEEN

While I'd been speaking with Sara Ingram, my phone had vibrated twice.

I checked and found one message from Grand. He wanted to know why I hadn't brought him my client. He told me to call him back. I decided not to do that, at least not for the moment.

I was surprised to hear the second message. It came from Sergio Villarreal, the portly diplomat at the Argentine consulate. I was getting quite popular, especially with people who hadn't wanted to talk to me before. First, Sara Ingram and now the envoy.

"Mr. Cuesta, could you please call me? I would like very much to speak with you again." He left me a cell phone number.

From uncooperative and even antagonistic, the vice consul had become downright cordial. Maybe they were starting to warm up to me. Or maybe the murder of Father Pérez had scared Villarreal, just as it had Sara Ingram.

The number looked vaguely familiar. I checked my notebook first, then I rang him back.

"Mr. Cuesta. Thank you very much for calling me."

"The honor is mine. I know how busy you are and just how difficult it is to meet with you."

He let the irony slide.

"I would like very much to talk to you about the events of the past two days," he said.

"I assume you mean the murder of Father Francisco Pérez."

That was a bit too direct for the diplomat.

"Well, yes, it would include that. Where can I meet you?"

I had just reached my car. "In honor of you, why don't we meet in Little Buenos Aires. We'll get together at El Gaucho."

"I'll be there."

I pulled onto 71st Street a while later and, as I looked for a parking space, I happened to see Villarreal getting out of a car. Someone else was in that car because I saw the diplomat duck down and speak briefly to a person in the driver's seat. I couldn't see who it was. The diplomat closed the door and sauntered up the street toward El Gaucho.

I found a space farther up, and, by the time I walked back, Villarreal was arranged at an inside table. I asked for a Quilmes beer, and Villarreal, a vodka tonic. The hefty man was dressed in dark blue this time, with a white shirt, a sand-colored tie, and, again, a red carnation in his lapel. He was also acting more diplomatically, but I still didn't like him.

"I want to apologize for the brief nature of our meeting the other day," he said. "I thank you for bringing me the information you did."

I told him not to mention it. I knew that, given the murder of an Argentine citizen, he was surely getting urgent calls from his home office, the foreign ministry in Buenos Aires. His bosses would be demanding information. He, or someone else in the consulate, had obviously talked to Grand. He had told them of my contact with Father Pérez before the murder.

"So how can I help you today?" I asked, coating it with as much sugar as I could.

The wide-bodied man sipped his vodka judiciously. "I'm told that you met with Mr. Corral—or Father Pérez—just hours before he was killed. We would appreciate any information you could give us about that meeting."

I took out the photo of the priest and the soldiers and put it before him. He tapped the image of Father Pérez.

"That's the man who was killed?"

"That's right. Do you know who that is standing next to him?"

He frowned at the photo and shook his head. "Why should I?"

"It's Navarro, the guy who is missing. The guy I asked you about."

Villarreal studied the photo. Given how many Argentines had died mysteriously in recent decades, you had to wonder just what connections and decisions the diplomat might be making behind his blank gaze. You could see him weighing the practical and rational interests against the brutal fact of a homicide. They were calculations that had marked an entire generation.

"Did the priest help you find him?" he asked.

"No. In fact, the priest was protecting him. That's because they were buddies from the bad old days. Pérez was a military chaplain, a death squad chaplain, but I think you knew that already."

Villarreal conceded that fact, although grudgingly. "Yes, I had heard of him back when all the facts came out. But I didn't know he was hiding here under another name."

I flicked my eyebrows at him cleverly.

"Just like you didn't know Navarro." I held up my cell phone and my notebook. "The number of your cell is in here from when you phoned me a while ago. It's the same number that I found on Navarro's rental application. I doubt you give your cell phone number to just anyone who calls the consulate. How did Navarro get it?"

He fixed on me with all the gravity of a man who represented an entire nation. Then he lied.

"I have no idea how he had that number. As I told you last time, many people know me."

"You also knew Fiona Bonaventura was here searching for the daughter of her sister Sonia. In fact, you were acquainted with the entire family way back when, weren't you?"

The fact that I had discovered that connection didn't surprise him.

"That's true. I worked with the father of the two sisters, Don Pablo Bonaventura, at the foreign ministry. A wonderful gentleman and a great patriot."

"Being a great patriot didn't keep the military killers from murdering his daughter and son-in-law. And you didn't just work with him at the ministry. You were on his personal staff. Were you still with him when his daughter died?"

He nodded. "He had left the government by then, but there were still issues on which we needed to consult him. I was the one assigned to do that. It was a terrible, terrible time for him."

"But you didn't mention any of that the first time I talked to you."

He arched an eyebrow. "You didn't name your client. I couldn't assume who it was you were representing."

I smiled at him again. I didn't believe that for a moment, but I wasn't meant to believe it. A bit of smooth diplomatic dodging was all it amounted to.

I put my elbow on the table and leaned closer to him.

"So you were working for the military government and were also close to the family at the very moment that Sonia and her husband were betrayed."

He was as stiff and still as if I'd pinned him to the sky with daggers.

"Many civilians remained at their government positions during that period, Mr. Cuesta. Many of us felt maybe we could do something to help offset the horror."

"You didn't do a very good job in this instance did you? And you were the only government employee who Manuel Navarro, one of Sonia's killers, named as a reference here in Miami. I'm wondering, Mr. Villarreal, how many more of the old gang might be here."

I was clearly including him in that murderous gang, and he didn't like it. I had offended his diplomatic dignity. He stood up.

"Excuse me, but I have another appointment."

"I bet you do."

I stood up as well, tossing bills on the table to cover the check.

"You're a diplomat, and you have certain international protections, Mr. Vice Consul. But you're not protected from covering up the kidnapping of a child in Argentina, or from concealing information about a murder here. If I find out that's what you're doing I'm going to let people know, and there ain't no diplomatic status going to help you."

It wasn't very diplomatic on my part, but I turned on a heel and left him standing there. I had a reason for doing it.

I stalked off down the sidewalk in the opposite direction of where I was parked. As I passed Villarreal's car, I glanced in.

Sitting in the driver's seat was the same hatchet-faced man with the wild hair I'd seen leave Villarreal's office at the consulate. He seemed like a very strange partner for the dapper diplomat.

As I passed, he spotted me as well. If looks could kill, I'd be a dead man now. But given what I do for a living, if looks could kill, I would have been dead a long time ago.

CHAPTER TWENTY

I circled the block, got back in my car, but I didn't move.

Villarreal had known Fiona was in town. The question was how he'd found out. Had someone in Buenos Aires informed him, maybe someone Estevez had consulted? Or had he been told right in Miami? Who else might know about Fiona's supposedly secret quest?

Just having to pose that question made matters all the more urgent. I had to get Fiona and the girl out of the crosshairs and into the courts.

As I drove away, I called Dr. Sanger at the DNA lab. They put me on hold long enough for the doctor to discover a whole new genetic code. He finally picked up, and we exchanged greetings.

"So what's happenin', doc?

"The stock of labs like mine is going up. That's what's happenin'."

"Is that right?"

"Yes. We just got the results. Your client, Ms. Fiona Bonaventura, is definitely related to the person whose hair you brought me."

"There's no doubt?"

"The helixes don't lie. These two women share the same blood."

I didn't respond right away.

"That's good, isn't it?" Sanger asked

There was no doubt now that the girl, Elena, was one of the legendary "children of the disappeared." It would be necessary to get her away from Navarro. But first someone would have to tell her just who she really was. I was trying to picture what went on in a person's mind and heart in those circumstances. What would she feel when she heard her real mother had been killed, possibly by the man she called her father? As Alice had said, it was going to be traumatic, to say the least.

"Are you still there?" Sanger asked.

"Yes, I'm here."

"Do you want me to call your client to tell her?"

"No, I'll take care of it."

I thanked him and hung up. I decided not to call Fiona Bonaventura, but to deliver the news in person. The more urgent question was how to tell the girl.

Fifteen minutes later I again was sitting in the cafeteria of Miami College of Art and Design, sipping a *café con leche*.

On the wall behind me hung a painting of what appeared to be a rain forest. When you looked closely, the leaves were various denominations of dollars. The roots of the trees morphed into the limbs of dead people lying beneath the ground with their eyes closed. It was macabre.

I didn't spend a lot of time looking at it. I was keeping an eye out for Elena Navarro's boyfriend. I had decided that he was my best bet for getting to Elena in a way that wouldn't scare her. If I were to walk up and try to tell her what I knew, she might freak.

I was on my second coffee when I saw the young guy cruise in by himself and get in line. He wore the same baseball cap, a T-shirt, paint-stained jeans, and he carried a book. Elena was not around. I watched him buy something to drink and walk out again.

I followed him out the door and down the hall, where he sought out an empty bench and sat down. I waited a minute, saw that nobody joined him, wandered over, and sat next to him. I saw his T-shirt bore a pen-and-ink self-portrait by Rembrandt. It went well with the baseball cap.

"Excuse me," I said, " but you're an acquaintance of Elena Navarro, aren't you?"

He took a sip of his drink and shrugged with schoolboy indifference. "Why?"

I reached into my shirt pocket, pulled out the old photo of Sonia Bonaventura, and handed it to him. He frowned, but then he focused on it. I saw recognition bloom in his eyes. He turned to me as if I were someone trying to trick him.

"Who is this?"

"That's the real mother of Elena Navarro. The people pretending to be her parents are not."

His eyes went big. "Both of them?"

"Yes."

He fixed on the photo. "Where is this woman now?"

"She's dead, murdered in Argentina soon after Elena was born."

He gazed at the photo intently, as if by doing so he would see something that would disprove what I was telling him. But he couldn't find that something.

He turned the same intense gaze on me. He was trying to figure out what my game was.

"Who are you?"

I told him. I also explained that I was employed by Fiona Bonaventura, who I now knew for sure was Elena's aunt.

"You want to hear something?" he asked me.

"Just about anything."

"Elena already knows that Manuel Navarro is not her father."

"Really?"

"Yes."

Of course, most kids had that kind of thought at one time or another. He seemed to understand that as well.

"I don't mean she thinks that sometimes. I mean she knows it. Her mother told her."

Felicia Navarro suddenly swelled in my imagination. "Really?"

"That's right. Elena hates Manuel Navarro. She's always hated him. A couple of years ago she told her mother that she couldn't stand the fact that she was his daughter. That it made her crazy. It made her want to kill herself. That's when her mother told her the truth."

"Is that right?"

The kid nodded. "She said Elena could never tell Navarro because he might kill both of them. Now it turns out she isn't her mother either."

He seemed dazzled by the duplicity. I couldn't blame him. Latin families had gone through all kinds of convulsions during the last decades. But the families usually went through those problems together. People at least knew who their real relatives were. He turned that same befuddled gaze on me.

I asked him his name.

"I'm Nelson. Nelson Cruz."

He looked back at the photo of Sonia Bonaventura. "This is going to be hard for Elena. She loves her mother . . . or at least the person she thought was her mother."

"I know it's going to be hard. That's why I figured you might help me."

"And she's already going through a lot of stuff lately."

"You mean the sudden move and having to drop out of school?"

"Yeah. It's happened before. They left Argentina, like from one day to the next."

"How do they explain that to her?"

"They told her some people are after her father because of a business he was in down in Argentina. That they want him to pay some money and he says he doesn't owe them. Navarro says they want to persecute him and stuff."

"I see." And I did see, except the business Navarro had been in was the military. The crimes he had committed had less to do with money and more with torture, murder, and child stealing.

I told Nelson Cruz the accurate story, and he absorbed it in disbelief.

"She never knew any of this?" I asked.

"No, nothing."

Life was very strange indeed. Given her paintings, you had to wonder if somehow her unconscious hadn't hooked up to her mother's tragic life.

I also told Nelson about the death of Father Pérez and the connection it had to Elena, that Pérez was the person who had first handed Elena to Felicia. That news of the priest's murder left him mute.

"If you want to help me, you can begin by introducing me to Elena tonight," I said. "If you're there when she hears some of this history, it will help her deal with it. Later I may need your help to get her away from Navarro."

He stared at the photo one last time, as if it were a trick question on a test. But the resemblance was obviously too much to argue with. Finally, he nodded.

"I'll do it."

CHAPTER TWENTY-ONE

I was home, just watching the television coverage of the killing of Father Pérez, when Grand called back. The footage showed the body, now covered with a sheet, surrounded by all those doors. It was like a cross between the news and a game show where you had to find the prize behind door number two.

"Hello, sergeant," I said, as sunnily as I could. "I'm just watching you on the tube. You look good."

"You're sounding chipper for a guy in the middle of a murder investigation, Willie."

"I thought the people in the middle of a murder were the guy who got wasted and whoever did it."

"Right, but since I don't know who did it and I do know you, you're the guy in the middle for the moment. Why didn't you return my call?"

"Did you call?"

"You know I did. I want to speak to your client, the one involved in this case."

"I'm not sure she's involved at all in this case."

"I'll decide that after I talk to her. What's her name?"

"Just let me notify her. In fact, I'll bring her to you."

"You said that this morning. I haven't seen her."

"Well, right now, I don't know where she is."

"So why don't you call her? In fact, why don't you give me her number and I'll call her. "

"Because she's here from out of town and doesn't have a cell phone."

"Then give me her land line."

"It's out of order."

"You're out of order, Willie."

I was thinking of Grand getting Estevez on the line instead. Neither I, nor Fiona, nor Estevez was ready for that. I wasn't sure what

Estevez's involvement was with Father Pérez and Navarro. But I had visions of the girl and her mother caught in the crossfire.

"Be patient, Grand. You'll get what you want."

"Tell me this, Willie. What kind of car does your client drive?"

"She doesn't drive any car, as far as I know. I told you, she's here from out of town. She's using cabs. Why do you ask?"

"Because this morning, after the news about the priest reached the radio, we got an anonymous call. A guy speaking Spanish said a big black SUV-type vehicle pulled away from the realty office right around the hour that the priest got popped."

"Well, it wasn't my client." It didn't sound like Estevez either, but I couldn't be sure.

"I want to ask her myself."

"Tomorrow, Grand."

"No later than that, Willie."

"Have a nice day."

The phone fell quiet, and I finally found time to dive into the databases. I needed to know who owned the house in Coral Gables where the Navarros were camped. I typed in the address and waited for the machine to do its alchemy.

The name that came up was Arno, Arturo Arno. According to the data, he had bought the place about a year earlier for a tidy sum. I wondered how he had made that sum, so I typed his name into a business database for the firms in the state of Florida.

I found that Arturo Arno was the owner of an air cargo company named Southern Hemisphere Air Transport, based at Miami International Airport. The company had a satellite office in Rosario, Argentina.

Using yet another database, I confirmed that Arno held a commercial pilot's license.

The moment I saw that, I got a nasty feeling in my gut. I quickly shut down that screen, brought up the website for the Argentine war criminals, and surfed the A's.

I reached "Arno," and a familiar visage popped right out at me. On the screen was a long, thin face, with a straight, narrow nose and weird, wired eyes. The photo was at least twenty years old, but it was the same ugly cuss I had seen with Villarreal, both at the consulate and on 71st Street.

Unlike Navarro, he hadn't changed his name. Maybe he'd been forced to keep his real name in order to retain his pilot's license. In any event, there he was in all his glory.

He had the look of a drinker or a druggie, which was a perilous thing for a pilot to be. But I started to read his resume and even worse fears were fulfilled.

According to the files, Arno had held the rank of captain in the Argentine Air Force. He had been attached to *Grupo de Tareas 332* and "was known to have served on flights during which opponents of the military government were taken from detention centers and dropped into the Río Plata or the Atlantic Ocean far from shore. It is believed that hundreds, possibly thousands of individuals were disappeared in that manner."

I looked at his scary face and wondered if Arno had flown the plane when Sonia Bonaventura had been dropped into the sea. I had managed to temporarily lose Elena, and she had ended up in the clutches of a man who might be one of her mother's actual murderers.

History, a very bloody history, seemed to be repeating itself. I was apparently helping it.

I called Fiona Bonaventura, and she answered herself. I decided not to tell her about Arno. Not yet, and maybe never.

"Is your husband there?"

"No, he's not. He has a business meeting."

"Will he be gone long?"

"All afternoon."

"Then stay put. I'm on my way."

"Have you heard from the laboratory?"

"I'll be there soon enough."

She answered the door wearing black slacks and a white blouse. The maid was gone, so she was alone.

Fiona led me onto a balcony that overlooked the beach and the sea beyond. We sat down in canvas chairs facing each other. Her hair was ruffled slightly by an onshore breeze.

"What did the doctor say?"

"He said the girl is your family. There's no doubt."

She had been expecting the news and took it calmly. She nodded once and for the next minute was lost deep in her thoughts. She might have been tracing her movements over the past two decades all over Argentina: the death of her sister, the long search for the child, the false leads and the frustrating dead ends, the reticence of her husband, right up to the moment on that balcony and to the words I had just uttered. She had waited twenty years to hear them.

Despite her self-control, there was no mistaking just how much the moment meant to her.

"You've done it," I said to her. "You've found your sister's child."

She frowned at me and shook her head. "I should have helped save my sister all those years ago. She should have gone into hiding much earlier or left the country altogether. I could have convinced her if I had put my mind to it, but I didn't do it."

She stared out at the depths of the sea. "Instead, like my husband, I was just angry with her for causing me worry. If I had acted then, I wouldn't have to do this now. Sonia would be alive. She would never have known the inside of a detention cell or a military plane. The main cause in my life is one that never had to be."

It was a statement that echoed not just with irony, but with a terrible emptiness. Many people in similar situations felt what had come to be called "survivor guilt." But this gorgeous woman was going further. She was saying that her whole life was a wash, or even less. You sensed she carried that detention cell around inside her. Part of her was locked up inside it, the way her sister had been. Maybe the girl Elena, had the key that would allow her to get out.

Maybe Fiona was thinking the same thing right then. She fixed on me.

"When can I go tell my niece who I am? When can we get her away from those people?"

"We can't just walk in there because that might lead to bloodshed. In fact, we can't tell the police about it yet because the same thing might happen. That's the last thing we want."

I told her about my meeting with Elena's boyfriend, Nelson Cruz. I explained that we needed an intermediary, not only to make contact with her, but, possibly, to get the girl away from Navarro without getting her hurt.

I also said it would be better if I held a first meeting with the girl to explain the history to her. I could then arrange a reunion between the two of them.

"When can you have that first meeting?"

"Tonight. Nelson is working on it."

"And when will I see her?"

"If all goes well, tomorrow."

I saw hope in her eyes.

"Please tell her that I love her very much."

I said I would.

CHAPTER TWENTY-TWO

Nelson Cruz called early that evening. Just enough heat had gone out of the day that I was sitting on my back porch overlooking the garden, drinking a cold Presidente.

On the CD player, Rubén Blades, the great Panamanian singer, had found the woman of his dreams and delivered the perfect seduction line: "You are the song I've always wanted to sing, my love."

That's what he said. It was a beauty.

While I listened, I ruminated on my case.

I kept wondering what it was like to be Elena Navarro. I thought back to when I was twenty-one years old and trying to figure out a life in the midst of so many possibilities. One moment I thought I'd spend my life in Miami. The next instant I wanted to hop a freighter for Madagascar or Timbuktu and lose myself in the trade winds.

I traveled a bit, but in the end my destiny was determined by an onshore wind and I stayed. I'm glad I did.

Elena wasn't just caught in the swirling, disorienting winds of youth. She had to deal with deception, duplicity, and those sudden, unexplained displacements. She was suspended in a spiderweb of lies.

When I was her age, I didn't know exactly where I was going, but I always knew where I came from. Not Elena. In her case, that would be decided by a complex, scientific process involving the most modern technology—genetics, helixes. I wondered if suddenly discovering her true past would change the way she lived her future. That all seemed much more complicated than any coming of age I'd had to do.

I sipped my Presidente and that's when Nelson called.

"Is that you?" he asked.

"Yes, it is. Did you speak with Elena?"

"Yeah. I told her I met someone who knows some things about Navarro. She says she wants to meet you."

"That was smart of you."

"Where can we meet?"

"How about at Caliente?"

"The nightclub?"

"The same."

"I'm in school. I don't have that kind of money."

"You don't need money. My brother owns it."

"You're shittin' me."

"Not in this instance. There are back rooms that are quiet. We can use one of them."

"This is going to be heavy for Elena." He sounded very young indeed.

"That's why it's good you're going to be there."

We arranged to meet at the club at ten. That meant everyone necessary was on board, except for one person.

I changed clothes and drove straight to Alice's place. She had just gotten home from the gym and still was wearing tight black Spandex shorts and a black sports bra. She sat on her balcony overlooking the river, drinking cold white wine.

I complimented her "six-pack abs."

"You're probably just thirsty. Pour yourself a beer."

I did. Then I settled down next to her.

"So what happened today?" she asked.

First I told her about the DNA results, and she gave me a high five.

"I'm still batting a thousand with those helixes. I've never struck out. Did you tell your client?"

"Yes. She's happy, but she's also worried."

"Smart woman. You can never tell what will happen in highly emotional terrain like this."

Then I told her about the meeting I'd arranged with Elena.

"It would be good if you came with me tonight."

She stopped in mid sip. "You think so?"

"Yes. First, the presence of another woman will make her more comfortable. Second, you're a compassionate soul. And after the initial shock, she may have some questions that will require legal advice."

Alice arched an eyebrow. "And third, you'll need somebody to dance *merengue* with after the meeting."

"You have a deal, counselor."

In the spirit of the evening, I took Alice to dinner at yet another Argentine restaurant over in Coral Gables. We ate flank steaks with chimichuri sauce, drank Argentine cabernet and cappuccinos, and arrived at the club shortly before ten.

I left the car with Esteban, the chief valet. It was nowhere as luxurious as most of the vehicles he parked, but he didn't sneer at it the way some valets did. Maybe it was my natural air of authority. Or maybe it was because I was the owner's brother and head of security.

He, the other valets, and the doorman—a big Cuban named Pujols— all greeted us warmly. They were accustomed to seeing Alice around. Multicultural doyen that she is, Alice dances a mean *merengue* and, for a white girl, a sensational *salsa*. I also know she has found more than one Cuban lover in the club over the years, but we don't discuss that.

I told Pujols I was expecting a couple of kids and gave him the names of Nelson and Elena.

My brother's club, in all modesty, is the best Latin dance club in the hemisphere. At each end of the dance floor, Tommy has built a bandstand and the very best Latin musicians in the world have played there: Celia Cruz, Willie Colón, Tito Puente, Juan Luis Guerra, Oscar d'Leon, La Ley, Shakira . . . you name 'em.

The club features amphitheater seating, four levels surrounding a large central dance floor. Everyone can watch the dancing and everyone can see who else is in the house. If you're looking for someone to dance with, talk to, eventually snuggle up to, you scan the levels for the lady or lad of your choice. Any Latin club worth its salt is not just about dancing. Many Latins will tell you their parents first got close on the dance floor.

As head of security, the layout works for me and my staff. I can look down at the dance floor from the top tier and determine if anyone is getting out of hand. Maybe it's a drunk whose dancing has turned sloppy. Possibly he's traipsing on other people's toes or twirling out of control. I can often spot such a whirling dervish before he does any damage.

The seating arrangement allows me to watch out as well for "pony express riders." That's what we call thieves who wait for couples to hit the dance floor, then cruise by their table, and, without breaking stride, pluck a purse or expensive jacket from a chair. They then tuck it away under a loose-hanging *guayabera* or sport jacket and hightail it for the exit.

We also keep a lookout for hookers trying to do business on the premises, as well as anyone who makes an unusual number of trips to the bathrooms, which usually means they're pedaling drugs. If you make too many visits to the john, you get invited to leave. We can refer you to a local proctologist or gynecologist if you really have a problem, but you have to abandon the premises.

Every once in a while political differences in the Hispanic world spill over into the club. Lots of people come to Caliente. Individuals on opposite sides of one issue or another inevitably run into each other. I've had to separate some patriots before they pulverized each other, but those instances are unusual. In general, people leave their politics behind when they come to dance.

The disturbances and crimes are more likely to occur when the club is full. The crowd doesn't even start to show up until midnight. When Alice and I walked in, it was still very early and the place was quiet. At 10 p.m., a Latin dance joint might as well be a library.

I found my brother Tommy sitting at his usual table near the bandstand. He's older, stocky, and light-skinned. I'm thinner and a bit darker. He's good with money, and he says I'm better with people. That's why he handles the cashier's booth and I take care of the drunks.

He gave Alice a kiss. She and I both ordered lime daiquiris and listened to the latest news about Tommy's wife and kids, my godchildren.

The band hadn't started yet. A Juan Luis Guerra CD played softly over the speaker system. He was sending smoke signals to his beloved, declaring his desire, but they were swept away by the Caribbean winds. He was having a rough time getting through to her.

A few minutes later I saw Nelson Cruz and Elena Navarro enter the club. He was dressed as he had been earlier, but she wore a short black dress. I alerted Alice, we excused ourselves to Tommy, met them just inside the door, and I made the introductions. The girl greeted us demurely, tentatively. All things considered, I couldn't blame her.

I led them all across the empty dance floor to one of the private dining rooms under the stadium seating. The one I chose had wine-red wallpaper, Oriental sconces, a black lacquered table, and subdued lighting. We call it the Shanghai room.

A waiter took our drink order. As we waited for him to come back, Alice chatted up Nelson. I watched the girl, who sat silently. She was even more beautiful up close and resembled the photo of her late mother even more than I had realized. It was a bit spooky.

The waiter brought the drinks and left. Alice and Nelson knocked off the chatter, and everyone was left looking at me. I had planned to tell Elena the whole story: about being hired by a woman from Buenos Aires, the tragic history she had related to me of her sister who was killed, an Argentine friend spotting her on the street twenty years later.

But I didn't. When the moment came, I simply removed the photo of Sonia from my pocket and placed it before her, the way I had with Nelson. It was a hunch I had.

She stared at the photo a long time, and everyone stared at her. Presenting a person with a new explanation of where they come from is a bit like participating in a blood transfusion. Or, in a more modern sense, an act of genetic engineering. The sense of that person's heredity goes through wholesale change in a matter of moments, as if the chromosomes themselves were changing under the skin.

We all watched her closely for any outward signs of the transformation. Like Nelson when he had seen the snapshot the first time, her facial expression changed. But hers didn't become agitated. It became becalmed.

"This is my mother, isn't it?" she asked finally, still staring at the face.

"Yes, it was."

The word "was" made her eyes narrow. "So she's dead."

"I'm sorry. She has been dead for a long time."

"Yes, that was what I thought. She was very beautiful, wasn't she?"

"Very."

I told her about her father, Mario Murillo, as well. When she spoke, her voice was still calm, but tears had welled up in her eyes. One of them slipped down her beautiful right cheek.

"Did Manuel Navarro kill my mother?"

"Navarro was an administrator at the prison where your mother was detained. It was from there that they sent her to die."

I pictured the last sad moments of Sonia Bonaventura, and once again they brought to mind the portraits of suspended human beings painted by her daughter. But I didn't give Elena any more detail on her mother's terrible death. She had no need to hear it right then.

Nelson had sat in stunned silence until then. Now he put an arm around her.

"You knew," he said.

She shrugged. "When my mother . . . I mean when Felicia told me that Navarro wasn't my real father, that meant she couldn't be my real mother. She is so scared of him, she would never dare to make love to another man. Never. Never."

She fixed on me. "Whatever it is you're doing, I don't want anything to happen to Felicia. She has always loved me."

"I don't want any harm to come to her either."

That was the best I could say. I didn't know for sure what would happen.

"What is it you want me to do?" she asked.

"I want you to meet with the sister of your mother—your real mother. Your aunt has spent years looking for you. She hired me to help her."

That scared the girl a bit, but she nodded. "Yes, I'll do that. When will I meet her?"

"I can arrange it for tomorrow."

She squeezed Nelson's hand as if this other life, this new family, was already trying to pull her away from him.

"Before we finish I need to know something else, Elena. After you and Felicia and Navarro left the apartment, you went directly to the house in Coral Gables. Is that right?"

"Yes."

"Do you remember if Navarro went anywhere the next night?"

She thought about it and shook her head. "No. He didn't leave the house all that day or night. None of us did, except for the man who owns the house where we're staying."

"Arturo Arno."

"That's right."

"Do you know anything about Arno?"

"He's a pilot, and he and Navarro are mixed up in business together."

"What kind of business?"

She shrugged. "It has something to do with where Navarro works." I thought of the warehouse where they armored vehicles. "IPS?"

"Yes. It involves some kind of shipments, but I think it must be illegal. There is another man who is also involved. The three of them never let you hear what they are talking about."

"Who is that other man?"

"I don't know his full name, but they call him Oscar. He's ugly and very crude."

I described Oscar Porta, the owner of the tango club on the Miami River.

"Yes, that's him." She was surprised that I knew him.

"Who else would come and speak to Navarro?"

"Corral, the one who was killed. He rented us the apartment. And there was another man always there, but he isn't Argentine."

"Who's that?"

"My uncle, or at least the man I called my uncle. The husband of our cousin Sara."

I pictured the red-faced gringo from Glades Springs who played polo.

"You mean David Ingram?"

"Yes, he was there. He's one of them."

CHAPTER TWENTY-THREE

A half hour later Alice and I were on the dance floor. We were engaged in a very subdued, but rhythmic *merengue.*

I had invited Elena and Nelson to stay. Understandably, the girl had preferred some peace and quiet—time to consider her new identity.

"So, that was quite something," Alice said over the music.

"Yes, it was." I was still reeling about the involvement of Ingram.

"That girl is certainly carrying a lot of baggage."

"Everybody is, after a certain point in their lives."

"Yes, but she's very young to be hauling that particular luggage. It's very heavy."

"I appreciate your contribution tonight."

She separated her cheek from mine, exactly in rhythm.

"I didn't say a word."

"Yes, but Elena kept looking at you for feminine understanding, and you were there."

"It's the only kind I've got, feminine that is." She pressed her cheek to mine again. "Who is this Ingram guy she talked about?"

So I told her about the visit to Glades Springs and my near run-in with a riding crop.

She removed her cheek again.

"Oh, he sounds delightful. What could he possibly have to do with Navarro and his buddies, besides being married to his cousin?"

"I have no idea. But I'll have to go see him at some point."

"Well, you better figure out who he is first. If I were going to see a guy who had those kinds of friends and who wanted to take a whip to me, I'd find out who else he might have whipped in the past."

"An excellent point, counselor. I plan to do that. But first I need to get Fiona and Elena together and have both of them sit down with you and those DNA results. We need to get this girl to an immigration judge before something happens to her."

116

THE LADY FROM BUENOS AIRES

"Exactly. If I can squeeze the whole story out of them tomorrow, I can write the brief Sunday. First, I need Fiona to tell me about the disappearance of her sister and about her search for the child. Then I need Elena to give me the story from the other side, all the running and hiding and those meetings Navarro held with nefarious types, like the late priest."

She tapped my chest with her long, skinny finger. "Finally, I need you to put together what you have on Navarro's past, his connection to the death squad killers. With the priest having just been killed, I should be able to convince a judge that Elena is in imminent danger and that she needs the protection of the courts, even though she has no claim to legal U.S. residence or citizenship. That might make it tricky, but we'll handle her legal status later. We need to get that girl away from Navarro."

"Not only away from Navarro, but from Arturo Arno as well."

"Who's that?"

I filled her in on the pilot who owned the Coral Gables house. I didn't have to connect the dots for her: girl, plane, killer, and the entire Argentine military legacy. Alice comprehended the nasty possibilities.

"We don't have to wait for the judge to rule in order to get her out of that house and somewhere safe, Willie."

"That's what I'm thinking. I'm going to tell her to leave tomorrow, along with Felicia, her stepmother. If they can just sneak away, we won't have to risk the police going in there with guns drawn."

Alice patted my cheek. "Good thinking. You can hide them with me for the time being."

"Then what happens with Navarro and Arno?"

She thought that over for about six beats of *merengue* rhythm. "We'll send immigration agents to pay them a visit. To get into this country, you have to check a box on your application that says you have never deprived anyone of their human rights. Those two guys obviously lied about that. They lied big time. They can be deported back to prison in Argentina, that's if they aren't put away right here for murdering the priest."

I could hear a jail door clanking behind them. I told her that sounded fine to me.

We finished that *merengue*. Then I left Alice so she could graze among other Cuban guys who wanted to dance with her. I visited with my security operatives.

By shortly after midnight the place was packed and the dance floor was dense with swaying female hips, double-jointed and, in some incredible cases, triple-jointed. The job had its distractions.

A while later we spotted a hooker working the bar. She had poured herself into an outfit in a snakeskin design. It was so tight, it looked like she was laminated. Ladies who visit the club often dress provocatively, but this girl had crossed the border into crass commercialism.

I approached her, and it was clear she didn't know who I was. She flared her eyes at me in what she considered a lascivious manner.

I asked her to dance and halfway through the tune recommended we go somewhere more intimate. She agreed and showed me the tip of her tongue between her teeth.

I ushered her outside, helped her into a cab, closed the door behind her, and told the driver to take her to the next club.

She pouted. "I thought you said we were going some place more intimate?"

"The back seat is empty except for you, sweetheart," I said. "That's intimate."

About two a.m., Alice got tired of dancing and also of fighting off hot-blooded Cuban guys. I had one of the valets drive her home and told her I'd be in touch later in the day.

The rest of the night unfolded without any fights or major incidents. It had been a night of music, of love not war, at least until that point.

I left at four a.m., putting Pujols in charge until the place emptied out, which would be around five. I drove home with the music from the club still working its way out of my body, dancing just a bit behind the wheel.

I parked the car. Then I did what I always did on late nights. I went to the all-night coffee joint a block away and bought a loaf of freshly baked Cuban bread. They always pulled loaves out of the oven about that time. I'd toast a couple of slices and eat them before I went to bed, to soak up the daiquiris.

The loaves smelled like heaven as they slid out of the oven. I paid and was headed back toward my place, the only person on the street. There is no quiet like the quiet after a whole night listening to Latin trumpets. And four a.m. is also about the only time it isn't hot during a Miami summer. I enjoyed the stroll.

I was a few feet away from my door when a red SUV with tinted windows pulled up. The passenger side window was lowered partway, and a guy asked me for directions. I didn't hear him clearly, so I stepped off the curb, walked over, and asked him to repeat himself.

I was about a foot from the door when suddenly he threw it open. The edge of it caught me hard on the side of the head.

The bread went flying, I went over sideways and hit the ground. Before I could react, he and a guy from the back seat jumped out and came at me. I kicked at them in my best Bruce Lee/Jackie Chan imitation, but the second guy rapped me in the shin with a crowbar, momentarily paralyzing me and leaving me speechless with pain. That ended my attempt at kung fu.

They quickly dragged me to the SUV, tossed me facedown onto the floor of the back seat, frisked me, and threw a wool blanket over me. That way I couldn't see or be seen. Then they both jumped into the back, their feet on top of me, and the van lurched off with a screech.

We started straight down *Calle Ocho*, the main drag of Little Havana. I tried to lift my head once to see, but the guy with his feet on my shoulders kicked me on the side of the head with his heel. So I lay still.

They were efficient, I'll say that. Clearly, this was something they had done before. They didn't speak, and I had no idea what they looked like. It had all happened too quickly for me to get a look at their faces.

What I did know was I was being kidnapped in exactly the same way many people in Latin America, including Argentina, had been kidnapped during the dirty wars. Sonia Bonaventura had been snatched from a house, but many others had disappeared this way—grabbed off a public street.

I also knew that the majority of those people hadn't lived to tell the tale. That thought made me squirm. The same guy who had kicked me in the head stomped me in the ribs, driving the breath out of me. Then he smacked me across the back with the crowbar, rattling my spinal cord. I struggled for breath. The air in the car had a strange smell to it, like fertilizer. I wondered if they were going to use it to plant me somewhere.

Seconds later the vehicle made a sharp turn to the left, rolling me over on my side. Then it made another left. That meant we were heading west in the direction of Coral Gables.

The radio was on, and a woman sang in Spanish about how she was tired of falling in love:

I want no more sadness
and I'm tired of madness.

I felt the same way.

The driver kept his speed down. The car slowed and stopped from time to time, apparently at traffic lights or intersections. For all appearances they were a group of law-abiding friends cruising home after a night on the town. With a kidnapping victim aboard, you wanted to be very careful not to attract cops.

I couldn't count on the police pulling them over, but the fact that they were obeying the rules of the road might give me some kind of chance to escape.

If I were going to do that I had to do it soon. Given how long we traveled, we had soon left Coral Gables behind, which meant they weren't taking me to the house owned by Arturo Arno.

Where we were heading was in the direction of the Everglades, which had served as a dumping ground for numerous unloved and unwanted individuals over the years. Once we got there, no one else would be around. They could do their dirty work and bury me. Everything grew very quickly in the Everglades. Within a few weeks I'd be pushing up ferns, especially if they used the fertilizer I smelled.

The thought of that provoked me.

"I'm a former policeman. You won't walk away from this."

They weren't impressed by my resume. Their answer came in the form of a kick to my ribcage. It left me breathless again. This time I batted the corner of the blanket away from my mouth to get more air.

My head was pressed against the left-hand back door of the car. When I moved the blanket I was looking right at the lever that controlled the back seat. Above it was a release. Apparently you could fold the seat back to create cargo space.

I eased my hands from my sides up near my head, but did it slowly so I wouldn't get kicked again. Then I braced my feet and waited.

We were far out on 8th Street, where the stops grew farther apart. We had passed a couple of joints that spilled loud Latin music out onto the street, but now it was quieter. We traveled a ways, and then the vehicle started to slow down, apparently for a light or a stop sign. When it was about to stop I made my move.

I arched my back suddenly, bucked their feet off me, reached with my left hand for the lever, and, lunging in that direction, slammed upward on the release with the palm of my right hand.

The vertical cushion of the seat flew backward and with it the guy who had been grinding his heels into me. He shouted as he tumbled backward. That caused the driver to slam on his brakes.

I grasped the handle right above me and managed to throw open the back door. Scrambling and pushing hard with my feet, I flung myself out toward the street. Someone tried to grab my leg, but I kicked at them and fell out of the van.

I landed right into a curbside puddle of water, rolled through it, got up, and found myself stumbling headlong into some kind of park. Sprinklers were on at full force for night irrigation, and I passed right through them. I wasn't worried about getting wet. I was worried about getting dead.

I tried to get my bearings. I was almost exactly where I'd thought, on the western end of the city in an old, blue-collar Latin neighborhood called Sweetwater. I had worked cases there in the old days, and I knew some local Nicaraguans and Hondurans. But right then they couldn't help me. No one was in sight.

I heard a shout in Spanish and a screech behind me. I turned and saw the SUV jump the curb and race toward me. They were going to run me down.

I ran, weaving around several banana plants and hurdling an arica palm. The SUV didn't bother to avoid them. It went right over them and closed ground to about thirty feet of me.

I swerved, sprinted through another sprinkler, and at the far corner of the park saw several tall palms and a poinciana tree. I jumped a low jasmine hedge, ran right toward the trees, and then between them, where the SUV wouldn't fit. As I did, I slipped on the wet grass and fell.

I looked up and saw the SUV skid wildly, spin and careen off the poinciana. That created a snowstorm of bright orange blossoms that slowly fell to the ground and all over the vehicle. But it was a tropical snowstorm, not the kind that would stop them. The passenger window slid down, a hand came out, and a gun muzzle flashed. A spray of bullets threaded between the palm trees and slammed into the palmetto grass next to me. I jumped up and took off.

A narrow alleyway ran off the park, and I sprinted into it. The backs of squat brick apartment buildings gave onto that alley. People lived there, Latin people. A battered and exploded piñata—formerly the Lion King—lay near a back door like a sleeping guard animal. I also caught a tantalizing aroma of food, maybe *arroz con pollo* or a *pollo rostizado* that somebody had cooked that night for dinner. I wanted nothing more than to have my knees underneath that table.

But it was four-thirty in the a.m. now, the *comida* was over, the diners were tucked into their beds, and the windows were all dark. I yanked desperately at three back doors, banged on them, and cursed in loud Spanish, but they wouldn't budge.

The SUV had looped around the palm trees and roared into the alleyway.

I ran toward the end of the short cul-de-sac. I had no other choice. A chain-link fence about eight feet high stood there separating me from the next street. Parked right next to it was an old car up on blocks, a small, tattered Cuban flag hanging limply from the aerial.

I sprinted right at it, timed my stride, hit the front fender of the car with my left foot, and managed to catch the fence with the toe of my right shoe. My shirt ripped on a prong at the top, and I lost a shoe, but I scrambled over. I hit the ground hard and looked up to see a sign on the other side telling me not to trespass. It was too late now.

The driver was timing the fence too. He revved up, popped the clutch, raced down the alley, skirted the junked car, and slammed right through it. The SUV ripped apart the links, wrenched the anchor posts from the ground, and dragged them across the macadam in a shower of sparks. From somewhere in the buildings across the street a disturbed sleeper swore. "*Mierda! Hijo de puta!*"

The driver, unaffected by the name calling, backed up to get loose from the metal posts. That gave me time to jump up, run, and reach the corner. I sprinted around it and found myself on a commercial strip. I pulled off my other shoe, tossed it, and sprinted down the middle of the street in my socks, searching for some place, any place, that might be open.

Many of the business signs were in Spanish and I might have been in some poor, outlying neighborhood of Buenos Aires twenty years earlier, running for my life. And I had to keep on running. Every storefront—every *restaurante, gasolinera, médico,* and *banco*—was dark and shuttered. There was no one to help me. The SUV skidded into the street behind me, and I heard it closing in.

Then I saw a person.

It was a woman with bleached, almost yellow hair, and she was standing alone on the next corner under a streetlight. At first I thought she might be waiting for a cab. I hoped one would come right then, and we could both jump into it, but no such luck. As I got close, she turned and I saw in the cone of streetlight a smile break out on her heavily rouged face. Her hand went to her waist, she cocked a wide hip, so that I saw a lot of thigh emerge from a skirt that was slit up the side.

"*Buenas noches, mi amor,*" she called to me as she opened her arms. "You're in a hurry to have me."

Her smile widened to reveal discolored teeth, and I realized she was an aging hooker trying to pull her last trick before the sun came up. She was the only one in the neighborhood open for business.

I turned, saw the SUV closing in, and realized the woman wouldn't do me any good. They wouldn't hesitate to gun her down with me if I tried to hide behind her.

Instead of negotiating for her charms, I pushed her down as I ran by. She cursed in vivid Spanish. As I rounded that corner, more shots rang out.

I was on a straightaway now with no side streets, and the SUV would surely catch me before I got far. I ran as hard as I could in my stockinged feet toward an overpass about a hundred yards ahead. The kidnappers screeched around the corner behind me and started closing in again.

It was then that I saw my guardian angels.

In the tunnel of that overpass stood three young men. They were all facing the wall. At first I thought they had stopped to pee after a night of beer drinking.

But they were all making strange swirling and looping gestures with their arms, and I heard a curious hissing noise. It took a frantic moment, but I realized I had run into graffiti artists. They were using the cover of night to tag the underpass.

I was no more than a hundred feet away when the headlights of the SUV, closing in behind me, hit the three of them.

"*Policía,*" I yelled at the top of my lungs. "*Corran!* Run!"

The three kids turned toward me, flinched, let their spray cans clatter to the pavement, whirled, and took off. I already had a head of steam, so by the time they got up speed I was in the tunnel and right with them.

We ran up the weedy bank next to the overpass and sprinted across the street above, just as the big SUV roared up an access ramp and wheeled into view. It came toward us, but a half block down, we cut between a Caribbean cigar shop and a religious articles store with a life-sized statue of the Virgin staring at us from a show window. We dodged into a narrow alley where the SUV couldn't fit. I heard it skid to a stop behind us, then go roaring up the street. They meant to cut us off on the next block.

But my running mates knew the neighborhood. We cut sharp right, ran through several backyards, one of which contained wire pens holding fighting cocks and another where I had to jump over a pit that was used to roast a Hispanic family's Christmas suckling pig. We cleared two ficus hedges, crossed a narrow side street, and a minute later dove into a large clump of croton bushes. My lungs were burning.

I listened, but all I heard were throbbing insects in the nearby vegetation. The screeching tires of the SUV were no longer within earshot. My three saviors listened too. They were Latino kids no more than seventeen. They had dropped their spray cans, but their hands were still covered in fine mists of phosphorescent paint—one red, one bright orange, and the other bright yellow.

They looked me up and down, a guy who looked old for a graffiti artist.

"My tag is Miguel 7," said the one with the red hands. "What's yours, man?"

"Willie," I said. "8th Street Willie."

CHAPTER TWENTY-FOUR

We laid low for a while, and then the kids helped me find a cab. I was covered with mud, my shirt was ripped, and I was barefoot. I had to dangle a fifty-dollar bill in front of the cabbie's nose before he'd let me in.

The driver dropped me in front of my place just as the sun was coming up. The Cuban bread was still lying in the gutter, and I picked it up, but it was cold by now.

I went around back, let myself in quietly, tiptoed barefoot to my kitchen closet, grabbed a spare gun I kept hidden there, and made sure no one else was home.

Then I showered, probed at my different bruises, and climbed into bed. But I didn't sleep. I lay with the gun on the night table next to me, keeping an eye on the street, in case they decided to visit me again.

I tried to snatch from all the chaos any demonstrable clue as to who had shanghaied me. But they were good. Apart from the red vehicle, which I was sure would disappear, there was no hint. Not one word had been spoken, not one face seen. They were a long way from Buenos Aires, but they still knew their business.

I couldn't call the police anyway. It would set off the kind of attention that could get Elena Navarro hurt. I also decided not to frighten Fiona Bonaventura any more than she already was. I wouldn't tell her, or Alice Arden for that matter. I wouldn't tell anyone. I didn't want to spread the fear.

But it was too late.

Just before eight a.m., the phone rang. It was Fiona.

"Someone just called here, a man who whispered into the phone. He said if I didn't go back to Buenos Aires, I would die and my niece would die as well. He said we would end up like my sister Sonia."

I winced at her words, but she wasn't finished.

"Now that I know she's my niece, I don't want her hurt, Mr. Cuesta. I don't care about myself, but I can't put her in danger."

I told myself that the girl was already in danger, given that her keep-
ers were Navarro and Arno. I hadn't told Fiona about the pilot and didn't
tell her now.

"Leave your condo, find another phone, and call me back."

"Why?"

"Please, do what I'm telling you."

She hung up. I couldn't be sure what her husband's involvement
was, so I couldn't take a chance that he was there or that her phone was
tapped. If he wasn't one of them, then how had they gotten Fiona's
number?

It also occurred to me that the men who had kidnapped me had
probably followed me from the club. I wondered if they had staked the
place out earlier and spotted the girl and Nelson. I wondered what they
knew and didn't know and who they had in their sights.

The phone rang and it was Fiona.

"Why are we doing this?"

"Because we have to. Is your husband home?"

"No, he isn't. He went out early."

"How early?"

"An hour ago."

"Was he out late last night?"

"No, he was here. Why?"

"I want you to go back upstairs and pack a bag. Walk down two
blocks to the Fontainebleau Hotel and take a cab to a hotel farther north
on Collins, called the Driftwood House. The cabbie will know it. Check
in there and wait for me. I'll bring Elena there to meet you as soon as
it's safe."

"And my husband?"

"Don't phone your husband and don't leave him a note. Just go."

She didn't respond. She understood exactly what I was implying.
Her silence was the same silence that existed at the heart of her marriage. Questions unasked and unanswered. Buried suspicions so awful
they had left her mute.

That silence lasted a long time. Then she hung up.

Next I phoned Nelson Cruz on his cell.

"Is that you?"

"Yes, Nelson, it's Willie Cuesta."

"Oh, wow!"

"Why wow?"

"Elena talked to me for a long time last night after we left the club."

"About what?"

"About how she suspected all along through her life that Navarro and Felicia weren't her parents. She told me about every time they had to move. She told me her whole life."

"She must trust you a lot, Nelson."

"I guess."

"I'm going to trust you too. First, I need to know if you were followed last night, either on your way to the club or the way home."

"Followed?"

"Yes, in a car."

"I don't think so."

"Or at least you didn't notice. Well, today I want you to bring Elena to meet her aunt, and I want you to be absolutely sure you're not being followed."

"Okay."

"That means checking your rearview mirror, making a couple of U-turns. You get what I mean?"

"Like the movies."

"Exactly. Then I want you to bring Elena out to Miami Beach, a place called the Driftwood House at 95th and Collins. Get there at noon. I'll meet you in the lobby."

"Okay."

"If there's any problem, if Navarro or anybody else tries to keep her in the house, you call me right away."

"If he does, we'll make up a story or she'll sneak out. Don't worry, I'll bring her."

"Good."

"There's something else you should know."

"What?"

"After I dropped her off last night, Elena called me back. She heard Navarro and the other guy talking."

"Arno?"

"Yeah. They're leaving the country, and they'll take Elena and her mom with them."

"Where are they going?"

"I don't know."

"When?"

"They said they had to get out of Miami soon. Elena doesn't want to go anywhere, Mr. Cuesta."

"Don't worry, just bring her."

I hung up and stayed staring at the phone. Arno was a pilot. He could leave any time and head just about in any direction, although it would probably be south. They would disappear into Latin America somewhere and take the girl with them. I pictured jungle engulfing them and covering their tracks for all time. They might let Elena and Felicia live, and they might not.

Sonia Bonaventura had died after getting on a plane with Arturo Arno. I knew I could never let that happen to Elena.

CHAPTER TWENTY-FIVE

I glanced at the clock. I had time before I needed to be at the Drift-wood House, time enough to visit the torture victim, Miguel Méndez. It was important I see him. If he could link the priest and Arno to the detention center the way he had Navarro, that would help before a judge and might help put away the members of GT 332.

I left my house by the back door, made sure my buddies from that morning weren't waiting for me, and found my car. I made for the MacArthur Causeway and hurried down to South Pointe. It was mid-morning, but the streets were empty except for glaring white-hot sun-light and the hum of air conditioners. It was as if the cityscape itself was buzzing.

I reached the gate of Méndez's complex. The same guard was there and recognized me.

"Tell him Fiona sent me." It was a lie, but I was getting good at that.

It took a while for the guard to get an answer. He finally did, and he flagged me through.

Méndez opened the door only a crack as he had the last time. He wore a robe and his hair was tousled. He had probably finished his all-night "technical help" shift at the computer a couple of hours earlier, and I had woken him. But the moment he set eyes on me he was wide-awake and worried.

I held up my empty hands. "It's Willie Cuesta, Miguel. I called on you two days ago with Fiona Bonaventura."

He nodded warily. "What do you want?"

"I need to talk to you. I have here two more photographs for you to look at. Can I come in?"

His face stormed over. Speaking to me with a chain between us was already more than he wanted to do. He glanced at the photos that I had downloaded and that were now clutched in my hand. I didn't show them to him.

The standoff lasted about ten seconds, and then his curiosity about monsters out of his past got the better of him. He closed the door momentarily, removed the chain, let me step in, closed it again, and locked it.

That was as far as I got. Méndez stopped right there, and so did I. The curtains were closed, and the condo was dusky and barely furnished: same tea gourd on the desk, same computers with chess games in progress, exact same reclusive and menaced solitude hanging in the air.

Behind the door, in a corner I hadn't seen before, stood another desk and two more computers. One had a chess game on the screen, the other had what appeared to be e-mail. A television sat on the floor next to it. There seemed to be screens everywhere—almost as if I was looking out the windows in a submarine, as if Méndez lived underwater, like Captain Nemo.

I brought out the snapshot of Father Pérez taken with the soldiers and held it up. Maybe it was the sight of the uniforms, but the photo alarmed Méndez right off the bat. After my experience of the night before, I could better understand his fear.

I tapped the figure of Father Pérez.

"I want to know if you recognize the man dressed in the priest's robes. I think he might have been at the detention center at the time you were there and when Sonia was killed."

One of his birdlike fingers pointed at the priest.

"He's the one murdered, isn't he? The one on the television."

"That's right."

I watched his hooded eyes widen. The priest had once been an enemy. Now he was dead, but that didn't seem to be the issue. The killing had followed Méndez to Miami. That was the problem. That was the worry.

"Do you recognize him?"

He nodded more at something in his memory than at me. "Yes, I knew him. He was there."

"He was where?"

"At the detention center. I saw him there many times."

"What did the priest do?"

His voice dropped. "Sometimes the torturers went too far. People died. The priest gave last rites. Then they took the bodies away."

He spoke in the shorthand of painful memories.

"And you're positive it's the same priest?"

"Of course, I'm sure. I thought he would bless me someday after I died."

"Some of the others they threw from planes, didn't they, even before they were dead?"

"Yes, they say that's how Sonia died. He blessed them too before they were put on the planes."

I produced the printout of Arno's face and held it up. He didn't give me time to ask if he recognized the pilot. His finger jutted out again, trembling.

"Yes, he was there."

"Do you know what he did?"

He tried to remember, but couldn't. Of course, Méndez probably wouldn't know because he had never taken that last fatal flight.

"But you're sure you recognize him from the detention center?"

He nodded, fixed on the photo. "Is he here?"

"Yes. But I don't think you have anything to worry about."

Méndez didn't believe me at all. Every time I showed up, I gave him more murderers right in Miami to worry about. After all the years and the miles he'd traveled, I was bringing them back into his life.

Behind him, on a computer screen, one of his chess partners made a move. A piece jumped several spaces, stopped, and the computer chirped.

A question occurred to me that had been lurking in the back of my mind since the first time I'd been there with Fiona. She'd told me that only family members and a couple of the closest confidants had known where Sonia and Mario were hidden before they were kidnapped. I asked Méndez if he was one of them.

He nodded.

"I did know, but I didn't go there. I was afraid. Mario was being hunted. I'm not proud of it, but I cut my ties with them. To be with him was to risk being killed."

"After you were captured, did you tell where they were?"

I didn't use the words "under torture," but he understood where I was going.

He shook his head hard. "No. They detained me the day before they captured Mario and Sonia. I have no idea how they discovered where I was, but they did. They didn't question me until the next day. By then they had already found Mario and Sonia. They never asked me. Never."

"Is there anyone else from your group that knew and might have told?"

"The ones who knew the hiding places all were discovered and all of them died. Mario, Sonia, Roberto Guzmán, María Teresa Montejo, Alberto Cruz. I'm the only one who survived."

His expression turned bitter, and an anguished torrent gushed from him that might have been blocked for years.

"Later, some people said I had betrayed them all. They said it behind my back, but I heard it. When others die and you live, people question your right to exist. They say I must have betrayed someone and that's why I have been allowed to survive. Very few survived the detention center. Why do you think I'm not in Buenos Aires? Do you think it is only fear for my life?"

I didn't answer. I let him do that.

"The members of military intelligence didn't leave me alive and release me out of mercy. They did it to torture me more, but only in a different way. It made my colleagues as afraid of me as they were of the killers. Can you imagine what that does to a person?"

I wondered if people really had those suspicions about him. Or was it that Méndez was suffering from a case of survivor guilt even worse than Fiona's. Did he lament that he was alive while all his friends had died? Would he rather be dead?

I tucked the photos away.

"Can you remember anything you might have heard about Mario and Sonia during those last days? Anything that might explain what happened to them?"

He shook his head. "I don't know. I heard nothing. For the last three days before they found me, I was in hiding. I talked to no one. Not one human being."

He was still hiding, even now. He opened the door and waited for me to step out. As I passed the one computer screen that didn't contain a chess game, I glanced down at it. On the screen was an instant message. It was short and obviously an answer to a message Méndez himself had sent.

It said only: "Tell him nothing! Nothing!"

I read it again and then tried to read the return address of the e-mail. Méndez quickly stepped in front of me, then reached down and turned off the computer. We stood staring at each other just inches apart.

"Trading e-mails with a buddy?"

"That has nothing to do with you. You leave now, or I'll call the guard."

I hesitated, and he reached his hand toward the phone. I took the hint and left.

CHAPTER TWENTY-SIX

At a few minutes before noon I entered the lobby of the Driftwood House. It was a boutique place right on the beach, small and select. The lobby was done in tasteful art, abstract tropical. A piece of driftwood hung over the lobby and it too was graceful. It was a very attractive hideout and a discreet place for a family reunion, as long as none of the bad guys found us there. Those guys weren't discreet or attractive.

I asked for Fiona and was directed to the in-house phone. The operator patched me through.

"Is my niece here?" she asked the moment she heard my voice.

"Not yet. I'm coming up."

I crossed the lobby and took the small stainless-steel elevator up to the third floor. Fiona opened the door and allowed me into a small but elegant room done in jade green. I found she had prepared carefully for this meeting, a reunion she had been looking forward to for half her life.

Old photographs of Sonia, Mario, herself, and, apparently, other members of the Bonaventura clan lined the bed. Most of the people depicted were dead, and it seemed as if they were gazing up at me from the bottom of the sea. It would be a crash course in family history, a tragic history, but part of the curriculum necessary for the "children of the disappeared."

Fiona looked at me, and her eyes were full of anxiety. I sat next to her on the bed.

"What's wrong?"

She shook her head. It was clear that again she was worried about what the child would think, feel, and, in the end, do. Would the girl like her? Would Elena feel abandoned? Betrayed? Scared? The amount of emotion one might expect from the girl was enough to frighten anyone, a bit like a time bomb.

"She knows you've been looking for her a long time," I said. "I've told her. That means you care about her and are prepared to love her. She knows that too."

133

"I should have done much more to save her mother. Maybe she will figure that out too."

I grew stern with her.

"Don't start that again. You're the closest family she has. The only real family she has. Don't spoil it by blaming yourself for something you didn't do. Give her a chance to love you. She needs it. You do too."

I left her and went back downstairs to the lobby. Minutes later Elena and Nelson walked in. The girl was back to her usual jeans and small backpack. Maybe it was just me, but I saw even more little girl in her right then. And she looked even more nervous than her aunt.

I instructed Nelson to wait for me, and I escorted Elena upstairs. It was the moment I'd been working toward since the first day.

When the elevator door opened on Fiona's floor, the girl hesitated, as if she were tempted to go back down to the lobby, to continue the life she knew, no matter how false and unsettled it had been. What she was about to do would be even more disorienting and, to a delicate young psyche, maybe more frightening.

In the end, she walked resolutely down the hall with me. I knocked on the door and Fiona opened. The two of them gazed at each other across a twenty-year gulf of estrangement, pain, loss, tragedy, but also shared history. And hope too. The distance between them was an emotional minefield.

Neither of them said a word. Fiona's eyes were as full of love as any two eyes I had ever seen. Elena's were gripped in trepidation, but that was to be expected.

I told them to come find me downstairs when they were finished, and I left. I heard the door close behind me.

I found Nelson lying on a chaise lounge in a shady spot near the pool. I stretched out on the next lounge.

"After this meeting, they have to go see my friend Alice." I wrote the address on the back of a business card. "She's going to take their statements and prepare the paperwork that will be presented to an immigration judge. We're going to ask the courts to protect Elena and Felicia."

"That's good."

"You're going to drive them to Alice's. After that you need to take Elena home, have her talk to Felicia, and bring them both back to Alice's house. We need to hide them until we can go before the judge."

"Okay."

"If Navarro and Arno aren't there, then they can each pack a bag. If those guys are in the house, then they'll have to sneak out. But we have to get them out of there. It's too dangerous."

"And what happens with Navarro and the pilot?"

"We're going to report them to immigration, have them deported and put in prison back in Argentina. Hopefully they ll rot there."

Nelson liked that idea. So did I.

Alice Arden had once called me a "neat freak." I didn't understand what she meant. I'm not a slob, but my apartment doesn't simulate Martha Stewart's jail cell either.

"I mean you like to settle accounts," she said. "Call it justice, if you please, but in your case it isn't revenge as much as neatness."

She's the only person to ever call me neat.

Nelson and I eventually talked about baseball, art, and more baseball.

After almost three hours, the two women appeared. Elena had red-rimmed eyes. Fiona wore those tortoise shell shades, but they couldn't mask the fact that she'd been crying.

They stood before us, the aunt with her arm around the girl.

"You're sure you want to go through with this?" I asked Elena.

She nodded without hesitation. "Yes, I want it."

"Then I'll call Alice and say you're on your way. Nelson and I have also made plans to get you away from Navarro."

"I told you I won't leave without Felicia."

"I know that. We'll get her out with you."

I filled her in on my conversation with Nelson.

"It will be easier for us to escape either late at night or early in the morning," Elena said. "Navarro went out late last night, and he slept all morning. I heard him say he was going out tonight again."

I twitched. "How late was he out last night?"

"Very late. I heard him come home with Arturo Arno, the man who owns the house. It was around dawn."

I was willing to wager I knew where he'd been: playing bumper cars in the western end of the county. But I didn't discuss it. She already had enough to scare her.

"Nelson will leave his cell phone on and so will I," I said. "You and Felicia will pack some clothes if you can, and you'll go to Alice's house. Fiona will find you there and meet Felicia for the first time."

We all looked at Fiona. She seemed to understand why.

"Felicia and I will be fine," she said. "I know she has always loved Elena very much."

It was a statement that many people in Fiona's position would never have been able to make. It was one of those leaps of humanity that only those severely tested by life ever had to think about. I was proud of her.

Alice would need at least two or three hours with them, so I took the opportunity to go home and get some shut-eye. I propped chairs under the knobs of both my front and back doors, set the alarm clock, put my gun on the night table, and tucked myself in.

Two hours later I got up even before the alarm went off. I showered, got dressed, and headed for Alice's place. On the way I put a call in to my FBI friend Jeff Callahan, who had once worked in Buenos Aires. It was Saturday, and he was fishing somewhere out in Virginia, but he answered his cell phone.

"How are they biting?"

"They're not, which is why I'm answering the phone. What can I do for you, Willie?"

"In your days in Argentina, did you ever run into a guy called David Ingram?"

"You mean Captain David Ingram?"

"Are you saying he was military?"

"If it's the same guy. He was the military attaché, an Air Force officer, serving at the embassy back before I got there. I heard his name quite a bit because he was famous for his good contacts in the old military government. In fact, between you and me, people said he was more than just a military guy."

"You mean he was CIA?"

"You didn't hear it from me. Anyway, he really got around."

It certainly seemed that way. Ingram had gotten around to meeting Navarro, marrying his cousin, and forming part of private meetings with bad guys even twenty years later. It made me wonder what Captain Ingram had been involved in all those years ago during the "dirty war."

"You still there?" Callahan asked.

"Yes. Anything else you can tell me about the former captain?"

"Did he retire?"

"Yes. He's not in uniform now."

"What is this all about? You didn't really tell me last time."

So I clued him in. When I got to the name Mario Murillo, he stopped me.

"So it has to do with the Martin case?"

"Martin?"

"Yes. Mario Murillo's full name was Mario Martin Murillo. He was the son of an American father who lived in Argentina for a time, a guy by the last name of Martin. His mother was Argentine, and Mario used her last name. But he was also an American citizen. The embassy was still looking into his killing when I was stationed there."

It took me about ten seconds to think that all out.

"Because anyone who had a hand in killing him could be charged here in the United States with the murder of a U.S. citizen. Is that it?"

"Yep."

Callahan let out a yelp.

"I've got one! Gotta go."

The line went dead, but that was fine. I "had one" too. I now understood why Father Pérez had perished. I also comprehended why everyone in Miami who might have been involved in the deaths of Mario and Sonia was running for his life.

CHAPTER TWENTY-SEVEN

I found Alice Arden sitting on her balcony overlooking the lower stretch of the Miami River. She was watching the slow flow of the current, the same way that Oscar Porta had watched it two nights earlier. But we were farther downriver now and so was my case.

Fiona, Elena, and Nelson were not in evidence. Alice's eyes were puffy, and it was apparent she had been crying, which was highly unusual for her.

"They left a while ago."

"And?"

"It's a long, amazing story, Willie. What Fiona went through over the years to find that girl is absolutely astounding. Both in Buenos Aires and then later in another city, Rosario, she just barely missed them. Elena talked about leaving those places on a moment's notice with the Navarros, and Fiona was always just minutes away. It's incredible."

That made me wonder just where Estevez had been when those near misses occurred. Had he been tipping them off even then?

I told Alice what I had learned about Mario Martin Murillo's U.S. citizenship.

"Oh, yes. Fiona told me. She just happened to mention it, as if it didn't mean much. Of course murder is murder no matter what the nationality of the victim, but that makes Elena an American citizen. When I get to a judge, I can say I'm trying to protect an American citizen. It transforms the case."

"It changes the status of the crime these guys committed as far as the local police are concerned," I said.

"Absolutely. They killed an American. They won't just get deported, they'll be sent to the slammer here. Maybe even face the death penalty."

"Do you have everything else you need for now?"

She crossed her bare feet on the edge of the railing. "Yes. Between the story, the DNA evidence, and the testimony of her stepmother, Felicia, we can prove that Elena was the victim of a kidnapping when she was just hours old. Nelson says he'll bring them tonight. All we need to do is keep them both safe until I can get to my judge tomorrow."

"I'm with you. One of the ways we can keep them safe is to keep an eye on somebody who might want to do them harm, right?"

"Absolutely."

"So get dressed. We're going to a polo match."

An hour later we were driving north and west of Glades Springs on a winding two-lane road in the direction of the Everglades. As we drove, the vegetation grew more and more luxuriant. So did the walls around the gated communities. These gates were higher than the ones I'd seen in Glades Springs, and the pretensions were also more inflated. The enclaves had names like Mariposa Manors, Everglades Empire Estates, and the Grand Eucalyptus Villas.

Around the next bend we found a sprawling, three-story Tudor-style manse sitting on what had to be a man-made hill, overlooking a long green polo field. It was so out of place on the edge of the Everglades that it was a bit like making a bend in your imagination and finding a magic castle. There couldn't be many Tudor mansions in the world surrounded by stands of tropical royal palms, but I'd found one.

Alice also was impressed. "Well, shut my mouth, I think we're in Shangri-la."

That mansion was surrounded on three sides by a parking lot. Cars were pulling into it in preparation for the polo match. Valets in pure white were sprinting here and there, docking Silver Clouds, Jaguars, Rolls, Bentleys, and bevies of BMWs.

Stepping out of those royal carriages were the cream of the American aristocracy—ladies in wide-brimmed hats and flowing, colorful frocks, next to men who, given the temperature, had forgone tweeds in favor of pastel-colored blazers. But the gents still looked like they'd stepped out of old Brooks Brothers ads.

Alice wore a straw hat with an orange hibiscus tucked in the band, a bright white blouse, very tight jeans, and boots in honor of the horses. I was in an old white jacket, black jeans, and a tropical shirt in honor of the tropics.

"We appear to be a bit underdressed," I said.

"Yes, but we make up for it in sex appeal."

I waited for the Porsche in front of me to move, and I pulled up under the porte cochere. The look my car attracted from the Latin valet was even more corrosive than the one I'd received at Fiona's condo. But Alice got out of the car, and he was temporarily dazzled by the length and languor of her. I snatched the valet ticket from him, let Alice take my arm, and we waded into the horse world.

The inside of the Tudor polo palace was as richly and royally appointed as it appeared from the outside. It was all broad, varnished beams, chandeliers that were made to look medieval, and coats of arms that, by necessity, had been imported from the British Isles. The only royal lineage that had emerged locally were the royal palms, the local alligators, and possibly a golden panther or two that roamed the nearby Everglades.

The walls all around us were hung with large, vintage, black-and-white photographs of polo matches—lots of wild-eyed horses and grimacing guys in helmets wielding polo mallets the way old medieval knights wielded maces.

A young man in footman's livery, wearing the green-and-white colors of the club, stood at the entrance to the main salon. Unlike the décor, he didn't look very British.

"There must be a shortage of help," I said. "That looks like a Puerto Rican footman."

"No. He's distinctly Dominican," Alice said as we sauntered by. You didn't argue with an immigration attorney about such things.

Another Caribbean footman approached holding a tray of brimming champagne flutes. Alice and I accepted the bubbly and barged on. We passed large round dining tables set with brilliant white tablecloths and real silver. At the center of each stood a bottle of Argentine wine, apparently in honor of the visiting team.

We were working our way through the crowd when I spotted Sergio Villarreal standing near the long mahogany bar. He was more splendidly dressed than usual, decked out in a gray cutaway.

But even more interesting than his attire was the company he was in. The diplomat was in deep conversation with another Argentine, Eduardo Estevez. They were cheek to jowl, and whatever Villarreal was telling him had Estevez worried.

I was worried as well. I didn't like the linkage I was seeing. As far as I could tell, Villarreal was connected to the killers of Sonia Bonaventura. If he was an intimate of Estevez, then Fiona was extremely vulnerable, even more so than I'd thought.

"The vice consul of Argentina is in attendance," I said to Alice.

"Does that mean he's the consul in charge of vice?"

"I've yet to determine that."

She gave Villarreal a glance. "I think I'll leave him to you. I'm going to find me a real polo prince."

She drifted off into the sea of CEOs and I headed right at the two Argentines. Villarreal had me in his sights halfway there. He said something. Estevez spotted me and moved away into the crowd before I could get to them.

I sidled over to the diplomat, despite the fact he obviously wasn't pleased to see me.

"Mr. Vice Consul, you are very grandly dressed today."

"Mr. Investigator, an Argentine team is playing an American team here, and it will be my honor to present the cup to the winners."

He was able to assume false bonhomie almost instantly, like a good diplomat. In a way it was the same ability he'd shown twenty years ago: the capacity to continue in the service of a government that was disappearing thousands of his countrymen.

I looked in the direction of the departed Estevez.

"Interesting conversation?"

He shrugged. "I am the representative of my country, and I am available to all the Argentines, as I told you the last time we met."

I smiled some more. "I see. Did you know Estevez back in the days of the 'dirty war,' when you were a worker bee for the military government?"

He didn't like my tone, but didn't say so.

"Of course, I knew him. He was the son-in-law of my superior, Don Pablo Bonaventura. I would go to the house, and he would be there, but we never knew each other well."

"By which you mean he didn't confess his sins to you."

His eyebrows went up. "I didn't know he had sins to confess."

"Did Don Pablo Bonaventura, your boss, ever talk to you about Estevez?"

The diplomat squinted, as if he were reading very small print on a policy document. "What do you mean? What would he have said?"

"Did he ever think that Estevez might be a traitor, might represent a danger to his daughter Sonia and her husband?"

Villarreal arched an eyebrow. "You didn't know Don Pablo. He was a man who had walked the corridors of power in my country, and he was, by nature, conservative. If he considered anyone in that house a betrayer of the family, a danger, it was the other son-in-law, Mario Murillo. It was Murillo who made trouble at that very dangerous moment."

I sipped my champagne. "Yes, but I understand Don Pablo was trying to keep Murillo alive, if only for Sonia's sake. In the end they were betrayed, and I'm wondering if there wasn't a person in that house with certain political interests who might have been less intent on keeping them alive."

Our eyes locked for a long silent pause. He understood that the description I'd just enunciated might apply to Estevez, but also might be applied to Villarreal himself. The chess pieces were moving behind his dark brown eyes.

"Don Pablo was a very astute judge of character," he said. "He would not have made the mistake of having such an enemy in his house."

His answer made me smile. He was exonerating himself, as well as Estevez.

"Yes, Mr. Vice Consul, but even a political veteran like Don Pablo might have made a mistake at that moment. It was a very treacherous time, full of treacherous people."

His eyes narrowed, but he didn't take the bait.

"The people in the house weren't the only ones who knew where Sonia and Mario were hiding. I'm told some of the members of their political movement also knew."

"But why would a member of their own movement betray them?"

"Maybe the moment came when they were afraid for their lives. You get mixed up with the wrong people and you can get killed, Mr. Cuesta. Sometimes people realize that and they repent, they change sides, before it costs them their lives."

His tone was explanatory, even diplomatic, but it was also clear that my life was being threatened by the representative of the Argentine government. First I'd been grabbed off the street, and now this portly penguin in the cutaway was getting rough with me.

"You'll have to excuse me," Villarreal said. "I have official duties to perform."

With that he drained his champagne and disappeared into the crowd.

CHAPTER TWENTY-EIGHT

I washed his threat down with some champagne and got the bartender to top me off again. Then I went in search of Eduardo Estevez. I wanted to know what he and Villarreal had been discussing so very strenuously, and, between the two of them, who might have been threatening whom.

The crowd started to course down the stairs of the clubhouse toward the playing area. They filed past the outdoor grandstand and the polo green, and then they entered a large building, somewhat like an airplane hangar, which stood next to it.

I fell in with them and found myself in an indoor polo arena, something I'd never known existed. It was about five stories high, the roof was made of whitewashed glass, and the field, a bit larger than an American football field, was covered in some kind of mulch, not grass. The playing area was ringed by a wall about waist high, presumably to keep the ponies from trampling the paying customers. The seats ascended from the top of the wall on all sides.

It was air conditioned and at least twenty-five degrees cooler in there than it was outside. Summer polo in the South Florida heat would have been considered cruelty to animals, and to me too.

Bright orange goalposts stood at both ends of the field. At each end, a team of three men each was warming up the polo ponies and passing the ball to one another. The Argentines were in blue jerseys and helmets, the Americans in bright red. All wore the same white riding britches I'd seen on David Ingram. They wielded their long-handled mallets, swinging them in perfect sweeping arcs, and picking the white ball neatly off the ground.

The Americans were at the same end where I had entered. As a galloping pony skirted the wall, I looked down and recognized the rider. It was former Captain Ingram under the red-brimmed helmet, in the red jersey with the number 3 stenciled on it, atop a pony with the red leggings.

He tracked down a rolling ball, cut the pony into position expertly, swung the mallet, launched the ball across the field, and galloped after it. The pony never broke stride. I don't know anything about polo, but I was impressed.

The general admission section of the grandstand, the upper-level seats, were already full with the general public. Just above the surrounding wall were private boxes, furnished with fan-back wicker chairs, and the crowd from the clubhouse, la crème de la crème, filed into those choice seats.

Just above those private boxes was a small section marked "V.I.P. Box." Ensconced there were two people who appeared to be from India, or maybe Pakistan. The gentleman was bearded, wore a white turban and a seersucker suit. The lady with him was dressed in a Western manner, but her hair and shoulders were draped in a diaphanous red veil. Seated with them was Villarreal. In his tails, he looked like their butler.

A public address announcer told the crowd that in attendance were "the Maharaja and Maharani of Jaipur, great proponents of polo from India, where our beloved game was born." The couple waved to the crowd and were warmly applauded.

He also introduced the Argentine vice consul, who drew a small smattering of applause.

I found one available seat in the grandstand just above the private boxes, near the Indian royalty. I was Cuban-American royalty and could hold my own.

The two teams assembled near the center of the field, and the public address announcer introduced them all, including Ingram. Each player waved his mallet at the crowd. Moments later they and their horses surrounded a referee in a striped shirt who threw the ball down between them, and the mounted scramble was on.

The players poked at the white ball with their mallets, the horses jostling and rearing, until the ball finally came out of the scrum and they galloped after it. I turned and watched a blue-shirted Argentine player lead the pack down the field.

Following his progress, I turned almost completely to my right, and that's when I happened to spot Sara Ingram.

She was sitting about six seats down, on the opposite side of Mr. and Mrs. Maharaja and Villarreal. She wore a flowered dress, white shoes, and a plastic visor.

She appeared to be by herself, so I inched my way in her direction, excusing myself to the others in that row. I finally squeezed in next to her.

"What a pleasure it is to find you here, Mrs. Ingram."

My sudden appearance startled her. She made a face. It was clear she didn't share my enthusiasm for the encounter.

"What brings you here, Mr. Cuesta? You're of Cuban descent, aren't you? I didn't think Cubans played polo."

"We don't. In fact, I've never been to a polo match before in my life. But when I saw your husband was competing, I had to come. He certainly seems to be a very good player."

She watched me suspiciously. "David is a distinguished player. He is actually quite good for an American."

A pinch of national pride had entered her tone.

"I take it the Argentines are better."

"Most experts consider Argentines the most accomplished players in the world."

"And your husband learned the game from them in Argentina."

"That's right," she said, following the action.

The ball had ricocheted off the wall just beneath us, and the players pursued it in a pack. You could feel the concussion of the galloping hooves right through the bleacher seats.

Captain Ingram, very much in the middle of the scramble, gained control of the ball and led the mad dash toward his goal. The commentator who was doing the play-by-play over the loudspeaker commended him for a brilliant "break out." Sara Ingram's eyes followed him down the field.

"Did your husband learn the game while he was stationed at the U.S. embassy as military attaché, or was it afterwards?" I asked.

She didn't take her eyes from the field, where the players played fast and furious, but I could tell she was now following the thoughts inside her own head. They seemed to be just as furious, although her calm tone belied them.

"He started to play while he worked in the embassy, yes, and he has continued ever since."

"You didn't mention your husband's military background when we spoke before."

"I didn't think that mattered."

"Didn't it? Didn't your husband, given the position he held, have considerable contact with the Argentine military. In fact, I wonder if he didn't meet your cousin Manuel and you because of that position."

She turned and met my gaze. "David and I met at an Argentine Defense Ministry reception. My cousin brought me there. What importance does that have?"

"You told me Navarro and your husband had nothing to do with one another. You told me your husband knew nothing of your cousin's problems."

"I have a home, a family, children, Mr. Cuesta. I cannot let the past—not my past, but another person's past—follow me here and destroy everything my husband and I have worked for. Would you want your children to know that the man they call their uncle had participated in . . . "

Her voice trailed off.

"In disappearances, torture sessions, and killings," I said. "No, I guess I wouldn't want the children or the neighbors in Glades Springs to know that. But I'm not asking you to stand up in front of the PTA or the Ladies Club and talk about those terrible times. I only want you to tell me."

"What do you expect me to tell you? I was only a student, a schoolgirl."

"You were a young woman who was the cousin of a war criminal and the girlfriend of a man who had reason to know what was happening inside military intelligence."

She shook her head. "Don't say such things about my husband. He didn't know anything about what Manuel was doing."

"Excuse me, Mrs. Ingram. Your husband wasn't the cultural attaché. He wasn't the embassy landscaper or the cook. He was the top military man and . . . maybe even more than that."

I didn't want to say that Ingram was CIA and I didn't need to. She knew where I was going.

Just then a well-dressed older woman, a polo maven, walked by just beneath us and greeted Sara Ingram as she passed. Mrs. Ingram flashed an artificial smile at the acquaintance and exchanged a pleasantry. The woman moved on, and Sara Ingram turned back to me, all business again.

"You're trying to destroy my family and my life."

"No, I'm not. I'm trying to unite another family. You should be able to understand that. I have the results of DNA tests. Elena Navarro definitely belongs to the family of my client."

The pack of ponies roared by us. I felt everyone in the crowd around me turn to follow them, everyone but Sara Ingram and me. Moments later the Argentines scored a goal. One young Argentine cried out, "Go-o-o-l!" The others cheered, but Sara Ingram didn't seem to notice.

"From the time that Manuel and Felicia came to live here two years ago, I knew trouble would follow," she said. "I knew that even hidden there in Glades Springs, our lives would change."

She turned and looked me in the eyes. "Please, don't let anything happen to Felicia, Mr. Cuesta. Manuel has treated her badly. She would have left him many times, but he threatened to go to the authorities and tell how they got Elena. Felicia was terribly afraid that Elena would be taken away from her."

"That's why she has stayed with him?"

"Oh, yes. For that and no other reason. My cousin Manuel has made her run with him, everywhere he has had to go to avoid the human rights police."

"So she knew he was a war criminal, and he knew her child wasn't hers. So they had each other blackmailed."

"I don't think Felicia ever would have told anybody about Manuel's past, unless he tried to harm the child. That was why he never physically harmed Elena. In that sense, Felicia blackmailed him but only to protect her daughter."

It sounded like an absolutely hellish arrangement, but they had lived with it for twenty years. At the moment, Sara Ingram herself looked like an inhabitant of hell.

The polo period ended—or the "chukker," as the commentator called it. The players dismounted, and fresh ponies were paraded out to the field. We watched in silence until Sara Ingram turned to me again.

"You know there are people in my country who say some of these so-called revolutionaries weren't disappeared at all, weren't killed. That they are alive, but just ran off to other countries. The disappeared, that's all made up. That's what they say."

Even as she said it, I could tell she didn't believe it. It was exactly the kind of rumor some people wanted to believe so that they would not have to face the brutal truth about what had occurred in their countries. It was like people who denied the Holocaust had happened.

"Mrs. Ingram, we both know your cousin was involved in kidnappings, tortures, and murders. Now the priest is dead and Navarro's hiding the girl. He is still a very bad individual and deserves to be in prison."

I saw her momentary resistance slowly drain out of her. She became resolved to the wretched truth about her cousin. Her eyes narrowed, and she seemed to bring him into focus.

"I was remembering this morning how Manuel used to disappear for days at a time and nobody would know where he was. Not Felicia, not me, not anyone in the family. I was studying then and I lived with them in Buenos Aires. After days away, he would simply come home, sometimes in the middle of the night. I would wake up in the morning, and he would be there at the breakfast table as if he had never been away. I would ask him where he had been and he would only say, 'I was working.' He never said anything else, and we never found out what he was doing."

She frowned at her own words, as if she herself didn't believe them.

"But you eventually knew," I said.

She nodded. "I know that at the same time he was gone we would hear of people being kidnapped from the streets and their homes. I would hear the rumors, and I would put two and two together." She shook her head in disbelief at her own life. "Have you ever had to wonder if such great evil lived in your own home, Mr. Cuesta?"

She turned and let me see her fear.

"I know you need to find Elena. I know that Manuel will eventually end up in prison. But please, please, keep the rest of my family out of it."

"I'll try my best, but given you and your husband's connection to your cousin, I can't promise you that, Mrs. Ingram."

My answer didn't make her happy. For the first time I saw in her eyes, mixed with all that maternal instinct, a flash of anger. It lasted only a moment. Then she got up, edged her way down the aisle, and left the arena.

CHAPTER TWENTY-NINE

The players changed mounts again, played another "chukker," and after a while a horn went off declaring halftime, with the score tied at three. The break gave the crowd a chance to refill their champagne glasses at the bar beneath the grandstand.

Some of them then wandered out onto the field and began replacing the divots of mulch ripped up by the dashing horses. It appeared to be polo tradition—the public acting as groundskeepers, a democratic impulse on the part of the princes and princesses of American society. Landscapers sipping champagne.

I got myself some of that champagne, but skipped the gardening. Instead I kept an eye out for Estevez. I didn't see him, but I did see Alice, who stood near the bar, huddled with an attractive, silver-haired gentleman in a coral-colored blazer.

She stepped away from him and approached me.

"You've attracted a very flashy admirer there," I said.

"His name is Antonio, and he's from Argentina. You can't tell the Argentine millionaires around here without a scorecard."

She glanced at Antonio, who was watching her closely. He raised his champagne glass in a starry-eyed toast. Alice answered in kind.

"I didn't know you were intent on marrying money," I said.

"I'm not, but I'm also not avoiding the good life if it gallops my way."

She leaned closer to me. "Antonio says all of high society in Argentina had the same opinion on the deaths of those two kids back then."

"Mario and Sonia?"

"That's right. He says everyone believed it was someone inside the girl's family who betrayed them."

I frowned. "Somebody inside the Bonaventura family sent Sonia to her death?"

She shook her head. "The feeling was that whoever told the military intelligence agents where the couple was hiding thought that only the husband, Mario, would die."

"Really."

"Yes. They didn't know the girl would die as well. There must have been a deal with the military, and it somehow went wrong. At least that was the gossip among the affluent."

She smiled at Antonio, who was still watching her.

"I better get back to him. He's giving me some pointers on polo."

"Ask him if he knows anything about Number Three on the American team, David Ingram."

"Will do, chief."

She wandered back to the wealthy Argentine, and I went searching once again for Estevez.

I stepped into the passageway between the two grandstand pavilions. Grooms were leading fresh ponies onto the field for the second half, and others were ushering sweaty ponies back to the stable.

One of the grooms walked right toward me, leading a pony with a white blaze on its face and wearing the blue saddle blanket of the Argentine squad.

He was a slight, willowy, middle-aged man, with shoulder-length sandy hair, and somehow he seemed familiar.

I tried to take a closer look, but when he noticed me looking at him, he turned away and shifted to the other side of the horse. Another groom spoke to him in Spanish, addressing him as Pedro.

I followed him a few steps and watched him head back toward the stables. As I did, a breeze brought the smell of the place to me. For some reason, that aroma also aroused my memory. Somewhere else, recently, I'd encountered that distinctive smell.

And then suddenly I knew. On the back floor of the SUV, I thought I'd smelled fertilizer. Now I realized it might also have been horse manure on the bottom of a boot.

I stood there with my nose twitching, not just to catch the aroma, but to understand just who I was surrounded by.

Of course, that aroma didn't explain why the man seemed so familiar. I hadn't seen any of the kidnappers' faces. I stood stock-still, staring at the groom's back as he walked away.

Then I reached into the inside pocket of my sport jacket and brought out the photographs I'd collected. I focused on the shot of Father Pérez and the soldiers. Standing next to the priest was Manuel

Navarro. Just over Navarro's shoulder, in the background, was a young, thin, light-haired soldier with a boyish face, a cow ick, and a look of consternation.

The photo was twenty years old, but he hadn't changed that much. It was the same slim, sheepish man, the groom who had just passed by me.

I walked away from the arena and followed him, headed for the stables. As I did, play resumed out on the polo field, and I heard the crowd cheer.

The stables sat slightly uphill from the arena and looked like a sprawling Spanish colonial villa with a barrel tile roof. In polo country, even the ponies lived like royalty.

I found grooms in each stable wiping off overheated horses that had come out of play. The horse's names were hanging from nails above each stall: Warrior, Armageddon, Hannibal, Khartoum. They were ponies to take into battle.

In one of the last stalls I found the fellow I was looking for. He was wiping down the pony with the blaze, whose name was Pericles. Pedro had placed the saddle over the wrought-iron gate of the stall, as well as the reins and other tack. He stroked the horse with a large round sponge.

I stood in the door of the stall, just feet away from him, but he pretended I wasn't there.

"Hello, Pedro."

His head came up, and he frowned. He didn't like the fact that I knew his name.

"It's good to see you again," I said.

"I've never seen you before," he said sullenly.

"Oh, that's not true at all. Don't you remember the tour of Sweetwater we took just last night. I'm sorry I had to leave early."

"I don't know what you're talking about. You must have me mixed up with someone else."

He moved to the other side of the horse, trying to hide. So I stepped into the stall.

The horse nuzzled me a bit, maybe sniffing for a carrot or a sugar cube. I stroked its blaze.

"Do you recognize me now, Pedro? I recognize you. In particular I remember those boots resting on my rib cage."

"I told you, I don't know what you're talking about. I was not in Sweetwater last night. In fact, I've never been in Sweetwater. I was here last night taking care of the horses, preparing for the polo match. I'm a groom and have duties."

"So you weren't with some of your old friends last night?" I held up the photo with Father Pérez. "Old friends such as these?"

He stopped stroking the horse and stared at the photo.

I tapped the image. "That's you, Pedro, along with the good *Padre* Pérez and also your superior officer, Manuel Navarro."

Right then Pedro looked pretty much as he appeared in the photo, like a deer in the headlights, only twenty years older.

"Of course, Father Pérez is no longer with us. But I believe you knew that. Still, the U.S. immigration authorities will be interested to hear that a former member of Argentina's GT 332 is living here. You're supposed to declare that sort of old indiscretion when you enter this country. But I doubt you did that."

By now Pedro was sweating as much as the horse. He looked at me desolately, his face resembling even more the spooked young man in the photo. When he spoke he sounded on the edge of tears.

"You have to understand I was forced to serve in that unit. I didn't want to do it."

"Is that right?"

"Yes."

The horse turned and gazed at him, as if it understood the conversation and was no longer happy with his keeper. Pedro peered outside the stall, afraid someone would hear us. Then he turned back to me.

"I was a simple boy from the countryside. They took me into the army and made me be part of terrible things."

"What kind of terrible things, Pedro?"

He hesitated.

"I can send the immigration investigators to question you about it."

He flinched as if the horse had kicked him.

"No, please don't put me through that."

"Then, tell me. You were involved in kidnappings, disappearances, killings, weren't you?"

He shook his head hard.

"Not killings. I never killed anyone."

"But you were part of GT 332, weren't you? You kidnapped people from their homes and from the street."

"Because I was under orders to do so. I would be dead if I refused."

"Were you involved in the disappearance of Mario Murillo and his wife? You were, weren't you?"

"Yes, I was there."

"What happened?"

He stared at the hay under his feet. I went around the horse and crowded him.

"What happened?"

"The same thing that always happened. We broke in the door. The woman began to cry. The man wanted us to take him and leave the woman, but we had orders to take her too."

"Specific orders?"

"Yes." He threw his head back in despair. "She was pregnant, very pregnant. I said to the lieutenant we should leave her, but he said those were the orders."

"From who?"

He shook his head hard. "I don't know."

"From Navarro?"

"Maybe, I don't know. But the lieutenant told me that both of them were going to be killed. They never told us things like that. We never knew for sure what would happen once we turned them over. Some lived, some died. This time we knew."

He had backed into the corner of the stall, as if cornered by the ghosts of those he had captured during those years. I advanced and boxed him in there.

"And how did you know where to find them?"

He bridled at the question. I grabbed him by the shirt.

"Tell me."

"Someone they knew betrayed them. I don't know who, but that's why they had to be killed, so they wouldn't tell who it was."

I tightened my grip on him.

"Tell me who it was!"

"I tell you that I don't know. I never knew."

"Then tell me who was with you last night when we went for that little ride."

His eyes were as big as horses' eyes now, and he shook his long hair.

"I can't tell you. They'll kill me."

"Who'll kill you?"

Another groom stood in the door of the stall and called out Pedro's name. The polo period had ended, and it was time to change mounts. I turned toward the voice and that's when Pedro made his move.

He broke from my grasp and pushed me so that I toppled over into the hay. A pitchfork stood propped against the back of the stall. He grabbed it and raised it above his head, about to skewer me like an hors d'oeuvre.

But in grabbing the pitchfork he had placed himself directly behind the horse. Pericles suddenly reared up onto his forelegs and kicked at Pedro with all the strength of his hindquarters. One of the hooves caught the groom right in the rib cage. The kick was so hard I thought I heard a bone break.

Pedro hit the back wall of the stable, screamed out in pain, dropped the pitchfork, and grabbed his side. He wore the agonized look of a trapped and wounded animal. But the shutters right next to him were open. He put one hand on the sill, vaulted out of the stall, and started running, with his right hand holding his ribs.

A large field behind the stalls met a tree line about a quarter mile away. He was injured but he was also frightened. He had disappeared into the trees before I covered even half the distance. The way he was galloping he looked like he would run all the way back to Argentina.

CHAPTER THIRTY

I brushed the hay off of me, stopped at the stall to thank Pericles for saving my hide and to pick up the photo I'd dropped. Then I made my way back to the arena. One of the bad guys had gotten away from me. Also, Sara Ingram hadn't returned to her seat. It seemed I had put her off her polo altogether.

But neither of them was as interesting to me as Eduardo Estevez, who was still nowhere to be seen. I decided to hold my ground and keep an eye out for him.

The match was mostly chaotic scrums, with horses milling and bumping, and players poking the ground with their mallets trying to gain possession of the ball. But every once in a while a player was able to break loose, launching the ball down the field, galloping after it ahead of the pack, and knocking the ball through the bright orange goalposts. When the ponies got going, they ran like the wind and were beautiful to behold.

Ingram was not so beautiful. He was an aggressive player, constantly in the middle of the melees. Once he knocked an Argentine from his horse, but it didn't do much good. In the end, "the Aggies," as the crowd called them, won 8-5.

Afterward, the players mingled at mid field. Villarreal presented the Argentine captain with a silver cup.

I kept my eyes on Ingram. He and Villarreal did not exchange even a word. When the ceremony was concluded, the crowd emptied out. I watched the former Air Force captain head for the tunnel under the grandstand where I sat. He didn't look up at me.

I saw him enter a door marked "Locker Room," along with the other players. I figured it would be too crowded in there to talk to him.

So I stayed where I was, waiting for him to come out. He did so just a few minutes later, dressed only in a black terry cloth robe and flip-flops. He headed down the tunnel away from the field and entered another area.

I followed him and found a frosted-glass door marked "Polo Spa and Health Club." I waited, but none of the other polo players followed. So, I did.

The foyer was walled in rich green marble. A small gold plaque just inside the door pronounced, "Members and Guests Only." An attendant's desk stood next to it, but no one was on duty. So I kept going.

The green marble and the gold fixtures continued all through the facilities. Hanging on walls, here and there, were more black-and-white photos of polo ponies, apparently legendary mounts in their later years. They were studs posted there to remind the members that they too were studs.

I heard voices and stuck my head into a massage room. A large black man was massaging a flabby, balding white man on a green marble table. It looked like he was kneading greasy dough and preparing to make a very large and unhealthy loaf of white bread. It wasn't pleasant to witness.

Ingram wasn't in there, nor in the gym, which was jammed with the latest in exercise machines and technology. That left only the sauna and the steam room.

I headed farther into the facility, and that was when I encountered the attendant, a muscle-bound, blond fellow in an Everlast T-shirt.

"Can I help you?"

"I'm looking for Captain Ingram?"

"Are you a guest of his?"

"Yes, I am."

He pointed farther back. "He's in the steam room, but you can't go past this point in street clothes."

He pointed me to a locker and a tall pile of white towels, and then he went about his business. I obliged him, stripping down, hanging my duds, donning a towel with a "PC"—Polo Club—monogram, and padding back to a clouded glass door.

The room was suffused with billowing steam, and at first I couldn't spot anyone. But the draft created when I opened the door stirred that mist and that was when I saw Ingram. He was sitting on the upper bench for maximum temperature. A towel was wrapped around his waist, and his normally florid face was now a dangerous red. He was speaking to a man sitting on the lower bench, who was also wrapped in a towel, his back to me. They were the only two people in the place.

Ingram also recognized me through the swirling steam. He grimaced.

"I don't believe you're a member. What are you doing here?"

The second man turned. It was Eduardo Estevez.

Our eyes locked for several long moments. He was as surprised to see me as I was to find him there.

I approached them. "What am I doing here? Right now I could ask your guest the same thing."

In other circumstances, I wouldn't have been so surprised. That a wealthy Argentine might have friendly relations with a former American official was not big news. But in this case, they both had connections with a kidnapper and killer, Antonio Manuel Martínez Navarro, and maybe they'd had them for a long time.

Ingram stood up.

"You get out of here now, or I'll have the attendant call the police and have you thrown out."

I stood my ground.

"I don't think Mr. Estevez would want the police on the premises, especially since they already want to talk to him about the murder of Father Pérez."

That made Ingram pause. More steam billowed from the vents. Nonetheless, the situation was getting clearer to me, not cloudier.

"What do you want to know?" Ingram asked.

"I think I just learned everything I need to know."

"What the hell does that mean?"

"It means Mr. Estevez here is supposedly looking for his niece and has been for years. But he's had a direct connection to Navarro all along, through you. So he hasn't really wanted to find the girl."

"That's not true," Estevez said. "I've wanted to locate her, if it could be done. I just didn't want to waste my life on a mission that would prove impossible. I told you that the last time you accused me of being an accomplice to murder."

"Did you two know each other all those years ago down in Argentina during the dirty war?"

"Yes, we did," Estevez said, "but only socially."

"Did socializing include plotting the deaths of your brother-in-law and sister-in-law over cocktails? Or did you do it between periods at the polo matches?"

Estevez got exercised now. "That statement is going to cost you. I'll speak to my attorney tomorrow."

"You're going to need an attorney, but it won't be over a slander suit, it will be over the killing of the priest."

"I had nothing to do with that. I didn't see Pérez after I left his office that afternoon. I told you that."

"And you came up north here and had a drink with a friend that night. That's what you also told me. I assume Captain Ingram here is your alibi."

"That's right."

"So you're going to arrange alibis for each other. I wonder if you're also going to supply alibis for one another when it comes to what happened twenty years ago. What sort of information did Estevez here supply you, Captain, that you passed along to your amigos in GT 332?"

Despite the steam, Ingram was now cool and collected. He was the old intelligence officer with ice water in his veins.

"For your information, I had no direct connection to GT 332 at any time. As military attaché it was my job to keep in touch with members of the Argentine armed forces. And Don Pablo Bonaventura, Sonia's father and longtime public servant, was aware of that.

"When things were at their worst, he sought me out at an embassy reception, and I agreed that his son-in-law was apparently in a very dangerous situation. He then asked if I could assist in getting both the son-in-law and his daughter out of the country as soon as possible and into the United States, where they would be safe."

That surprised me, and he could see it.

"You didn't know that, did you, Mr. Cuesta?"

"And you could do that because Mario Murillo's father was an American, and he was technically a U.S. citizen."

"That's right. I could have done it anyway, but that made it easier."

"So what happened then?"

"We met once and only once. Murillo refused my help."

"Refused? How so?"

"Just that. At Don Pablo's request, and also as a favor to my friend here, Eduardo, I went to the family house to meet with them one evening. The meeting didn't last long. Murillo said he didn't want to have anything to do with the American embassy and never would."

"When was that?"

"A day before they went into hiding."

"So three or four days before they were kidnapped. Did you have any contact with them after that meeting?"

"None. I told you, they didn't want to know me. Not then, not ever. Don Pablo and his wife were scared and angry over that decision. They wanted to save their daughter. But that's the way it was. I didn't go back. Anyone who worked at the embassy back then, who's still alive, can confirm all of this. We tried to save them, but they wouldn't let us."

"He's telling you the truth," Estevez said. "We tried to save them."

A new cloud of steam was emitted by two vents in the corners. I stared at Ingram through it. His story was as murky as the mist. Mario, Sonia, and Fiona's parents were all dead, and Fiona apparently had no knowledge of that attempt to save Sonia. I didn't know enough to accuse Ingram and Estevez of lying.

"And once Sonia was in custody, there was nothing you could do to save her in those ensuing days?" I asked. "Her child was technically an American too."

"Nothing. If we could have saved Sonia, we would have saved a lot more people too. We couldn't. Our connections went just so far. They didn't reach inside the detention centers."

I shook my head. "Navarro was one of your in-laws, Captain. He was in military intelligence. Don't tell me you never suspected he was involved in the disappearances."

"Did I ever suspect it? Yes. Did I ask him? Yes. Did he ever tell me anything about that work? No. Not once. And he wasn't one of my in-laws back then either. Sara and I were married just before I was transferred out of Argentina."

"And even though you knew the Bonaventuras all those years ago, you never suspected that Elena Navarro was really the daughter of Sonia? Even though she looked like her twin, just twenty years younger?"

"I was rotated out of Argentina shortly after Murillo and Sonia disappeared. I never knew where Sonia's child had ended up or even if it had survived. It wasn't until Manuel and Felicia moved here, years later, that I saw the girl and realized she might be Sonia's daughter. I'll admit it was a shock the first time I saw her."

"But you didn't say anything to anyone?"

"Her real parents were dead. Felicia was a devoted mother. Manuel is my wife's cousin, and I had no proof he had anything to do with any deaths. What was to be gained by telling anyone? The girl would only go through things that no child should go through."

"The girl deserves to know the truth."

"The truth is her parents threw their lives away."

Ingram's tone had grown even more steely. He was glaring at me, as if I were an innocent who had stumbled into lives that were too complicated for my simple means of understanding.

That was always the "cold warrior" rationale, that most Americans were too innocent, too idealistic to understand the way the world really worked. Some people, like Mario and Sonia, made bad political decisions and that got them killed. Period.

I wondered if by walking into that steam room and accusing those two men of murder I had done the same. They were both looking at me as if they wished I were dead. Lucky for me, all they had on them were towels.

I decided to cut my losses.

"I'm sure we'll speak again before this is over, gentlemen."

I left them there to sweat together. My case had just gotten murkier, and it wasn't just the steam.

CHAPTER THIRTY-ONE

I rinsed off quickly, dressed, and made my way back to the club-house. There I rescued Alice Arden from the mourting ardor of her silver-haired Argentine.

"You got here just in time. He was talking about breeding, and I don't mean polo ponies."

We headed back to Miami. Along the way I briefed Alice on my encounter with Pedro, the groom, although I left out the pitchfork. I also told her about my steamy meeting with Ingram and Estevez and their claims of trying to save Sonia and Mario.

Her lovely eyes narrowed. "Maybe, but maybe not. My admirer, Antonio, says everyone knew that Captain Ingram was CIA and that he had very close contacts with the Argentine military. Later, when the U.S. State Department turned against the Argentine military govern-ment, some journalists and human rights activists looked for Ingram, but he never spoke to anyone."

"Are you suggesting he might be lying to me, counselor?"

"I know it's a shock, but it's a possibility."

As we drove I checked my messages. I hadn't picked them up since early that morning, and I found one that surprised me. It was a raspy voice speaking heavily accented English.

"Cuesta, this is Manuel Navarro. I know you are looking for me and I need to speak with you. It is extremely urgent. Please call me." He left a cell phone number.

I found two subsequent messages from the same number, both of them aborted, with nothing more than a phone hanging up on the other end. All three calls had been made in the past two hours.

I tried the number, but it didn't answer. There was a voice mail recording, and I left a message.

"What is it?" Alice asked.

I told her.

"Do tell. What do you think *he* wants?"

161

"I have no idea, but he sounds worried."

She thought about that a moment. "Maybe it's good. Maybe he wants to turn himself in. Then again, maybe something is happening with Elena that we don't know and it isn't so good."

"I'll keep calling him back. Meanwhile, I need to deal with Ingram and Estevez."

I had told Sara Ingram that I couldn't keep her family out of it because I had already decided what to do. I had to give Grand somebody, or he would come after me. And I also needed to keep Estevez and Ingram busy so that they wouldn't have time to cause trouble.

I found Grand's number on my cell, hit the callback button, and moments later heard his gruff voice.

"It's Willie."

"I know who it is. Where's your client today?"

"I don't know where she is. I told her you wanted to talk to her and the next thing I know she disappeared."

I heard Grand gear up for a shout, so I cut him short.

"But I have something better. I have the guy who argued with Father Pérez just before he was killed."

"What do you mean you have him?"

"I have his name, address, and phone number. And I know for sure it was him because he admitted it to me."

"Did he admit killing the priest?"

"No, but I'm not the police. I could only press him so far. Maybe you can get it out of him."

"What does he have to do with the dead man?"

"I'll let him tell you that when you pick him up."

"And what does he have to do with your missing client, if anything?"

"He's the husband of my client."

"So maybe he can tell me where she is."

"Maybe. See how much I always keep your interests in mind, Grand."

"No, I don't see that yet. I better see it soon for your sake."

Of course, Eduardo Estevez wouldn't be able to tell him where to find Fiona.

"And there's another guy you should talk to at the same time, by the name of David Ingram," I said.

"Who's he?"

"An old friend of Estevez and a former American Air Force captain."

I gave him Ingram's address and also that of the polo club. I told him to check both places for Estevez as well.

"What does this Ingram have to do with all this?"

"Again, I'll let him tell you that."

"And what if these two guys don't tell me the truth? Then what?"

"Then you can arrest them for obstruction of justice instead of me. You get two for one. Not a bad deal."

"I want to see your client, Willie."

"As soon as I find her, Grand."

"You're not usually the kind of guy who loses clients."

"There's always a first time."

"There's always a last time too."

He was talking about me losing my investigator's license.

"I'll be in touch, Grand."

CHAPTER THIRTY-TWO

On the drive back to Miami I dialed Navarro's number twice more, but got no answer. For somebody who had seemed in a hurry to talk to me, he was suddenly very distracted. I started to think about where I might look for him.

I chose a route that took me through Coral Gables and cruised the house of Arturo Arno. Navarro's car was nowhere to be seen.

I kept going and dropped Alice off at her place just after dark. I told her to call me the moment Nelson showed up with Elena and Felicia.

"Where are you going?"

"I'm heading upriver."

"What does that mean?"

"I'll tell you when I come back."

I took South River Drive, following the bends in the Miami River, and headed in the direction of the San Telmo Tango Club. Elena had told me about the "business" Navarro had been involved in with Arno and Oscar Porta, the owner of the club. She didn't know what it was, but it had something to do with Navarro's place of employment—International Protection Services.

I took the last curve, reached the club, and cruised by slowly. Lights were on, and it was open for early dinner business. In the weedy lot next door stood the white IPS container I'd seen the other night.

I was several miles from the IPS factory and nowhere near the deep water of the Port of Miami, where containers went out. The fact that a big metal box was laying halfway between the two locales was certainly strange.

I cruised by it slowly. Tucked behind the container, at the very edge of the river, was exactly what I was looking for: Navarro's old black car.

I drove another block along the dark road and then pulled over. It was Saturday evening, and all the shipping companies and warehouses along that stretch were closed. Boats were docked along the river, but the crew members were ashore, pursuing their pleasures. Not a person was in sight.

I parked under a large sea grape tree just beyond a spill of street-light, killed my lights, put my penlight in my pocket, and got out. The air smelled of brine and summer heat. I popped the trunk and grabbed the crowbar and work gloves I kept next to the spare tire. I removed my jacket and left it in the trunk. Then I headed up the street.

The chain-link gate at the entrance to the lot was padlocked. I glanced at both ends of the street, stuck the crowbar in my belt, climbed the fence in two steps, and dropped to the other side.

I went quickly to the container, which was padlocked too. I assumed Navarro and Porta were next door, so I would have to keep an eye out. But it was dark on that lot and the tango music which already sounded from the club, would provide me with cover. I took the crow-bar out of my pants, jammed it between the door and frame of the con-tainer near the ground, and started to pull.

It was like trying to open a can of tuna fish with a toothpick. But I put my back into it, and the corner started to bend. A tugboat motored by in the middle of the river, downstream. I stopped, waited until it dis-appeared into the dark, and then went back to prying.

All I needed was enough space to squeeze through, and after about ten minutes I had it. I looked around, saw nobody, kneeled down, turned sideways, and nosed my way into the dank container.

My hips got caught momentarily, and I heard fabric rip near the pleats of my pants. My wardrobe was taking a beating on this Argentine business. I managed to wriggle free, pulled my legs in, and stood up so that my head almost touched the metal top.

The air in there was hot, humid, and fetid. I blew out of my nostrils to try to clear the smell. Only then did I turn on the penlight.

Squeezed in there with me, just barely, was a big, brand-new, silver SUV with tinted windows. I was pretty sure I'd seen it when I had vis-ited the IPS warehouse, amid all those sparking welding irons.

In fact, an acetylene tank and torch were in the container as well. The torch lay near the open door on the driver's side. I inched over that way and saw that the interior door panels had been removed. Someone had been reworking the armor. You had to wonder why anybody would mess with the armoring after it already had been cleared for shipment to foreign shores.

I squeezed along the wall of the container, went to that open dri-ver's side door, and shined the penlight inside. Lying on the front floor, next to the keys, was a pile of weapons—several AK-47s, at least one Uzi, and a selection of Mac-10s and Tec DC-9 assault pistols, some with extra-long ammunition clips.

I flashed the light on the passenger side door and saw that some of the weapons already had been installed cheek-to-cheek with the armor plating. They were waiting for the interior door panel to be refitted. Once that was done, nobody would know they were there. In other words, the weapons would be ready to smuggle into the countries where the cars were headed.

I opened one of the back doors, took the crowbar, and pried loose the door panel. I found more weapons secreted there. Even if the receiving countries x-rayed the cars looking for contraband, they would never see the arms through the armor. It was very neatly done.

The AK-47s were standard issue these days for all kinds of criminals. The Mac-10s and Tec-9s were the weapons of choice for drug organizations and kidnapping gangs down in South America.

I was sure that once the vehicle arrived in Argentina, the weapons would be removed before it was delivered. Navarro and company were not only sending armored cars down there for the well-to-do who were afraid of kidnappers and carjackers, they were also smuggling the very weapons that would be used by kidnappers and carjackers to attack those cars. It was a perfectly circular business. They supplied both the victims and the perpetrators. They made good money off both and constantly created more customers.

My admiration for the scam froze me for a minute. In that time I realized the discovery was also good for my case. The child stealing had occurred in Argentina. But this gave me something concrete, right on Miami soil, which I could take to Grand so he could go after Navarro, Arno, and company.

I thought of calling Grand right then from inside the container. Instead, I flashed the penlight into the rear cargo space of the SUV. A long package of some kind lay diagonally across that space, wrapped in canvas. It looked like it might be more weapons. I figured I'd give Grand a full accounting when I called. I popped the rear hatch and unfurled the canvas.

Manuel Navarro gazed up at me wide-eyed and motionless. He seemingly was as surprised to see me as I was to see him.

But Navarro was very dead. In fact, he had a bullet hole right in the middle of his forehead. The expression on his face indicated that the shot had taken him by surprise. Given who he hung out with, I couldn't imagine why.

Sticking from his pants pocket was his cell phone. I eased it out. It said he had missed four calls, all of which had come from me. I now understood why he hadn't called back, and it was through no fault of his own. The time between his call to me that afternoon and my first call to him, later in the afternoon, would provide police with the estimated hour of the crime.

I was still returning his stare when I heard a chain rattle out near the street, and the rusty gate swung open on the other side of the lot.

I made out footsteps approaching, more than one person, and I clearly heard exclamations as the new arrivals noticed the bent corner of the container. Porta was certainly one of them. I recognized his gravelly voice.

Your chances of finding an effective place to hide in an already crowded shipping container are fairly slim. Since I was standing right next to Navarro, I thought at first of wrapping myself up in the canvas with him. But, one, it disgusted me; and two, it probably wouldn't work.

I heard keys jangling and had one moment to act. I decided there was only one way out of there.

As the chain on the metal door rattled, I slipped into the driver's seat of the SUV, pulled the door closed, tilted the rearview mirror downward, took the keys from the floor, slipped the indicated key into the ignition, and then slumped down.

The container door swung open. It was dark, but in the tilted mirror I made out Porta and his bartender, both with pistols in their hands. They were cautious, standing on either side of the container and peering in.

"Who's in there?" Porta called out. "Is that you, Cuesta?"

I stayed still.

They waited. I waited.

Porta stepped into the container and then his sidekick. They were quiet, cautious, as if they were afraid of waking up Navarro. I heard the latch of the hatchback open as they checked to make sure the dead man hadn't gone anywhere.

I held back until they were both directly behind the car and gazing down at the bundle that was Manuel Navarro.

I suddenly sat up, turned the ignition key, slammed it into reverse, looked over my shoulder, and hit the gas.

The bartender didn't jump fast enough. In the red-and-white illumination of the backup lights, I saw the left rear bumper catch him square and send him flying into the weeds. Porta, on the other hand, jumped back, dodged to the right, threw himself to the ground, rolled out of the way, and shot at the vehicle.

Unfortunately for him, the SUV was armored, and also I had him outgunned by a good bit. I picked up a Mac-10 lying on the passenger seat, squeezed the trigger, and emptied half a clip through the open window. The shots went into the ground within a foot of him.

I wasn't trying to kill Porta, just making sure he didn't kill me. That half clip convinced him. As I turned the wheel and the SUV fishtailed to a stop, he jumped up and ran back out the gate.

I jammed the SUV into drive, made a U-turn, and roared after him. He turned the corner into his parking lot and made it through the front door of his club before I could clip him with my bumper. I jumped out still holding the Mac-10 in my hand and chased him inside.

Several couples had arrived early. So absorbed were they with their dancing that, despite the rattle of shots next door, they were still locked in tight tango embraces. Now they watched Porta dash onto the dance floor. Halfway across he turned. He was illuminated by an old, rusting chandelier.

When the women saw the gun he held they screamed, and everyone started to run. They wanted to make-believe they lived dangerously, but not that dangerously.

As I came through the door, Porta was the only one standing. He made the mistake of lifting the pistol, just like one of the tragic tango ruffians of legend. He had listened too well.

What I did was pure reflex. I squeezed the trigger of the Mac-10, and the burst caught him right in the chest. Porta was blown from under his fedora, ten feet across the dance floor, where he crashed into a table and fell.

For the next moments, nothing moved. The profound quiet that descends after a gunburst fell over him like a shroud.

The only sound was that of a tango crooner in the background. He was singing about a lost love, which he defined as "a long walk without dawns." He might have been describing Porta's situation as well.

By the time I knelt over Porta, he was gone. The gun he'd dropped lay nearby. I wondered if it had been used to put that hole in Navarro's forehead. I used my handkerchief to pick it up, and I dropped it into my pocket.

I retraced my steps to the lot next door and found the guy with the hook still alive and groaning.

I put the Mac-10 down, dialed Alice, told her what had happened and where I was. Then I dialed 911, but also called Grand and left him a message. After that, I sat on the back bumper of the silver SUV and waited to be detained on suspicion of murder.

CHAPTER THIRTY-THREE

Which is exactly what happened.

Minutes later the club and the lot next door looked like a law enforcement convention. At least ten cruisers, all with their roof lights flashing and spinning, were crowded onto the properties. The dark surface of the river reflected them like a liquid mirror in a funhouse.

They found Porta and Navarro and confirmed they were dead. They shoveled the guy with the hook into an ambulance.

They handcuffed me before anybody else got hurt, pushed me down into a chair in the tango club, and read me my rights. Alice showed up, stood at my side, and had them do it again in her presence, just in case I didn't understand the first time. She grimaced at the outline of Porta under a sheet a few feet away.

"Who is that?"

"You didn't know him."

They also interviewed some of the tango dancers, who reemerged from the shadows now that the shooting was over. They no longer looked tough.

Grand arrived a little while later. He inspected both the deceased, conversed with the Miami cops briefly, and then came and stood over me.

"Now you're in top-notch trouble, Willie."

I glanced at the corpse on the floor. "This guy and his friend with the hook tried to kill me after I discovered their enterprise out there in the container. Just look at the bullet holes in the SUV. And the fellow wrapped in the canvas was also part of it. His name was Manuel Navarro."

Grand's eyebrows went up. "The guy you were looking for? The guy who supposedly kidnapped the baby from Argentina twenty years ago?"

"So you talked to Estevez and Ingram?"

"Estevez spoke with me. Ingram said he didn't know anything about anything and never had."

"That's not surprising."

"Estevez told me he and his wife are your clients and the story of searching for the kid. You should have told me all this a long time ago, Willie, and you better hope nothing happens to that girl. It'll be on you when the time comes."

"Thanks for telling me."

He helped me up and led me to the SUV. Alice was right with us. Navarro's body still lay there. Alice didn't like looking at him any more than she'd enjoyed Porta's company.

"So this guy kidnapped the kid years ago and killed the priest just a few days ago?" Grand asked.

I wrinkled my nose. "I thought he might have killed Father Pérez, but at this point I doubt it."

"He's got a bullet in the head, just like the priest," Grand said. "We'll do ballistics. It's getting awfully dangerous to be from Argentina, isn't it?"

"It was like that twenty to thirty years ago, and, yes, it's getting that way again. At least around here. What else did Estevez tell you?"

"He told me that he doesn't know where his wife is, and he thinks you've hidden her somewhere."

I shook my head. "I didn't hide anybody. Maybe she's hidden herself. Maybe she's scared of him."

"Or maybe she's dead too."

I shook my head. "I don't think so."

"Why not?"

"I just don't think so."

"You're still holding out."

I said nothing. I wanted Elena and Felicia safe before I came clean to Grand. Once I had them, I'd sing like a songbird.

Grand gazed at the dead man again.

"The question is why these two people were killed, this guy here and the priest? What does it have to do with the girl?"

"Not much. I think it has more to do with her mother and father and how they died years ago."

"How many years ago was that?"

"Over twenty."

Grand grimaced. "Seems like a long time to still be killin' people over it."

"Amen."

"Why don't you tell me about it, Willie?"

So I did. I had plenty of time to do it because they kept us there a long time. It turned out that the Miami police had already been making a case on Porta: drug dealing, pimping, and fencing smuggled goods. To that they could add international arms smuggling. The tango dancers had also seen him lift the gun in my direction—attempted murder.

Alice ragged Grand about me acting in self-defense. And Grand knew I wasn't a flight risk.

Still, when he told me I could go, I was surprised. I think he knew if he locked me up, he would lose all contact with Elena, her mother, and her kidnappers. No dummy, Grand. He warned me again that I was obligated to produce my client.

"By tomorrow morning she'll be in front of you. This time, I promise, Grand."

I got out of there fast before he changed his mind.

CHAPTER THIRTY-FOUR

Alice and I quickly made for our cars. When she reached hers, Alice stopped, closed her eyes, and took a deep breath. I put an arm around her.

"Are you alright?"

"Maybe you're used to this kind of thing, but I've never gotten used to it. That guy tried to kill you."

"I don't do this every night either. I've only shot one other guy in my life, when I was on the force, and the situation was the same. He had a pistol barrel he wanted me to stare into."

She opened her car door. "Please try and get back to my place without finding any more trouble."

I told her I would catch up with her. After dragging myself on the ground to get into the container and ripping my pants, I needed to change again. I would do it quickly. It was getting late, and Nelson would be bringing the two women to Alice's place. I wanted to be there when they arrived.

But I never got there.

I was still home, changing, when my cell phone sounded, and it was Nelson. He said two words:

"They're gone."

"What?"

He sounded shaken. "They're gone. The guy who owns the house, Arno, wouldn't let them leave. He pulled a pistol on me and told me to get out. He followed me outside with the gun and waited until I drove away. So I parked a few minutes and then drove back by there. His car is gone, and so are they."

"Elena and Felicia?"

"Yes. He took them, kidnapped them. I shouldn't have left."

"Where are you now?"

"I'm parked down the street from the house, near the corner. I thought maybe they'd come back."

"Wait for me there."

Nelson did as he was told and was still there when I pulled up behind him. From where he was parked he could see the house. The lights were on, but there was no sign of movement.

"You think there's nobody in there at all?" I asked.

"Nobody that I can tell."

"Let's go see."

We left the cars and walked the half block to the house. I went right up to the front door and rang the bell. When no one answered, I pulled out my Cuban coffee strip again, got the door open, pulled my gun, and in we went.

Nelson was right, the place was uninhabited. It was obvious they had left in a hurry. A television was still playing, and on the dining room table I found a half eaten plate of food. I left Nelson to guard the front door and climbed the stairs.

In two bedrooms on the second floor I found the Navarros' empty luggage and their clothes hanging in the closets. If the women had been moved somewhere else, they had been forced to leave almost all their belongings.

I figured that back in Argentina, during the "dirty war," many family members had come home to find scenes just like this one: the lights on, the tube playing, the artifacts of life all there, but the human beings gone. It gave me the creeps.

Of course, this was a different situation because the kidnapper occupied the same house. I found Arno's bedroom, and in a drawer of the nightstand I discovered a small leather briefcase that contained important documents. Among those was an old military credential that identified him as Captain Arturo Arno of the Argentine Air Force.

I also found two empty boxes of .38 caliber ammunition, but no gun. I didn't like that.

I pocketed the military credential and looked around for any sign of where Arno might have gone. I didn't find any, went downstairs, and told Nelson we had to clear out. He wasn't happy, and neither was I.

Not only had I lost the girl again, but now she was in the hands of a man who had helped drop her mother into the sea.

I calmed Nelson down the best I could, sent him home, and told him to call me right away if he heard from Elena. In reality, there was about as much chance of that happening as snow on South Beach.

I climbed into my car, kicking myself for not moving Elena out of there earlier, even if it had meant leaving Felicia behind. My assignment had been to save the girl.

I also wracked my brain trying to think where I would look for them this time. Nelson said Arno was planning to leave Miami soon. Maybe it would be that night.

I drove as fast as I could toward Miami International Airport and called information along the way. I needed the exact address of Southern Hemisphere Air Transport, Arno's company. I found it at the backside of the airport, on the dark, narrow service road, away from the illuminated passenger terminals.

I pulled up to a chain-link fence, behind which sat a single hangar that stood dark, quiet. A cargo plane, a somewhat larger version of an old C-47, was parked outside, empty.

I killed my lights and waited a half hour. I watched commercial flights takeoff and land in the near distance, but no one showed up at that hangar. If Arno planned to leave from there, he wasn't ready yet.

Reluctantly, I phoned Alice and relayed the bad news about losing Elena yet again.

She rattled off a few choice words. "Now what?"

"I don't know. When I figure it out, I'll call you."

I hung up, sat there a few minutes more, and then made the other call I had to make. I phoned Grand, who told me he was just leaving the tango club.

"What is it now, Willie? Another dead man?"

"I have a lead for you. I have a suspect in the two killings, the priest and Navarro. He also has the girl I'm looking for, as well as another woman."

"Who is this guy?"

I told him about Arno, his ugly background, and the cargo company he ran. I also told him where to find a photo of the pilot on the human rights website.

"And he owns the black SUV you were looking for, Grand."

"Where is he now?"

"He left where he was living, so I'd put out an APB on him. But he's armed and dangerous, and anyone who sees him should keep track of him, report it to you, and not risk the lives of the two women."

"Is that right?"

"Yes. And you should also send someone to his hangar out at MIA. He may be planning to fly out of the country."

I ended the call, and then I headed for the Driftwood House on Miami Beach. Fiona was sitting there, waiting to hear that Elena and Felicia were safe at Alice's place. Now that Grand and every other policeman in South Florida would be out searching for Arno and the two women, it would be just so long before it broke on radio and television. I had to tell Fiona what had happened before she found out on her own.

It was late, almost midnight. The night clerk wasn't behind the desk at the moment, and I went right upstairs and tapped on the door. Despite the late hour, I could hear her talking on the phone, and it took her a few moments to answer.

When she opened up she was surprised to see me.

"I thought you would call me, and I would meet you at Ms. Arden's house." She looked beyond me into the hallway. "Elena and Felicia aren't with you?"

I walked in and closed the door behind me.

"No, they aren't. In fact, there's a problem."

She knew right away. Her dark blue eyes narrowed as if she were focused on something cruel.

"Elena is gone again, isn't she?"

I didn't have to say a thing. After a moment, her body twisted with pain, and her hands formed anguished claws.

"How could you let this happen again?"

The last time that Elena had gone missing, Fiona had been distracted by anger at her husband. I had gotten off easy. I wasn't so lucky this time. Fiona had now met Elena, held her in her arms. The prospect of losing her again had to be maddening.

Her eyes shot to the other side of the room, as if someone else were standing there who she could appeal to. But no one was there, and she whirled around at me.

"My husband said I shouldn't have hired you. He said it was a mistake, and he was right. He says you have been too concerned with what happened twenty years ago and not enough with finding my niece."

"If your husband was the one who betrayed Sonia and Mario, then he wants you to forget the past. Doesn't he? And maybe he didn't want to find Navarro. Well, now it's too late because Navarro's dead."

That shocked her into silence. I told her what I had found in the container and then the call from Nelson.

"My God. So, we don't even know who has Elena now."

"Yes, we do."

I told her Arturo Arno's name, but had no plans to explain his frightening aviation history. It turned out I didn't need to tell her.

"Arturo Arno! His name is in the military files. He flew my sister to her death. You let him take Elena?"

The claws had contracted into fists, and I thought she would hit me. Instead, she pointed at the door.

"Get out of here. I don't need your help."

I didn't move. I couldn't argue the fact that I'd failed her. But this was exactly when she did need my help and my protection too.

Then she turned in the same direction she had before, toward the closed bathroom door.

"Come out here, Sergio. Please, come out."

I looked at the door. After a brief pause, it opened. Standing in it was the wide-bodied Argentine vice consul, Sergio Villarreal.

A pin dropping would have made a large racket in that room. The three of us stood staring at each other for a good ten seconds. It took me that long to get over my astonishment. After all, I had worked to keep Fiona's identity from the diplomat, a guy who had dealings with her sister's killers.

"I have Sergio's help," Fiona said, "and I don't want you interfering with him."

I didn't take my eyes off Villarreal. "He's going to help you get killed is all, Fiona."

"I told you earlier that Sergio had been an aide to my father. The truth is he was more than that. He was a close personal friend of my father. He is trying to find the people who killed my sister and made my parents die of broken hearts."

"At least he's telling you that's what he's doing."

Villarreal crossed to the dresser, poured himself a glass of water from a pitcher and drank. Then he sat in the chair in the corner.

"I did not know that Fiona was coming here," he said, "but the moment you told me you were investigating Navarro, I suspected you might be working for her. I used my contacts in Argentina to find out where she was staying here, and I told her I would help."

I turned to Fiona. "And you didn't tell me any of this."

"Sergio asked me not too."

"Of course, he did. That's because he's had dealings with every one of the members of GT 332: Navarro, Arno, and Father Pérez too. He's an honorary member of that military death squad."

Villarreal shrugged. "It's true I've had contact with all of them. For some time I've known that members of GT 332 might be here, the same ones responsible for the deaths of Sonia and Mario. I applied for this posting, in part, to find them. Since I was employed by the government during the military regime, I was a person they might trust, if they had to trust someone.

"I made contact first with Arno and asked him to fly cargo to Argentina for me. Later, through him, I met Navarro, but I never saw the girl. If I had, I would have known right away that she was Sonia's daughter, and I would have acted sooner.

"Meanwhile, Fiona contracted you, and you were able to accomplish something which I, as a diplomat, could never have done. You broke into the Navarro apartment and secured the DNA evidence. I also figured that with you pursuing them, they might confide in me. But everything began to happen too quickly."

Listening to him was like fast-forwarding a film and seeing all the scenes of my case at an accelerated clip. I finally arrived at the scene we were in right at the moment. I didn't know what to believe. That being the case, I didn't trust him. But Fiona had made up her mind.

"Sergio knows them, and he can make a deal to save Elena. You will only make them run, and then I'll never see her again . . . or maybe they'll kill her."

Villarreal was watching me, not victorious nor defiant, but more melancholy, as if he felt sorry for having vanquished me.

"I think you've done all you can do, Cuesta. I believe if Arno is planning to leave the country, he may be in touch with me before he does. I think I can convince him to give me the girl."

Fiona marched to the door and opened it.

"Please leave now and do nothing to interfere with us. I'm begging you."

I knew it wouldn't do any good to argue with her. I gave Villarreal one last withering glance. Then I walked through that door. When it closed behind me, I felt it closing on Elena's life—and maybe Fiona's as well.

CHAPTER THIRTY-FIVE

It was past midnight when I got home. I took a bottle of Haitian rum, some ice and lime out onto the back porch overlooking the bougainvillea. I poured myself one large drink and then a second. I brooded and tried to think.

I was remembering all those people who had contracted me over the years to search for lost family members. Some stayed missing, lost in the worldwide currents of immigrant smuggling. Others I had found alive, and many, too many, I had tracked down in morgues.

Those clients called me from all parts of the globe. Cuban families trying to find loved ones who had pushed off from the north coast of the island on a raft, but hadn't arrived in Key West or Miami. Those I never found. Almost certainly, they were lying on the floor of the Florida Straits, being caressed for all eternity by the currents of the Gulf Stream.

There were Haitian boat people whose overcrowded fishing trawlers had been swamped by sudden South Atlantic storms. Occasionally you found one who had made it ashore on Andros Island or Eleuthera, in the Bahamas, but most of them were gone. You could only imagine their terror as they had headed for the dark bottom.

Dominicans tried to hide in shipping containers on the docks of Santo Domingo and breathed their last before the ship landed at Miami or Port Everglades. Mexicans made for Florida to pick oranges, but died in the Arizona desert, killed by thirst, mirages, and terrible delusions.

I'd even received a call from a Chinese family, originally from Guangdong, who had paid thousands of dollars to cutthroat smugglers —snakeheads—to bring their loved one to the United States. He hadn't made it. I had found his body in a squalid morgue in Belize where he had drowned in the night surf. The captain had fooled him, and others, into thinking they were swimming for the bright lights of South Beach. It was a cruel world.

Those clients of mine had never seen their loved ones again. Fiona had at least laid eyes on Elena. Was that better—or was it worse? Would it have been more humane if I had failed her totally?

I had no way of knowing that and was getting nowhere by interrogating myself. In the middle of the night, I decided to get a few hours of sleep.

When I went to bed, I propped chairs under the doorknobs again and placed the pistol on my night table. I was living like a Mafioso gone to the mattresses.

I slept almost six hours. At one point during that doze, I dreamt about the late Oscar Porta. I don't know where we were, but the tango man was wearing his fedora and talking to me urgently. I had killed him in what was clearly self-defense. He had his own opinions on the matter. I didn't understand what he said. He was speaking the language of the dead, a tongue that, luckily, I haven't yet mastered.

But maybe some other ghost talked to me in terms I *did* understand, because by the time I woke up I had decided what to do.

It made no sense for me to go searching the countryside for Arno, Elena, and Felicia. Grand and his web of cops all over South Florida had a much better chance of flushing out the pilot.

Me, I needed to go back twenty years and close in on this case from the past. If I could figure out what had happened back then, I might understand what had gone down in the past few murderous days. I was the only one on that path. If I could traverse it quickly enough, it might lead me to Arno and the two women.

I got ready and drove right to Miami Beach, specifically Collins Avenue. I left my car with the scowling valet at the condo building, walked by the security guard who recognized me, took the empty elevator up, and pounded on the door of Estevez. It was just shy of eight a.m.

Nobody answered, so I pounded again. A few moments later, Estevez himself yanked the door open and stood staring at me, daggers in his eyes. He was wrapped in a short black robe, and his blond hair was tousled. I brushed by him into the condo. He closed the door and stalked after me.

"What are you doing?"

"I'm waking you up."

"Do you know what time it is?"

"Where were you last night?"

He glared at me. "I was here, recovering, after I spent all afternoon answering questions from the detectives. What are you doing involving me with police interrogators? I'm not paying you to put me in trouble with the police."

"As far as I can see you're not paying me at all anymore."

He brushed my words aside. "And where is my wife?"

"She's hiding from you. She finally figured out that she was sleeping with the enemy."

That made his face collapse in shock. It surprised me, but he seemed genuinely shaken by what I'd said.

"That's not true. I have never been her enemy."

"I think differently and so does she."

He cupped his face in his hands, then dug his fingers into his hair and stared desolately into nothing.

"You don't understand," he muttered.

"Then explain it to me, Estevez."

He looked at me, but didn't speak. He stalked away onto the veranda overlooking the sea. I followed him.

"You killed the priest," I said.

He whirled on me. "Why would I kill him?"

"Because Pérez knew something about the past you didn't want anyone to know. I'll ask you again, did you ever speak to Pérez, or anyone associated with him, about Sonia and Mario's political activities?"

He hesitated.

"Did you?"

He was pinned against the railing. As far as I was concerned he could answer or he could jump from the fifteenth floor. He seemed to understand my position. His answer exploded from him.

"I never told them anything."

"You never told *who* anything?"

"First Pérez, then others. Twenty years ago Pérez was sent to me by military intelligence. He said if I didn't tell them what they wanted, they would harm not only me, but Fiona as well. He warned me that I had to cooperate."

"What did they want to know?"

"They wanted any information on Mario. I told Pérez I didn't know anything about Mario's activities. Mario didn't trust me. He never spoke about anything when I was around. That was the truth."

"And it ended there?"

He shook his head. "No. Pérez kept arranging meetings with me and military officials. He told me if I didn't agree to the meetings, military intelligence would come for me and Fiona. So I went."

"Who were the military officials?"

"I didn't know who they were. They never said. That was one of the ways they terrorized you."

"What did they ask you."

"All kinds of things about Mario and sometimes about Sonia. They were mostly senseless things: what they ate, what they watched on television. I realized later they were trying to find out when Mario might be at the house. Of course, they asked me other questions about their political friends, but I always told them I knew nothing about that. Absolutely nothing."

"Then what?"

He ran his trembling fingers through his golden hair. "Then Mario and Sonia went underground. Two days later Pérez called. He asked if Mario was at the house."

"And?"

"And I said he wasn't there. I said he and Sonia had been gone for two days and were in hiding. I figured that would keep them away from me and Fiona and the rest of the family. They asked where they were hiding, but I didn't know. That is what I told them . . . That was all they asked."

"Then Mario was kidnapped and murdered."

"Yes, and Sonia was disappeared. It was horrible. Fiona and her parents were shattered. I went to see Pérez. I begged him for Sonia's life and that of the baby. He told me the same thing I had told him for so many months, that he knew nothing and there was nothing he could do. He closed the door of the rectory in my face.

"I figured I would never have contact with him or the others again, which was the only good aspect of it all. But I was wrong. Months later, one of them called me. It was this man who now calls himself Navarro. He said my information had been important, that I had helped them capture Mario by telling them that he was no longer in the house. They even managed to convince me of that for a time, that's how guilty I felt about having any contact with them. They said they would tell Fiona of my betrayal if I didn't pay them money."

"So you paid them. You let them blackmail you."

He nodded sheepishly. "Yes. From time to time, the phone rang and they asked me for amounts of money. They obviously had access to my bank accounts because it was always a sum that I could just barely afford. And they could still arrest me if I argued, or do something to Fiona. They let me know that."

"And after the military government fell?"

"That was in 1983, and I didn't hear from them for several years. But one day the phone rang again. It was Navarro. He demanded more money."

"But why would you give it to them? They were out of power."

"Because it turned out they had recorded my conversations with them. They had my voice telling things about Mario and Sonia. Worthless things, pointless matters. But it was still me, and I was speaking to them. They threatened to send copies of the tapes to Fiona. They didn't ask for as much as before, but I have been paying ever since, lately to a bank here in Miami."

"And so when Fiona heard her niece might be here, you knew Sonia's killers were here too, and you didn't want to come. You didn't want to risk that she would find out."

"That's true, but I didn't know that Navarro and his wife had Sonia's daughter. I asked Pérez, but he lied to me. He told me he didn't know what had happened to the child. If I had known for sure that the child was here, I would have acted differently. I know what finding her means to Fiona. You may not want to believe that, but it's true."

I did believe Estevez, for the first time since I'd met him.

"So if you didn't betray Mario and Sonia way back when, who did?"

He shrugged. "One of their political allies, I assume."

"Like who?"

He threw his hands in the air. "Like other students, other so-called revolutionaries, that's who." He pointed at me. "This man Miguel Méndez, for example."

"Méndez swears they didn't question him until after they were captured."

"Sonia's dead and he's alive, isn't he?" He pointed wildly away from the beach. "And how about this woman, the professor who taught Mario and Sonia and who is living here now."

"Which professor?"

"She taught Mario, Sonia, and Méndez at the university. She was one of the professors who helped turn them into radicals. People said she was a lesbian and was obsessed with Sonia." He struggled to remember. "Terán. María Terán. That was her name."

A face swam up out of my sleepy memory and clicked into place like a photo slide. María Terán was the woman I had met the first day at the Colonial Arms, where the Navarros lived. She had never mentioned knowing Sonia Bonaventura.

"This has nothing to do with me," she had insisted before she closed her door in my face.

Estevez was still glaring at me, his face apoplectic.

"None of this would have happened if it weren't for people like her. If you want to talk to someone about murder, why don't you talk to María Terán?"

CHAPTER THIRTY-SIX

Maybe I should have figured from the beginning that anybody now living in Miami who had been in Argentina during "the dirty war" would have some kind of connection to my case. It was starting to seem that way. There were no degrees of separation.

When I'd first met María Terán, we'd spoken largely of love and nostalgia. The second time, when I had pounded on her door, I'd been angry, but only because I thought she had innocently tipped off the Navarros and refused to admit it. Now I knew I'd been played for a dupe.

It still was quite early when I knocked on her door. I knocked hard and the sound echoed in the empty courtyard of the Colonial Arms. María Terán answered and recognized me right away, maybe because she knew I would eventually show up again.

"Yes?"

"Good morning, Professor Terán. I'm here to discuss a bit of political science with you, as well as some history. Your history with Sonia Bonaventura and other students."

She didn't get riled by the ambush. At least it didn't show on the surface. Her chin came up defiantly, the way it had last time.

"I told you before, whatever it is you are investigating has nothing to do with me."

"Fine. I'll just mention to the police that you knew both men who have been murdered this week. Father Pérez, who rented you this place, and your neighbor Manuel Navarro, who was found dead last night. Then I'll communicate your connection to Sonia Bonaventura and tell them that maybe that's where this whole case begins."

As I'd expected, the prospect of being visited by the police didn't appeal to her. She studied me carefully. Finally, she moved aside and let me in.

I hadn't entered her apartment before, I had only glanced in the last time we'd spoken. It turned out that almost the entire living room was lined with tall shelves crammed with books. She had brought her learning with her, if not her august position as a university professor. I wondered if she'd brought betrayal with her as well.

The only section of wall not covered with books was decorated with a painting. I recognized it right away as one of Elena Navarro's frantic and strangely suspended portraits.

Terán sat in a high-backed wooden chair right in front of it. I sat in a smaller chair across from her, like a student meeting with my advisor—except in this case I was going to do the grading.

"What is it you want from me?" she asked.

"I want to know what happened to Sonia Bonaventura."

"She was killed by Argentine military intelligence. Everyone knows that."

"Why was she killed?"

"She opposed the military government."

"Sonia's brother-in-law says it was you who led her into the opposition movement against that government, who taught her everything she knew."

She didn't answer right away. Just like Ingram, she looked at me as if I were terribly naïve, someone who knew nothing of real life. In that carved, high-back chair, it was she who looked like the inquisitor.

"Sonia was my student, Mr. Cuesta. At that time, being a professor at the university presented one with difficult choices. You were supposed to be availing your students of the truth, or at least helping them find their own way to the truth."

"Was it truth you helped them find, or death?"

She squinted right through me and into the past. "One could stick to the curriculum, teach philosophy according to the textbook, or one could look at the world right outside the window. In the end, it was the only thing I could do because the students cared about nothing else.

"It was not a question of making them believe certain things. It wasn't about turning them against the government. The government was killing off its opponents, and they knew it better than I did. Many of those dying were of their generation. One could only try and help them understand why it was happening."

"And why did it happen, professor?"

"For the same reason it happened in Nazi Germany or Fascist Italy or the Soviet Union under Stalin. It didn't just happen among us, the Argentines. In order to create a society, human beings bury other, less civilized sensibilities. But from time to time the demons emerge from under the surface of that civilization, and they wreak havoc, especially when the established order is challenged. In this case, the Argentine military felt challenged. You don't tell generals, whose power depends on hierarchy, that it is time for those at the bottom of the society to possess power. That is what many of my students believed."

Her eyebrows were already arched, but now they bent a bit more. "And it didn't help that your own government helped train military officials from all over Latin America in how to eliminate their political enemies. In Argentina all we know is that later many innocent people died."

I didn't argue political history with her. The demons I was interested in right then weren't those guys. I wanted to know about María Terán's demons. I was recalling what she had told me the first time we'd talked: "I came following someone I loved."

I also recalled what Eduardo Estevez had said about her being obsessed with Sonia Bonaventura. Twenty years later, she had lived right across a courtyard from Elena Navarro, who was the spitting image of her late mother. María Terán's current address was no accident. I remembered how she had reacted when she thought I might be romantically pursuing the girl. She had sent me packing with my tail between my legs.

The painting by the girl hung right over her head. The suspended figure might have been Sonia in her last moments. Maybe the girl had no way of understanding the connection when she had painted it, but María Terán surely had.

"I'm told you were close to Sonia, Elena's mother. More than just a teacher."

Her eyes narrowed again as she tried to assess just how much I knew.

"Yes, we were close. Sonia was a beautiful young woman, bright, vibrant, passionate, serious, interested in others. We spent many hours talking about ideas, about morals, about politics, and about love."

She reached into the bookcase next to her, pulled out a red leather photo album and flipped through it. She stopped at a page and handed me the album.

"Here we are just a few weeks before Sonia died."

The photo was taken outside what appeared to be a classroom building at the university. A sign hanging over a stone archway identified the building as belonging to the faculty of Philosophy and Letters. Sonia Bonaventura was the same as I had seen her in the other photo— somber and beautiful. And also visibly pregnant.

María Terán was twenty years younger, her hair devoid of gray, her olive skin almost unlined. She had her arm around the shoulders of the girl, and she was smiling, despite the terrible times they were living.

Other photos on that page and the following pages depicted a march—young faces full of anger and idealism. I saw Sonia and Mario in several of them, right at the front of the demonstration.

María Terán tapped one of the photos with her finger.

"That was one of the few protest marches during the military dictatorship," she said. "It came in the later years. Before that everyone was too frightened. Just days later Mario and Sonia went into hiding, and then they were disappeared. They were two of the last to die."

"When was the last time you saw Sonia?" I asked.

"She came to my office at the university one afternoon to tell me she was going into hiding. She said she had convinced Mario that for the sake of the child she was carrying, they couldn't take more chances. The next day she stopped coming to classes."

"And that was the last you heard from her?"

She shook her head. "No. She phoned me after that."

"From the place where she was hiding?"

"Yes."

"When was that?"

"Several days later. The night before she was found by the military."

My eyebrows went up.

"She called you at your office or your home? Wasn't she afraid that your phones might be tapped? That by calling you she'd be traced?"

She shook her head. "She called me at my mother's house. She knew I went there once every week, and she knew better than to call me anywhere else."

"Did she say where she was hiding?"

"No. I never knew that. But she said she was afraid—very, very afraid. It wasn't for herself so much, but for her child. She was afraid that she and Mario would be betrayed."

"By who?"

"I don't know. I told her she shouldn't worry because only the people closest to her knew where she was, and she said, 'That is the problem, professor.' I asked her what she meant by that, but she didn't answer. She also told me that they had been offered a chance to leave the country, and she was trying to convince Mario they should take it. But then Mario heard her speaking to me and ordered her to hang up."

I could sense in her, even twenty years later, a tinge of resentment toward Mario Martin Murillo, the man who had stolen Sonia from her.

I also wondered if the chance to leave the country had come from Ingram. Maybe the former CIA agent's story was true. Maybe Sonia herself had confirmed it.

"She didn't say more about leaving the country?" I asked.

"No. She hung up, and I never heard from her or saw her again."

Of course, years later she had seen Sonia again, but in the person of the dead woman's daughter: Elena Navarro.

"You knew the first time you saw Elena exactly who she really was, didn't you?"

She nodded. "Yes. There is no mistaking that she is Sonia's daughter."

"Did you know that she and the Navarros were here when you moved to Miami?"

She shrugged. "I had asked many people over the years. Finally I was told that some of the people involved in Sonia's death had left the country and come here. That was the rumor. I came. I found a job teaching Spanish. I went to Argentine restaurants, and one night I saw her."

"And you found out where she lived and you moved here to the Colonial Arms?"

We hadn't mentioned her unrequited passion for Sonia, but it was the subtext for everything being said. She knew that I knew.

"If you knew who Elena really was, why didn't you tell someone?" I asked. "Why didn't you try to find her real family?"

"Because it had taken me so long to find her, Mr. Cuesta, that I couldn't face the possibility of losing her again. In memory of her mother, all I've tried to do is help her, encourage her. You can believe that."

Given how far she had come to be close to Elena, maybe it was more than passion that she felt. Maybe it was an obsession, as Estevez had said. Obsessed people were capable of anything.

"Did you try and help her by killing the men who murdered her mother? Did you kill Father Pérez and Manuel Navarro?"

Her chin came up. "No, but maybe I should have."

I didn't know whether to believe anything she said after the lies she had told me. I had questions not only about what she might have done, but why she might have done it.

She could have killed the priest and Navarro because she knew they had killed Sonia. But it was also clear that she had been disappointed in her love for Sonia. Had bitterness led her to betray Mario and Sonia?

Had she turned against them twenty years ago? Did Father Pérez and Navarro know that? Is that why they were dead?

I, unlike the diplomat Villarreal, am not good at hiding what I think. She seemed to be reading my thoughts.

"I didn't kill anyone here, nor did I ever do anything in Argentina that led to anyone's death, Mr. Cuesta. They died because of their beliefs. I gladly would have died in Sonia's place."

My eyes fell again to the photo album and all those angry young faces. I studied them, trying to intuit the truth of what had happened. Dozens of marchers were pictured parading down a boulevard, carrying banners that demanded justice for the living and the dead. Mario and Sonia were at the forefront. Like all their fellow marchers, their mouths were open, chanting their young defiance at the dictators.

One of the people pictured suddenly popped out at me. I focused on that one face from twenty years ago. The hair was shorter now, the face more drawn, but it was definitely the same person I had spoken to more than once that week.

What that individual was doing in that crowd, I had no idea. My sense of what exactly had happened during that time was being turned upside down. It made my head spin. I understood that when I could make it stop spinning, then I would know who had betrayed Mario and Sonia, who had killed Navarro and the priest, and why any and all of it had happened.

CHAPTER THIRTY-SEVEN

I stayed a few minutes more and asked María Terán more questions about those perilous times. Then I left her.

Next, I made a quick stop that I'd been planning for two days. I parked on 69th Street and entered the convenience store with the Latin American long distance calling cards advertised in the window. Next door was the real estate office where Father Pérez had been murdered.

I introduced myself to the bespectacled middle-aged Latin woman who ran the place. Her name was Mrs. Chávez and, like most business owners who spent the day parked behind a counter, she kept a close eye not only on her store but on her neighborhood. She was a font of gossip and of knowledge. In between selling lottery tickets, single beers in small paper bags, and a calling card, she answered my questions. After ten minutes, I thanked her for her time and left.

I went to my car and was about to make a phone call, when my cell phone sounded.

It was Grand.

"You there, Willie?"

"I'm here, Grand."

"Well, you better get up here near Glades Springs where I am. There's been a shooting, and it involves those people from Argentina."

My heart—not to mention my lungs and stomach—skipped a beat.

"Was it the girl?"

"She was there at the Ingram house, but now she's gone. And it wasn't her who got shot. It was your friend, Eduardo Estevez."

"Estevez?"

"Yes. You better grab his wife, if you know where she is, and get up here to Hollywood West Hospital."

He hung up. I was just blocks away from the Driftwood House Hotel. I called Fiona and told her what had happened.

She was still angry with me from last night.

"You're making this up," she said.

"I'm afraid I'm not."

It took a moment, but she understood I wouldn't lie about that.

"How did it happen?"

"I don't know, but I'm heading that way right now."

Five minutes later, she came out the front door of the hotel, just as I pulled up. I did eighty to ninety on the highways all the way to the hospital. If the Florida Highway Patrol pulled me over, I had the perfect story: a man lay dying, and I was rushing his grieving wife to his side.

That wasn't a fabrication. Fiona was extremely upset at the news that Eduardo Estevez had been wounded. After so many years of marriage, no matter her recent suspicions, the loss of her husband would be a tragedy. Fiona already had lost enough people, all as a result of the same "original sin," the same betrayal more than twenty years ago. Now her husband had a bullet in him.

I pulled into the hospital lot in record time, and we hurried into the emergency wing. It was almost empty, just a couple of kids with skateboard wounds. More cops were there than patients. I told a uniformed sergeant from the Glades Springs department who we were, and he hurried us through swinging doors to a nurses' station. A nurse's aide ushered us into the pre-op area of the emergency complex.

We found Estevez in a corner room. He lay flat on his back, an oxygen mask over his lower face, a doctor and two attendants preparing him for surgery. His clothes lay on the floor, having been cut from his body. They were so saturated in blood that you couldn't tell what colors they had been.

Standing in the near corner was Sergeant Lester Grand. With him was a gray-haired guy in a suit who I figured was a plainclothes Glades Springs detective. Sitting in a chair between them was Sara Ingram. Her blouse and slacks were also liberally stained with blood, but it was probably from Estevez. She wore a dazed expression, as if she were in shock, but she didn't appear to be physically injured.

Grand stepped toward us. In a whisper, I introduced him to Fiona. He, in turn, introduced us both to Detective Dietrich of Glades Springs. Grand had been waiting quite a while to meet Fiona, but he didn't make an issue of it right then. Grand was a classy guy.

"I'm sorry we have to meet under these circumstances," he said.

Fiona didn't take her eyes from Estevez.

"How is he?"

"He has a slug in his upper left chest, below the shoulder and above the heart. He lost a lot of blood. Your husband tried to rescue the girl and the other lady and was shot trying to do so."

I crouched next to Sara Ingram.

"Who shot him?"

She came out of her daze, but only partially. "Arturo Arno."

"How did it happen?"

"Arturo came in the middle of the night with the two women. He had a gun, and he was acting very nervous. He wanted to speak to my husband. He said he needed help to get out of the country. Then a while ago he called Estevez. He demanded money from him."

I frowned and that stopped her. Estevez must have received the call soon after I'd left him.

"Go ahead," I said.

"Estevez arrived and told Arno he wasn't giving him any more money. He said they had blackmailed him, Arno and Manuel. They had lied to him and then blackmailed him for too long. I couldn't understand it all.

"Then Estevez said he was going to take the girl and the woman. Arno would have to shoot him to stop him. That is what Arno did. He shot him. Then he took the two women and left."

Moments later the doctor slipped the oxygen mask off Estevez's face and nodded in Fiona's direction.

She approached the bed. Grand, Dietrich, Sara Ingram, and I waited. Fiona whispered to her husband, and Estevez opened his eyes. He looked up at Fiona with a gaze that was calmer and more resolute than any I had seen in his eyes since I'd known him.

Fiona whispered again to him, and he whispered back. She stroked his head. Then the attendant stepped in, and Estevez was wheeled out toward surgery. Fiona followed him.

Grand turned to Sara Ingram.

"Do you know where Arno was going?"

Her eyes were still on the door through which Estevez had just left.

"Arno said he wanted to get back to Argentina or somewhere else in Latin America, that he could be safer there. I assume he'll try to fly one of his planes."

"Did Arno force your husband to go with him?"

She shook her head. "No. David went with him to try to help Elena and Felicia. David is also a pilot. He told Arno he might need someone to fly the plane. But he's hoping he can talk Arno into giving himself up before something terrible happens."

From the look on her haggard face, Sara Ingram didn't see much chance of that. I couldn't blame her. Neither did I.

CHAPTER THIRTY-EIGHT

Grand radioed the Highway Patrol. He had them update the APB and provide Arno's latest whereabouts. Then he took off for Miami. I would follow, but first I looked for Fiona.

I found her sitting by herself outside of surgery. She suddenly looked very, very tired, although still beautiful. She was deep in thought. I think she was trying to make a decision—whether she would stay with her husband if he survived.

Fiona had thought Estevez too interested in money. But in the end, he had showed he cared about other human beings more than he did his own safety. Yes, he was enraged at Arno, but if he were the calculating individual Fiona suggested he was, he wouldn't have risked his life. He hadn't stopped Arno, but what he had done might lead me or the police to Elena.

I decided there was nothing I could add to that, and I left her with her thoughts.

I was halfway back to Miami when my cell sounded.

"Cuesta?"

"Yes."

"It's Sergio Villarreal."

He was the last guy I expected to hear from. The guy who had stolen my client.

"Yes. What is it?"

"I just now received a phone call from Arturo Arno. He told me to contact the police and deliver a message."

"What message?"

"He says he is going to leave the United States today in one of his own cargo planes. He says he did not kill either the priest or Manuel Navarro, but he's afraid the police will accuse him. He says he won't go to prison for someone else's crimes.

"If he is allowed to leave, he will release unharmed the two women he is holding the moment he arrives at his destination. But if anyone tries to stop him, he will kill them. I hope the police will allow him to leave."

It occurred to me now that maybe Sergio Villarreal wasn't the villain I'd thought. At this point I had no option but to believe him.

"The police are already on the way to the airport," I said. "Whether they let him leave is another question. He just shot a man. He's wanted for one count of attempted murder, and I'm sure they'll want to talk to him about the two other homicides, Father Pérez and Navarro."

I filled him in quickly on the shooting of Eduardo Estevez. It shocked him.

"The police in South Florida aren't accustomed to letting murderers, or attempted murderers, just fly away," I said. "Arno is also traveling with an American who may be considered a hostage as well. And he's not just any American. He's holding a former U.S. intelligence operative. That will get the feds involved for sure, if they aren't already."

"Maybe I can convince Arno to let the American go," Villarreal said. "All the other individuals involved are Argentine citizens. No one else but Argentines have been killed or injured."

Grand wasn't going to care about the nationality of the two dead men. He simply wanted to arrest their killer or killers.

Villarreal interrupted my thoughts. "I'm going to the airport, to Arno's headquarters. Maybe I can intercede and negotiate some kind of agreement before something very bad happens."

"Be careful."

Villarreal beat me to the ramshackle hangar of Southern Hemisphere Air Transport. So did Grand and a good number of Miami Dade police officers, who had set up a perimeter just inside the gate. They were joined by two fire rescue ambulances, and even a couple of camera crews who had picked up the news on their scanners.

But we hadn't beaten Arno. His black SUV sat on the tarmac next to the hangar. The same cargo plane I'd seen the night before, bearing the company logo, stood in front of the corrugated metal building. A door just behind the cockpit was open, and steps had been lowered. It was ready to go, but I saw no movement inside the plane. I assumed Arno was still in the hangar with his three captives.

I was almost right. Just outside the gate I spotted Grand, surrounded by several uniformed officers and paramedics. I poked my head into that crowd.

Seated on a stretcher in the middle of them was Felicia Navarro. She was bleeding from a gash on her forehead. Her bleached blond hair was matted with blood at her hairline, and her pants were ripped at the knee.

Grand noticed me.

"She tried to grab his gun and save the girl. But Arno was too quick for her. He shoved her out on the road right here. The two men we had guarding the gate ran to help her, and Arno went right by them. They couldn't shoot because of the girl and the other hostage."

I looked toward the hangar. "So they're in there?"

"Yes. We've already called in. He says he's going to fly that plane out of the country, and he'll kill Ingram and the girl if we try to stop him. If we let him go, he says he'll let them live. But once he gets out of here and he heads for Argentina, he'll do whatever is convenient. We both know that, Willie."

Grand was gazing at the hangar. He was thinking the same thing I was. Once Arno got in the air, he might have no further use for his hostages. Elena Navarro could end up like her mother, being thrown from a plane over the ocean to the sharks waiting below.

Grand walked away to another group of cops, and I got closer to Felicia. I introduced myself and saw recognition in her eyes.

"My daughter told me about you."

Her eyes implored me.

"I'm afraid he's going to kill her, Mr. Cuesta. Someone has to do something."

She had sacrificed her life for Elena, living with the abusive Navarro for so many years to make sure she didn't lose the girl. Now she was facing the possibility that her sacrifice would end in tragedy. I wondered if she knew exactly how Sonia Bonaventura had lost her life and if she understood that it was a tragedy that had occurred once already all those years ago.

"Felicia, I need you to tell me anything that Arno said. We need to understand what he's going to do."

She shook her head, holding gauze over her wound. "I don't know, but the last two days he talked very much on the cell phone with somebody else. Somebody was telling him what to do."

"Do you have any idea who it was?"

Again she looked at me helplessly. "No."

"Felicia, I want you to think back. Did your husband ever tell you anything about who betrayed Sonia Bonaventura and her husband Mario? Do you remember those names? Did you overhear anything among him and his friends about their murders?"

She shook her head slowly. "I wish I could help you. But all I can remember from that time was how happy I was to have Elena and how much love I wanted to give her. I didn't know where she came from. I know nothing else."

Tears flowed down her face. With her bloodied head and ripped clothes, there was no doubt she had done all that was possible. Now I, Grand, and the assembled troops had to save Elena for her.

CHAPTER THIRTY-NINE

I left Felicia with the paramedics and found Grand again. He was standing with a uniformed police captain, discussing the possibility of rushing the hangar. But there was only one small window in the corrugated metal building, and Arno stayed away from it. They had no way of knowing where he was and if he had a gun to the girl's head, or to Ingram's. For the same reason, snipers had no way of getting a clean shot at him.

All we could do was wait. About an hour into that waiting, Dietrich, the Glades Springs detective, walked up.

"Estevez is going to be all right. They got the slug out of him. His wife came down with me."

He pointed a few feet away, and I saw Fiona. I approached, but she didn't give me a chance to ask about Estevez. Her relationship with her husband was obviously something that would have to be decided, but only later. She gazed toward the hangar.

"Elena is in there. We can't let anything happen to her."

"Everyone is doing what they can."

"I want to be sent in there to take her place. He killed my sister, and he can kill me if he wants. But we need to save the child."

I knew Grand wouldn't go for Fiona's offer and tried to tell her so. I was still standing next to her when the door to the hangar opened. Everyone on the tarmac froze. First, we saw Ingram pushed out, his red face overheated, his hands folded behind his head.

Then Elena came out in the same posture. Arno walked just behind her, dressed in the same bright blue jumpsuit I'd seen him in before, holding one handgun on Ingram and another to Elena's head. Even more than a hundred feet away, the terror in her eyes was painful to see.

Arno yelled in our direction.

"Don't try anything, or I will kill the girl."

He marched them toward the plane, and I saw Grand hold up a big black hand.

"Everybody easy. Hold your fire! Hold your fire!"

Arno pushed them to the foot of the stairs that hung from the side of the aircraft. When he arrived there, he and Elena climbed the stairs backwards, Arno holding her in front of him, until they stood in the doorway of the plane. Then he ordered Ingram aboard.

Once that was done, Arno placed Elena right in the open doorway and made her stay there. That made it impossible for a sniper to get a shot at him inside the plane.

The hatchet-faced Arno called out from over Elena's shoulder.

"We're going to get this plane ready to depart. If anyone approaches, I will shoot the girl."

He left Elena propped where she was and disappeared inside the plane.

I saw a police SWAT team in black coveralls and helmets deploy to each side of the airfield and even behind the plane. The FBI had troops there too. I could read their windbreakers.

They all kept their distance, at least for the moment. But I didn't like the looks of it. I doubted very much that they would allow the plane to take off with hostages, especially when the hostage taker was a guy like Arno, who was half crazed. I saw a violent confrontation coming, and I saw Elena getting caught in the middle.

I turned to Villarreal.

"Can you get Arno again? Is he on a cell phone?"

"Yes."

"Call him. I need to talk to him."

As Villarreal dialed I kept an eye on Grand. He wasn't going to like what I had in mind, so I wasn't going to tell him.

Villarreal told Arno I wanted to speak to him and handed me the phone.

"Arno? This is Willie Cuesta, I'm . . ."

His voice was gruff and loud. "I know who you are. What is it?"

"You don't have to do this. I know you didn't kill Navarro and the priest. I can prove it. And Estevez is going to live."

He said nothing, but a moment later I saw his grizzled face gazing toward me over the shoulder of Elena Navarro. One pistol was pointed at her head again.

"Where are you?" he asked into the phone.

I waved at him. He scowled at me and spoke into his cell.

"Come to the plane. Walk slowly and make sure you are not armed."

I told him I would. I handed both the phone and my handgun to Villarreal.

Grand was distracted, speaking on his radio. I ducked under the yellow crime scene tape, raised my hands, and started toward the plane. I got about a quarter of the way before the yelling started. Then I heard Grand.

"Get back here, Willie!"

I sensed the commotion among the other cops behind me and on each side. But I didn't turn around or glance to each side, and especially not in Grand's direction.

"I said get back here!"

Arno had thrown his arm around Elena's neck. He held the gun pressed to her temple to make sure no one else made for the plane. For the girl, there was no one in front of her but me. She was at the edge of that airplane door, the same way her mother had been in her last moments. Not thousands of feet in the air, but just as close to death. She was looking at me as if I were her only hope.

When I reached the foot of the stairs, Arno told me to stop.

"Turn around."

I did, and he could see I didn't have a gun tucked in my belt. I looked at the crowd that had assembled. Everyone—cops, camera crews, Felicia, Fiona, Villarreal—had their somber eyes glued to me as if I were already a dead man.

Arno growled behind me. "Roll up your pant legs and turn your pockets out."

I did that too.

"Now, don't do anything fast. Just get on board."

He pulled the girl back from the door just enough so I could climb the stairs, squeeze by them, and enter the cargo plane. He never took his eyes from me and never moved the gun from Elena's head. Once I was inside, he pushed her back into the doorway, trained one gun on her back, and jiggled the other one toward the bulkhead across from the door, just behind the cockpit.

"Get over there."

I did as I was told. The old cargo hold was empty except for several wooden pallets and straps used to tie cargo to rails that ran along the floor and sides of the aircraft. The only other thing inside that plane was heat. It was sitting in the sun, and it was as hot as an oven.

I pressed myself against the right bulkhead. Ingram sat in the cockpit, in the pilot's chair, watching all three of us. Sweat streamed down his bright red face.

"I need to talk to you," I said to Arno.

He pointed one gun right at my head.

"You don't do any talking. You're here because I need another hostage. I was going to use the other woman, but now I have you. If they try to stall me, I'll shoot you and throw you out the door."

"You don't need to do this, Arno."

"I said shut up!"

I heard Grand's voice crackle over a loudspeaker.

"Arno, we need to talk. Don't hurt anyone."

Arno scrambled back to the doorway and shouted from behind the girl.

"There's nothing to talk about. Ingram is going to fly this plane toward Argentina. You tell the tower to let us go, or there will be killing."

Arno moved back from Elena and waved a gun at me.

"You sit down right where you are."

I sat on a pile of pallets stacked next to me. Then Arno pointed the gun at Ingram.

"You get this plane ready to fly."

"They'll never let us take off," Ingram said.

"Do as I tell you. I want this plane in the air. I don't want to kill anyone. I haven't killed anyone yet, but I will do it. I'm not going to rot in a prison here for killings I didn't do. And if I'm going to die, I'll take all of you with me."

Ingram turned to the control panel. Arno pressed his back against the left bulkhead. That way he could watch Ingram and Elena with one eye and me with the other.

Another voice was heard outside. I could see through a porthole window and spotted Villarreal standing next to Grand.

"Arno!"

Arno grabbed the girl around the neck and again put a gun to her head.

"What is it?"

"It's Sergio Villarreal from the consulate. Please, release those other people. I've now received word directly from the presidential palace. The authorities there will let you land in Argentina."

Arno grimaced. "You're lying."

"I'm not. At least let the girl go."

"I won't release anyone until I land safely in a place only I know."

What exactly he meant by that, I had no idea. But again it occurred to me that once he was up in the air, Arno wouldn't need all the company. To lighten the load, and give him less to worry about, he would shove both Elena and me out that door. I gave the plane another quick look and saw no parachutes.

The fact was he wouldn't need Ingram either. He could fly the plane himself, land it on some dirt airstrip in the South American jungles, and just disappear.

Arno must have been thinking along those lines. He turned and yelled into the cockpit where Ingram was still fiddling with switches and gauges.

"Ingram, if they don't let us take off, right after I shoot Cuesta, I'll shoot you. So you better get this plane in the air now."

I watched Ingram process that information. Then he turned, flipped one switch, and cranked up the engines. The propellers started to move, hesitantly at first, but then they caught and began to spin. He gunned the engines until they were humming and then lowered the revs. It was still loud in the cargo hold.

Ingram picked up the radio microphone, called the tower, and identified himself, shouting over the engine noise.

"I'm going to be taking off. The man here with the guns is serious about shooting someone, either on this plane or outside the aircraft. Please clear the nearest runway for me to take off right away. I am taxiing there right now. Don't try to stop us."

Ingram signed off and turned to Arno. "Close the door and get everyone strapped in."

Arno advanced toward Elena, put his arm around her neck again so no one could get a shot at him. As the plane started to move, he suddenly pulled the chain attached to the hatch. It slammed shut, and he threw the latches. Then he pushed Elena away from the door, and she fell to the deck right next to me. I helped her up so that she sat with me on the pallets.

Ingram picked up speed and headed toward a runway. Through the porthole I could see uniformed police running after us, guns drawn, but no one fired. I thought they might try to shoot out the tires, but it didn't happen. They held their fire. Ingram taxied at greater speed than normal, and we left them behind.

Arno stayed standing, wrapping one of the cargo straps around him and lacing himself to a side rail, just as Ingram suddenly swung the plane into a ninety-degree turn and stopped. I could see past Ingram through the front windshield and found an empty stretch of runway staring us in the face.

Ingram talked into the radio again.

"This is Southern Hemisphere Air Transport. I'm taking off now."

A voice crackled over the receiver, ordering him not to, but Ingram paid it no mind. He gunned the engines, the old plane rattled around us like a boiler about to explode, and we picked up speed. Through the window I saw the police still running toward us. I picked out big Lester Grand doing a decent forty-yard dash, but we were too fast for them.

The radio squawked as a controller in the tower tried again to get Ingram to stop. He didn't answer, but kept his eyes glued on the runway. I grabbed one of the cargo straps, wrapped it twice around Elena, and tied her to the side rail. But I didn't have time to do the same thing for me. I just held on.

Moments later, Ingram lifted the aircraft off the ground. The engines strained, and the old plane shook, tilted, and rattled, but it flew. Some of the pallets shifted and slid toward the back of the plane, clattering and splintering in the tail section. Elena and I held onto the cargo straps to keep from sliding with them.

Ingram took her up at a steep angle. He probably was worried that one of the police snipers down below might make a last second attempt to bring us down. The three of us—Elena, Arno, and I—held on as if we were dangling in thin air. I thought of making a dive at Arno, but the moment I let go of the straps I would free-fall toward the tail of the plane.

Almost a full minute later, Ingram finally leveled her out. He turned his head and found Arno, with his free hand, pointing a gun right at his head.

I glanced out the porthole. The airport was no more than ten miles from the sea. We already had left Miami behind and were heading out over the aquamarine ocean. Elena looked out as well. I saw fear all over her face.

I had no idea what Arno planned to do, and I don't think he knew. He had been running and hiding, probably hadn't slept in days, and was coming unglued. Laced to the side rail, he looked like a madman who had been tied down in order to control him. There was one small glitch in that picture: he had a gun in his free hand. I noticed he had stuck the second gun into a nook between the rail and the bulkhead. But it was within his reach.

He saw me studying him and the storm on his face grew even darker.

"What are you looking at? Don't you try anything."

He lurched to one side, unlatched the passenger hatch, and kicked it open. The wind took it and slammed it against the outside of the fuselage. For a moment I thought the sky would suck him out of the plane. But he held onto a strut above his head and inched back away from the door.

"You make any trouble, I'll throw you out," he growled at me. "And I'll shove the girl out too."

The gusting air from the open door made dust and trash swirl all around us in the plane. It rushed over Elena, whipping her long hair.

I was still studying Arno. His scraggly hair stood on end in the swirling air.

"If you didn't kill anybody, why are you doing this?" I called to him over the roar of the engines.

He scowled at me. "I told you, because they'll blame me for killing the priest and Navarro. They're already blaming me. They said it on the radio."

"They're saying you're a suspect, but we can prove you didn't do it."

"Oh yes, mister investigator? How can you do that?"

I turned to Elena. "On the night the priest was killed, the night after you left Little Buenos Aires, did anyone leave the house in Coral Gables after 9 p.m.?"

She glanced at Arno, her hair blowing about like a Medusa. "No, none of us left."

"Not even Arno?"

She shook her head. "No. He went out earlier, but not at night."

"So if Father Pérez was shot sometime after 9 p.m., it couldn't have been Arno, could it?"

She thought about it for only a moment and shook her head. "No, it couldn't."

I turned back to Arno. "See, you have a witness."

That didn't satisfy Arno. He waved his gun in the air wildly.

"They'll still blame me for Navarro."

"But you didn't kill him either, did you?"

"No, I didn't kill him."

"No. The same person killed both the priest and Navarro, or at least the same gun. Almost certainly ballistics will prove that. When the priest was killed, an anonymous caller contacted the police and said they saw your black SUV leaving the scene. That person was already trying to frame you. The police will understand that."

Ingram had turned his head to watch, and Arno wagged the gun at him wildly.

"You fly the plane!"

Ingram turned away.

"So the call was a lie, wasn't it?" I asked Arno.

"Yes, it was a lie. The priest called me that night. He said you had come looking for Navarro. I said, 'But they haven't come looking for you. Just say nothing. I will hide Navarro.' That was the whole conversation. I never spoke to him again. I didn't leave my house that night."

"You didn't tell anyone beside Navarro about the priest's call?"

"No."

"Did Navarro tell anyone?"

Nothing pained Arno more than having to think, but he did it.

"Yes, he called somebody."

"Who did he call? Whoever it was almost certainly killed the priest."

His gaze slowly turned toward the cockpit, just as Ingram steered the plane into a banking turn and we all had to hold on tight. We were headed south now in the direction of Argentina.

Arno jiggled his gun.

"I don't know. Maybe he called his cousin. Ingram's wife."

"Or Ingram himself."

Ingram shook his head, looking straight ahead over the sea.

"He didn't call us. Cuesta is trying to fool you, Arno."

Arno turned and scowled at me. "You're trying to trick me."

I didn't take my eyes from Ingram. "No, I'm not. And it will be easy to check phone records to see who Navarro called that night."

Ingram turned his head from the controls and talked to Arno.

"He's lying to you."

"Oh no, I'm not," I said. "The priest was killed because he knew who betrayed Mario and Sonia. Didn't he, Arno?"

Arno was still gripping the rail with one hand.

"Yes, he knew. He didn't betray them, but he knew who did. He said to me once, 'I gave Sonia Bonaventura the last rites and she told me everything.'"

"But he wouldn't tell you who it was?"

"No. The priest was afraid, as always."

"And Navarro wouldn't tell you either."

"No."

"Not even near the end? That's strange, isn't it? I wonder why he wouldn't tell you. Navarro wasn't afraid like the priest. He must have had another reason." I fixed on Ingram's back. "Maybe it would have meant betraying a member of his own family."

The pilot didn't turn or say a word. Arno and Elena watched him as well.

"Twenty years ago Sonia Bonaventura was pregnant and desperate to escape Argentina," I said. "At first, Mario, her husband, refused to accept help from the American embassy. But Sonia was afraid for her child's life, and she begged him. If they were going to be in hiding, they might as well be out of the country.

"It was against his best instincts, but he, his wife and child were threatened by people even more dangerous to him than the Americans. Or at least that's what he thought. He finally gave in and asked for asylum from the embassy. He made the call from his hiding place, and who did he call but you, Captain Ingram? You already had connections to the family. You had already won the trust of Sonia's father."

Ingram turned to look at me and growled. "You're making this all up."

"You agreed to help spirit them from where they were hiding into the embassy. But you didn't do that. Once you knew where they were, you called your friends at GT 332 and revealed to them where Mario, the vocal anti-American student leader, and his wife Sonia were stashed. They crashed in and kidnapped them. It was a feather in your cap with your friends at GT 332, wasn't it? They didn't want Mario to get away and neither did you. You didn't like his politics any more than they did. They wanted him dead, and you helped them kill him.

"When Fiona showed up here in Miami and hired me, the twenty-year-old secret was no longer safe. Everything fell apart quickly. Father Pérez and Navarro were facing prison, both of them for child stealing and Navarro for torture and murder as well. They weren't trustworthy. They had to be eliminated, and somebody had to take the fall. That was Arno here. You called the police with the anonymous tip on Arno's vehicle. You're the only one it could have been. You betrayed Arno the same way you had Mario and Sonia."

Arno's wild eyes were now glued to Ingram. He was adding it all up slowly. Eventually he would come to the same sum that I had. But then Ingram made his move.

He was facing the rear of the plane, but his left hand still rested on the controls. Suddenly, he grabbed them and pulled down hard. The nose of the plane lifted and again was pointed almost straight up at the sky.

Arno lost his balance, fell hard, and slid toward the back of the plane. The gun he held smacked the side rail, came loose, and clattered to the deck, wedged against the base of a metal strut. Elena and I both hung on to the cargo straps so that we wouldn't slide with him.

We hung like that for long moments The plane strained as we climbed and the crate rattled. I thought the engines would choke and stall at any moment and then we would all end up as shark's supper.

But Ingram finally pushed the control lever back up and we leveled off. Then he made a dive for the gun. I went for it too, but Ingram was closer and would reach it before me.

I shot my foot out, hoping to kick it away from him. But I didn't catch it square and ended up nudging it right to him.

He reached down and grabbed it. He was still bent over when the girl, still holding onto the straps with both hands, kicked her legs out with all her might. She caught Ingram square on the shoulder and knocked him across the plane so that he backpedaled toward the open door.

Off balance, he pulled the trigger. A shot punctured the skin of the plane right above my head.

Before he could gain balance and take better aim, I threw myself at him. He pulled off another shot that buzzed by my ear and buried itself in the bulkhead behind me. My momentum carried at him and the heel of my hand caught him under the chin. I pushed and then I crashed to the deck.

Ingram tried to grab the frame of the hatch with his free hand. He managed to catch the rubber molding with his fingers, but the suction was too much for him. He toppled backward out the door. The back-wash grabbed him. He did one perfect back flip in the air, momentarily focused on the plane, and fired a wild shot toward me. Then he started to tumble again and again, drifted astern quickly, and cartwheeled downward in the direction of the dark sea.

The swirling sky wanted to suck me out too, but I managed to roll away from the door. By that time Arno had scrambled to his feet and was headed toward me from the tail section. He wouldn't face murder raps in Miami, but he had wounded Estevez, and he was still a war criminal wanted in Argentina.

The second gun was exactly where he had left it, wedged on the ledge of the side rail. I reached up, grabbed it, and pointed it at him. He stopped where he was, holding a strut above his head. His hair flailed around his head.

"You can get in the cockpit right now and fly us back to Miami, or I can kill you and try to fly this thing myself. You have five seconds to decide."

My chances of flying that plane were slim to none, but with me pointing a gun at him, Arno's prospects were even worse. He figured that out quickly. I moved aside, he stumbled past me and climbed behind the controls, just as the plane started to nose down.

He leveled the plane off, put it into a smooth arcing turn, and headed back north. I pulled the hatch closed and entered the cockpit. Keeping the gun trained on Arno, I raised the Miami control tower and told them we were heading back.

By that time Grand was in the tower, and he came on the radio.

"The girl's all right?"

"She's fine."

"And Ingram?"

"He's gone. Grand, I want you to do something."

"What's that?"

"Go to South Pointe, pick up a guy named Miguel Méndez, and bring him to the airport. Keep him out of sight."

I gave him the address.

"Why would I do that?"

"Just do it. You'll see."

I signed off. Then I went to Elena. She was shaking, but she was all right. I kept the gun pointed at Arno, but put my left arm around her. She lay her head on my shoulder and started to cry. She didn't say it, but I sensed she was weeping for her beautiful mother, Sonia.

CHAPTER FORTY

SWAT police, fire rescue teams, other uniformed types, the FBI, and Homeland Security were all over us the moment we landed. I helped Elena down the stairs. Arno was placed in handcuffs, but I told Grand that he only should be charged with shooting Estevez, not the murders of the priest and Navarro.

"What are you talking about now?"

"You'll see. Is Miguel Méndez here?"

"Miami Beach patrol officers just drove up with him."

We entered a waiting area in airport police headquarters, where Grand had set up shop. I handed Elena over to Fiona, and they fell into each other's arms.

Grand led me to Méndez, who was waiting in an outside hallway. He stood between two large patrolmen. Real flesh-and-blood people weren't his thing, especially not people in uniform. He looked scared to death.

I walked up to him. "Things will be all right, Miguel. I just need to ask you a few questions."

I pulled him aside and over the next few minutes asked him about the Argentine opposition movement and the last days before Mario and Sonia were killed. When he had answered all my questions, I thanked him, ushered him into a corner of the waiting area, and asked the two cops to take care of him right there.

I then had a member of the airport police lend me a computer in an adjoining office. My business there took me barely five minutes.

Sara Ingram sat on the other side of the waiting room from Méndez, still in the bloodstained clothes she had worn at the hospital. A paramedic, a female, was consoling her about the death of her husband. I took that woman's place. Sara Ingram's face was tracked with tears.

"How did he die?" she asked.

I said her husband had fallen from the plane during the struggle, although I didn't tell her I had given him the last nudge. I also advised her of the exchange between Arno, Ingram, and me that had led up to it.

She dabbed at her wet eyes.

"So now you know the truth. Now it's finally over."

I shrugged. "Possibly."

She didn't move a muscle or blink an eye. But I saw the surrender she had flashed a moment ago seep out of her. It was replaced by caution.

"What do you mean 'possibly'?"

From my pocket I took the photo of the demonstration that María Terán had given me. In the front line of march were Mario Murillo and Sonia Bonaventura. Just a few people away from them walked the young person who had looked so very familiar to me when I had first seen the photo. The hair was longer, the face was unlined, the clothes were different, but it was definitely Sara Ingram two decades ago.

"You weren't just studying in Buenos Aires, as you mentioned to me, you were on the same campus as Mario and Sonia. According to Professor María Terán, you were, for a time, very active politically and became particularly close to Sonia. Of course, back then you weren't known as Sara Ingram. Your name was María Teresa Montejo."

I took out another photo, one I had just downloaded from the computer and printed.

"Another photograph of you, under your original name, is contained on a website of students who were disappeared during the dirty war. You told me once that people in Argentina think some of the 'so-called revolutionaries' from those days were not disappeared at all and are still alive living in other countries. You wanted me to believe that might be true of Mario and Sonia. But the story you were telling me was actually your own, wasn't it? You were reported missing the very day that Mario and Sonia were captured. In fact, there were people who thought that, possibly, under torture, Mario or Sonia had given you away. That they had betrayed you."

I shook my head.

"But it wasn't like that at all, was it, Mrs. Ingram? The truth is quite the opposite. *You* betrayed *them*."

Her teeth were showing. "You're crazy. My maiden name is Sara Martínez. I have a birth certificate and passports to prove it."

"Yes, you have documents made by the same people who made Elena's birth certificate, and they are just as phony. If you want, I can bring Miguel Méndez over here to say hello to you."

I pointed across the room to where Méndez now stood watching us. His mouth was open, as if he'd seen a ghost.

The woman who called herself Sara Ingram stared back at him in stony silence.

"You went to see Father Pérez the day he died," I said. "The woman who runs the store next to the real estate office identified your photo and your red sunglasses. You and Pérez spoke out on the sidewalk. She said you argued with Pérez, but she figured you were just another real estate customer. You didn't look much like a murderer, and she didn't mention it to the police.

"After Pérez was dead, you made me think you suspected Navarro. But what really scared you was the possibility you had been seen."

She glared. "So what? Okay, I went to see him."

"Why?"

"Because Father Pérez was falling apart. He felt tremendous guilt about what he had done all those years ago, and he was also frightened at the fact that Sonia's family had found the girl. Manuel was afraid if anyone went to question the priest, he would confess everything. Manuel got very angry. I was afraid of what he might do."

"Like kill the priest?"

"Yes."

"And that's why you got involved? To save Pérez's life?"

She heard the doubt in my voice and didn't bother to respond.

"No, I don't think so, Mrs. Ingram. You went to see Pérez because you were afraid he would crack and tell the police the secret that would put you in prison for the deaths of Mario and Sonia. He knew you had betrayed them. When you saw how shaky he was, you decided you had to go back and kill him."

She shook her head. "It wasn't me. It was my husband who shot him."

"No, it wasn't. Your husband later killed your cousin Manuel because he also was cracking. Your husband was a cool customer. He killed Navarro, and then he went and played polo. But Eduardo Estevez told me that on the night Father Pérez was killed he spent the evening with Ingram. He was looking to give himself an alibi, but in the end he has supplied one for your husband. I'll bet it checks out. You're the one who doesn't have an alibi for that night."

Her teeth showed again. "First you kill my husband and now you try to take me away from my children as well."

"Just as you took Mario Murillo and Sonia Bonaventura away from their child. At first I thought that it was torture that had turned you, brainwashed you after you were captured. But that isn't true. You were a spy for Manuel long before Mario and Sonia died. You joined the student movement expressly to infiltrate it. You knew Ingram long before that too. You told me so. You hooked up with them to betray your own countrymen. You were always one of the traitors.

"It wasn't your husband who found out where Mario and Sonia were hiding. Mario never called him. He never asked for asylum. It was you who betrayed them. You were well connected in the student movement. You were part of the inner circle. You were one of the few people who knew where Mario and Sonia were. Sonia told you just before they went underground. Miguel Méndez couldn't figure out who in the movement it might have been who betrayed them and him because he thought you were dead just like everyone else.

"When you vanished, everyone figured you'd been kidnapped and disappeared as well. Your name was found on the same list as Sonia's, put there by your cousin, Manuel. Everyone thought you, María Teresa Montejo, had been dropped into the sea. But you were never in that detention center or on that death plane. You were never tortured. You were in hiding, and you eventually left the country with Ingram. You have a new name, shorter hair, a thinner body and face, different hair coloring, you hide yourself in Glades Springs and never come to Miami, where you might be recognized.

"Who on earth would look for you in Glades Spring, especially if they were convinced you had been disappeared? If they were convinced you were dead?"

Her gaze had hardened like water turning to ice. She looked at me the same way I'd been looked at on a couple of occasions already during my case, as if I didn't know anything about real life. When she spoke, her tone had turned to ice as well.

"Father Pérez was a weak man. But Mario Murillo and Sonia Bonaventura weren't weak. In fact, they were very dangerous people. They wanted to change the Argentine way of life, everything Argentines believed in: tradition, hierarchy, the church, relations between the social classes, the established order. We did what we had to do to save our country."

I could see she considered me a weak man too, even though I had tracked her down. I thought she was about to tell me so. Or maybe she was about to dig her long fingernails into my throat like the heroine of a tango tune. But she didn't have a chance.

Grand had been standing behind me for the last few minutes. He stepped between us and began reading her rights.

CHAPTER FORTY-ONE

Alice buzzed me in. When I stepped off the elevator she was waiting at the door with a tall glass of beer in her hand. I was dressed in the same clothes, covered with grime from the deck of the cargo plane.

"I saw you on television."

"Is that right? How did I look?"

"Dirty, but ravishing."

I took the beer, and we retreated to the terrace overlooking the river. I had been questioned for several hours. So had Elena. In the middle of it all, Alice called me on my cell. She was worried about me. I had told her to turn on the television and hang tight.

Grand and the immigration authorities had finally released us, and the three women—Fiona, Elena, and Felicia—had gone to stay at the Collins Avenue condo. I headed for Alice's in time to catch the early evening light on the river.

I sipped my beer and Alice her wine. Alice said she was already in touch with the immigration judge. Given the circumstances, there was no danger that the women would have any trouble with the authorities. Elena because she was an American by birth, and the other two because they would be needed as witnesses in the Arno and Sara Ingram cases.

"That scene at the airport was all over the tube all afternoon," Alice said. "Did you really fight with that guy, dangling from the door of the airplane."

"Yes, I did. I was hanging by one fingernail and clawed my way back aboard."

"My hero."

She sipped. "What was it like with the Ingram woman?"

"I'm not her kind of a guy."

"I didn't mean that. It sounds like quite a marriage she had. Two people who had sent innocent human beings to their death. Couples that murder together, stay together."

"Yes, but I wonder if after the deaths of Mario and Sonia, David and Sara Ingram didn't have each other blackmailed in somewhat the same way that Manuel and Felicia Navarro did. They shared sins in their pasts that would have made it difficult to trust each other if they had parted. Sara seemed as afraid of Ingram as Felicia was of Navarro."

"A strange symmetry between the two couples."

"Yes."

I sipped. "How could I blackmail you?"

"You can't. I'm clean as a whistle."

"We could do something about that."

"Yes, we could, but we won't," Alice said.

"We won't?"

"No. I don't think you should spoil your reputation. You've rescued a damsel in distress. You're like Sir Lancelot, a knight errant."

"I'd rather be a night to remember."

She chuckled wickedly and then we watched the last of the daylight sink into the river.